2,99 (3)

FORBIDDEN ALLIANCE

To Delyth

Enjoy!

Love Katrina

Also by Katrina Mountfort

Blueprint Trilogy
Future Perfect

FORBIDDEN ALLIANCE

BOOK 2 OF THE BLUEPRINT TRILOGY

KATRINA MOUNTFORT

Elsewhen Press

Forbidden Alliance

First published in Great Britain by Elsewhen Press, 2015
An imprint of Alnpete Limited

Elsewhen Press, PO Box 757, Dartford, Kent DA2 7TQ
www.elsewhen.co.uk

British Library Cataloguing in Publication Data.
A catalogue record for this book is available from the British Library.

ISBN 978-1-908168-80-1 Print edition
ISBN 978-1-908168-90-0 eBook edition

Printed and bound by CPI Group (UK) Ltd, Croydon, CR0 4YY

The Heath family

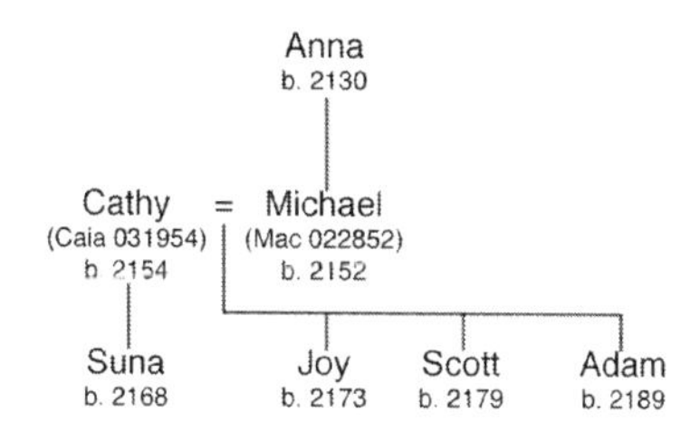

The Baxter family

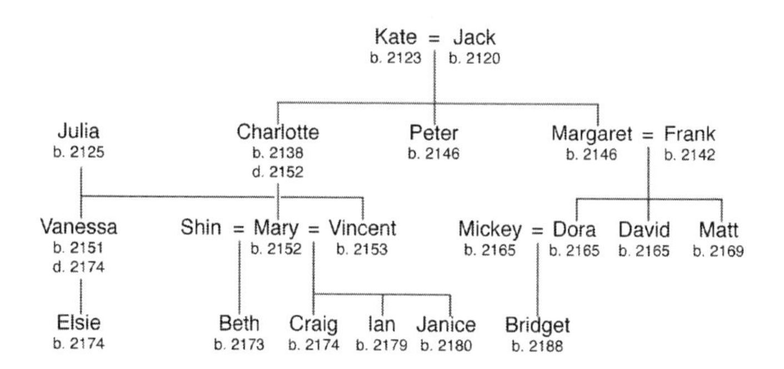

CHAPTER 1 – JOY

February 1 2189

"You look gorgeous. I'm so proud of you." Daisy tied the sash at the back of my dress, made of home-grown cotton dyed butter-yellow with rosemary, and the most beautiful garment I'd ever owned.

"You're the only one." I scowled.

"Joy, that's not fair! We all are," Daisy said.

"That's not what you said last week."

"Are we still talking about work? Course I was annoyed. Sometimes your mind's not on the job. And it frustrates me, because you're – "

"The brightest girl in the village. I know, I know." I rolled my eyes. "But the one who's useless at every job she tries. 'You're so clever, Joy, if only you'd apply yourself.' Do you know how sick I am of hearing that? Apply myself to what? Dishing out pig swill? I was born into the wrong time, you know. The late eighteenth century. That's when I should have been born. I've been reading about it. The Enlightenment, they called it. The golden age of art, music, philosophy."

"Yes, well none of them will put food on the table. Come on, birthday girl; let's have a smile. Sweet –"

"Ugh, don't say sweet sixteen or I'll puke. But I'm not sweet, am I? Unlike my perfect mother. Not easy growing up in the shadow of legends, you know."

Daisy sighed. "Let's not start the self-pity fest again. You know how it is when there's a new baby. No-one thinks of anything else. But the whole village is turning out for your party. Surely that's worth a little tweak of those lips?"

I shrugged. I should be excited at the prospect of my first adult party, but I already knew how the evening would unfold – everyone would stare at me, wondering whom I'd dance with first. Matt or Ryan. Ryan or Matt. And the only person I wanted to dance with wouldn't be there. I twirled my hair around my finger in disgust.

"Let me put a bit more of this in your hair; might make it shine more." Daisy brandished a jar of one of her home-made concoctions. "That's better." She combed a huge blob of gelatinous gloop through my hair, untangling it to the extent that it hung lower, now brushing my shoulders. "Matt and Ryan will be fighting over you."

"They can fight all they like. Why do they have to be my only choice? Huh, what am I saying; there's no choice at all." My voice turned into a chant. "I'm from a new bloodline. I'm the future of the village, and I'm going to marry Matt."

"Don't write off Ryan. He's a bright boy; I like him."

"So do I, but he's so spindly."

I did like Ryan, and I had the uncomfortable feeling that he liked me too much. He'd only been living here two months, a lovely guy with big blue eyes, but the body of an overgrown sapling. He'd been part of a gang who escaped from a Citidome down south and was our first new community member in over fifteen years – hardly anyone got out of those sinister bubbles. He'd been assigned to us because we don't have enough young people to work the land. That was the official reason, at least. But my best friend, Beth, and I knew better.

"Ryan's been brought in to breed with Beth," I said. "We know our futures. Heaven forbid we should have any say in it."

"You make it sound so bleak." Daisy grinned. "Well, it might not work out that way. I've been having a few chats with Ryan, and he's not interested in Beth. He's – "

"Don't say it; I can't bear to hear it. I'm not attracted to Ryan. Matt's cute but I've grown up with him; he's like a big brother."

What was that strange alchemy that transformed an ordinary person into someone's object of desire? Not that there was a single ordinary thing about the one I did desire.

"I know what this is all about. Still fixated on Harry, are you?"

"Don't say fixated. That trivialises it. Harry's the one I love. Always has been, always will be, but no-one will let me have him." I hoped my sigh conveyed the right blend of yearning and tragedy. Loving Harry came as naturally as eating and breathing. It had been three months and five days since I last saw him and already time had blurred the edges of my memories.

"You're way too young to be making any choices yet," said Daisy in that adult-appeasing-a-child voice that infuriated me. "But … don't set your heart on Harry. He'll never leave the canals. And it'd devastate everyone if you left the village."

I said nothing, because Daisy was right. I'd heard the arguments over and over. Harry lived a nomadic existence with his mum Dee, transporting goods on a canal boat. Harry's dad, Kell, had disappeared five years ago, so Harry would have to stay on the canals forever. And I couldn't leave the village because they needed a new bloodline. That's just the way it was. And it was breaking my heart.

I looked in the mirror and smiled; Daisy had achieved a miracle and de-frizzed my curls. I reached for the finishing touch, a wooden dolphin on a leather thong, cradled it in my hand and then fastened it around my neck.

"Ooh, that's gorgeous. Where did you get it?" Daisy asked.

"From Lynn at the market."

I was telling the truth – sort of. Lynn lived in Langley Mill, one of the canal trading points, and for years had exchanged messages and gifts between Harry and me. On Thursday she'd handed me the parcel.

"From Harry," she'd whispered. "There was a message too. Hang on, let me get it right… Teach a man to love, and he will have Joy for all eternity. Why he couldn't say happy birthday like everyone else, I don't know."

"Harry would never be so mundane." I'd laughed. I'd been rehearsing my message to him all morning. "Tell him… if you tame me, we'll need each other. You'll be the only boy in the world for me. I'll be the only fox in the world for you."

"You two are weird." Lynn had shaken her head, smiling.

Now Daisy was examining the carving. "Hmm, I've never seen anything like that on the market. Well, you look perfect. Let's go."

As we wrapped ourselves in woollen shawls and scarves to

brave the winter chill, I tried to recreate that perfect day, last October. Harry's image formed in my mind: nut-brown skin, chaotic spirals of black hair that hung over his huge eyes, dark as the canals on which he lived, framed by long, curling lashes. We'd walked along the beach and were heading back to the canal boat that was his home.

"What's on the other side of the sea?" I'd said.

And without any warning, he'd grabbed me by the waist and swung me around, the way he'd always done.

"A world of infinite Joy," he said, put me down and gave me that look, the one that made my legs shake and squeezed the air from my lungs. Could it be that, finally, we were about to make the transition from best friends to something I'd dreamed of for years? And although we'd vowed always to embrace originality, the kiss that followed had fulfilled every romantic cliché I'd ever read in novels. My heart pounded. The world around us disappeared. Then we'd heard voices and, to use another cliché, the shit had hit the fan.

"OK, I'm ready," said Daisy. "Let's pick up Anna along the way."

We stopped some fifty metres down the street and knocked on the door. Nanna emerged, together with Scott, my little brother. Everyone said he'd inherited my mum's dusky skin, but his colouring owed as much to encrusted dirt as it did to genetics.

"It's only me and Daisy, Nanna." As a kid I'd never liked the word Grandma so called her by her proper name, Anna, but it always came out as Nanna. This used to be a term of address for a grandmother, so the name had stuck.

"Good, I'll get my cloak," said Nanna. "Come on Scott, we're going to see the baby." She smiled.

Nanna looked from me to Daisy and her smile faded. "He's still not back?" I shook my head. "Well, let's see the dress." I parted the coat. "Oh love –"

I smiled and absorbed another wave of admiration.

Leaving the house, I noticed with a rush of pleasure that it was still light. My birthday marked the turning point of the bleakest time of the year, where the only thing to break the desolation was the singing of the sparrows. Just as I started to think winter would never end, the hours of daylight began to build. We passed the churchyard, and I cast my head towards the wooden crosses, so many new ones these last years: Ian and Jane, but they'd been old, James the farmer, only sixty-five. Worst of all was Paul, brother of Helen the health worker, at twenty-eight, two months ago, after a fall from a horse. Then my eyes rested on a weathered cross whose inscription always gave me a peculiar shiver. My mum's grave.

Cathy Brewer Died 1 February 2173

I must be the only girl in the world to have two living parents but both officially dead.

"The snowdrops are early this – " Nanna's words were cut short by the familiar sound of hooves, causing us all to turn round. The horse came to a stop and a man, smothered in a thick sheepskin shawl, swung from the horse. My spirits soared. He'd made it – the only man I loved more than Harry. The reason I could never leave this village. My gorgeous dad.

"About bloody time," muttered Daisy.

I hurtled into his arms. He enveloped me in the shawl and held me against the coarse fabric of his jacket for a full minute.

"My turn!" shouted Scott, jumping up and down, and Dad released me to lift him up into the air.

"Scotty, how can you grow so much in two weeks?" Dad said and then turned to us. "Sorry, there was a blizzard in Pontefract so I had to stay there for two nights. I've been riding all day. You wouldn't believe how sore I am." He rubbed his buttocks and winced. "How's Cathy?"

"She had the baby, this morning," Daisy said. "A boy. They're both fine."

"Shit – that's early. But –" Dad sounded pained. Good. He deserved to feel bad.

"She went into labour first thing. She was in a terrible state – horrendous pains. I had to get Helen." My voice was hard. A terror-filled ride to the next village wasn't the start I'd wanted to my birthday; Dad should have been here to look after Mum. "Helen's still with her, but she kicked us out. Said we had to let her rest. We've been at Nanna and Daisy's all day; we were on our way to see her."

"A boy." Dad's eyes glistened.

Was he pleased or not? Girls were more useful for breeding, and breeding was Dad's obsession. But boys made better farmers.

Now he looked at me. "Same birthday as you; how about that? And how's my birthday girl?"

"Pissed off. You messed up my big day."

Why couldn't Dad have a less important job and spend more time at home? He was president of the AOC – the Alliance of Outside Communities – which meant he travelled all over the country and could be gone for days at a time. Outside referred to the communities outside the Citidomes – that other world that I couldn't imagine. I'd only ever seen the nearest one, Tau-2, from a distance but Citidome complexes were dotted all over the country. They were so warm inside that you never needed a coat, which right now seemed the biggest luxury imaginable.

"So what's going on, Dad? What's so important that you had to go for ten sodding days, knowing Mum was almost due to pop?"

"Charming turn of phrase you've got. AOC business, I told you." But he didn't look me in the eye.

"Was it to do with Ryan's gang?" I had a feeling that the AOC had been involved in Ryan's escape; Dad had been away a lot more in the weeks before Ryan's unexpected arrival.

"Hey, why the interrogation? We'll talk about it later. Right now, all I want is to see your mum and your baby brother, and have a nice warm bath."

Something was going on; I was sure of it. Why did no-one tell me anything? I was too young to kiss Harry but not Matt. I was old enough to work, but not to vote on community decisions or be told exactly what Dad did. There was no consistency among adults.

"I'll take Bramble, you get yourself home," Daisy took the horse's reins.

"Thanks." Dad nodded.

We reached home. Helen smiled in that controlled,

unflappable way she always had, and I relaxed for the first time in ages. No-one had talked about it, but we'd all been living in a state of fear for seven months now, when Mum first realised she was pregnant.

"You're way too old," I'd said.

"I'm only thirty-four." Mum had looked outraged.

"B-but –" What had I wanted to ask? Was it an accident? Mum had explained to me and Beth all about safe times of the month, not that either had us had done the deed yet. I wouldn't mind, with Harry, but if one kiss caused all that fuss …

Luckily, Mum had saved my embarrassment. "No, we didn't plan it and yes, there's no reason why it shouldn't be safe," she'd said.

Except for the fact that Mum almost died having me, then had three miscarriages and a tough time having Scott, six years after me. And that childbirth was one of the most hazardous things that a woman could undertake and it wasn't unusual to die in the process.

Mum was propped upright on the bed, a tiny bundle in her arms. Dad was stroking her hair and I looked away – they were totally embarrassing when they were like this. When they'd stopped gushing over each other, I sat on the bed, flung my arms around Mum and cried so hard I could barely breathe, venting the tension I'd been holding for months.

"Hey, what's all this?" Mum said.

It took a few moments before I was able to speak. When I did, my voice was a whimper. "I was so scared."

"There's nothing to worry about. We're both fine. Do you want to hold your brother? His name's Adam."

As Mum placed the bundle in my arms, I stiffened. My love for my baby brother was so tied up with resentment that I didn't know how to untangle the two. I gazed into the solemn eyes of this new addition that we didn't need, the baby that had caused Mum to be grumpy for the last seven months, and tried and failed to feel the love I had for Scott. And now the baby had even taken my sixteenth birthday away from me!

CHAPTER 2 - CATHY

My exhausted eyes darted from Michael, then to Joy, holding Adam. Joy passed Adam to Scott, who held his brother as if he were an explosive device, before passing him on. Soon little Adam was resting in Michael's strong, capable arms. Ah, that was better. Maybe the baby would be the glue that joined us all back together. Or maybe he'd know that he wasn't wanted. The one thing I thought I could rely on was that indescribable rush of love when I first held my baby, the way it had been with Joy and Scott. But this time it hadn't happened. I felt frozen and wished someone else could look after this new burden. But how could I explain that to the gathering around my bedside? I flashed them a rictus grin, hoping no-one could read my mind.

"Sweetheart, I'm so sorry I wasn't here for you. Are you OK?" Michael asked.

"Apart from feeling I've been through a mangle? At least he popped out quickly. Only two hours this time."

"He looks small," Michael said.

"He's 2.3 kilos, according to Helen's ancient kitchen scales. About the same as Joy and Scott were. That's what happens when they're early."

"I should have realised there was a good chance he wouldn't go full term," he muttered. "No excuse."

At least that was one thing we agreed on.

"Took me a bit by surprise, too," I said, then looked at Joy, transformed into a beautiful woman in her new dress. Simultaneously I saw her as a baby; aged four, in her first party dress that she later tore playing football with Matt and Harry; and aged ten when she refused to wear a dress at all and insisted on wearing Harry's pants for her party. Tears pricked my eyes. "Sweetheart, you look stunning. I'm sorry I won't be there for the party."

"S'all right. But Dad, I don't care if you're exhausted.

You've got no excuse." Joy's half-smile said that it wasn't all right at all.

Poor Joy. We'd wrecked her big day. And I'd so wanted it to be special. Joy had lived up to her name in every way until the last year. Every new milestone had been a moment to treasure. But my relationship with her – and with Michael – had been ruptured since that business with Harry and I was struggling to repair them.

"I got stuck." As Michael embarked on yet another exasperating string of excuses for his late arrival at a major life event, my jaw tightened. The Alliance wasn't just a third person in our marriage, it was a whole legion of them. When he'd told me about this urgent trip, I'd wanted to scream – what about me? Would it be too much to ask for the imminent birth of our child to have top priority? But I'd bitten my tongue. After all, this trip was more important than most: one that might bring our dreams to fruition. Or destroy everything we'd worked to create.

"Cathy, he's gorgeous." Anna and Daisy were cooing over the baby.

He was a beautiful baby. Of course he was. I was just tired, wasn't I?

"And how's Mum?" Daisy winked.

"She's never bloody well going through this again," I muttered.

My names had defined my life. For eighteen years I'd been Caia 031954: the misfit, the rebel, the subversive thinker trapped in a world that starved my spirit. For ten glorious months I'd been Cathy Brewer, together with my soulmate Michael. In those short months I'd scaled heights of bliss and depths of fear that Caia wouldn't have believed possible. But on the day that Joy was born, Cathy Brewer had died. I marked the end of that phase of my life with a grave in the churchyard, in case the authorities came back.

We'd had to disappear, of course, and spent a blissful eighteen months travelling along the canal network with our friends Kell, Dee and infant Harry. During those languid months, the AOC was born. Eventually we'd decided that Joy needed a base, and had returned to the village we'd always thought of as home, changing our surname to Heath, a nod to

Heathcliff, my favourite fictional hero. But by then I'd become Mum. And being Mum was an all-consuming role, one that I thought was about to get easier until this latest invasion. No – I glanced at Adam – mustn't think like that. But oh, why couldn't I have done my child-rearing all at once, like normal people, like my friend Mary who'd had four children in seven years?

I turned my attention back to Joy. "Let's have a look at you in your full glory."

Joy stood up and gave a twirl. The dress enhanced her developing figure. She'd inherited my lack of height and curvy body shape, but luckily the latter was considered a desirable attribute among the villagers.

My heart tightened. "You're so beautiful."

"And very grown-up," Michael added. "You're making me feel old."

"That's because you are old." Joy giggled.

"Right, just for that, you're not having your other presents until I get out of the bath," he said, cuffing her head.

I smiled at the familiar teasing. It was always like this between Michael and Joy. That was what was making the latest row so hard. Joy was blaming us both for the whole Harry debacle, and couldn't see that I was on her side. Not that I hadn't been shocked to see them kissing in such an adult way. Early marriage and motherhood wasn't what I'd intended for her. But Michael was the one who was being unreasonable.

"It should hardly have come as a surprise," I'd said to him. "Remember when we used to put them to sleep in separate berths of the boat and find them in the morning curled up together like puppies? Her first word was Harry. I just wish they'd waited a bit longer. They're still kids. Joy should be embracing life, not pining over a boy she sees only twice a year."

"But, oh, I don't need to spell out the reasons."

"I can understand that you don't want to lose your little girl. But what if Harry came to live here?"

"Harry's never going to leave Dee and settle here and I don't want him to. I like the boy. I see him as my eventual successor in the AOC. But he needs grounding in reality, and so does Joy. They're a bad influence on each other, too fanciful."

"You've forgotten everything we used to dream of. A world where we could read to our hearts' content, appreciate beauty, fulfil ourselves. We were frustrated by our own education. Who are we to deny it to our children?"

"That's the kind of world I'm trying to create for them. But we're not there yet, and Harry's going to be an important part of the fight for the next few years. The cause has to come first, and it will for Harry. And Joy, well, truth is, I want more for her than I've given you. I know it's not easy for you all when I'm away for days on end."

At that, I'd softened. Michael could be infuriating, frustrating, obsessive, and I saw the same traits in Harry. Maybe I wouldn't wish that on Joy, but I wouldn't have exchanged my life with Michael for anything.

But he'd had to spoil the moment.

"She'd be far better off with Matt. He's a decent boy and nearly four years older; he'd be a steadying influence on her. And we need to find someone for him. Beth's too close a relation."

"You know what you're turning into. Fin."

"Fin?" At the mention of the man who'd imprisoned me while I was pregnant with Joy because his community needed a new breeding female, Michael shifted in his seat.

"Remember him? Obsessed with new blood? Not letting people be with the ones they loved? After everything we went through, I'd have thought you'd want your own daughter to make her own choices."

"She's just a kid! She doesn't know what she wants."

Now I looked at him and tried to take the accusation out of my eyes. He'd missed the birth of his son, and he knew how terrified I'd been. I'd always wondered whether my own fear had killed those three babies between Joy and Scott. Had I subconsciously expelled them from my womb because I was petrified to go through the process of childbirth, having almost not survived it the first time? No, there was no excuse for Michael going away so close to my due date. And he'd almost missed Joy's birthday party. Sensing the tension, Anna ushered the rest of the family downstairs.

"I should never have gone." His brown eyes sought mine and as ever, I was lost in them. It was impossible to stay angry with Michael for long. "You're sure you're OK? You look pale."

"You wouldn't look too good yourself if you'd pushed a baby out." I smiled. "But I wish the other two had come out as easily as that. I don't know why it's worn me out so much." I cast a guilty eye in Adam's direction. "Come on then, tell me about the trip. I'm itching to hear all about it."

"We were right; there are lorries going in and out of the correction camp complex marked with warnings that they contain flammable and explosive substances. We have to work out which factory they're going to, and the best way to detonate it. So November still seems like the best bet for Outbreaks 3 and 4: not so many people outside. I'll put it to the vote, but it looks like they're going to go ahead."

"That's good." I didn't have the energy to argue.

For the first time, we'd disagreed on an AOC decision. I thought that liberating a whole correction camp was too risky and I wasn't the only one. Debates had raged among the Alliance for almost sixteen years. The villages weren't subject to interference from the Citidomes on the tacit understanding that they co-existed peacefully with them. If we tipped the balance, how would the Citidomes retaliate? Helping twenty people to escape from the Citidomes was easy to hide from the authorities. But it was hard to believe that we'd manage to liberate a thousand Citizens without reprisal unless we could create a distraction that would allow the prisoners to escape of their own accord. Like an explosion.

"I'll freshen up, then let's give Joy her presents," he said. "How's she been?"

"Sulky and resentful until she broke down just now. Poor kid, I hadn't realised she'd been so stressed about me. Let's try and make the rest of the day about her."

I dressed and joined the others downstairs. By the time Joy had received her birthday presents from the rest of the family, Michael had emerged, pink from his bath, his beard trimmed to the short stubble I liked, gorgeous in his linen trousers and top.

"That's better; you don't look so much a wild man of the woods," Joy said. "David's coming to the party tonight."

I grimaced. Tensions ran high between our family and the Baxters.

"Great. I'll get ready for the snide comments." Michael shrugged.

"What gives you Citidome folk the right to dictate our lives?" sneered Joy in a good impersonation of David's mother, Margaret.

One of the AOC's aims was to keep each village renewing their population and to do that we needed to mix bloodlines among the village-born families. Five years ago, we'd exchanged a young man from Buxton for David. No-one had been forced, but Margaret still resented Michael's intervention. She'd never forgiven us for the banishment of her twin brother, Peter, even though Peter's betrayal had almost cost me my life. I couldn't think of that man without shuddering. It was another reason Michael wanted Joy and Margaret's youngest son, Matt, to be together, to heal the rift between the families. Poor Michael. Sometimes his job was tough. And it would be even tougher once everyone found out his plans.

"Now, present time," said Michael. "Happy birthday, sweetheart."

He gave Joy the smaller of two parcels. Her face lit up at the hand-knitted scarf and she flung her arms around us. This was more like it. I had never met a more physically affectionate human being than Joy. As a child she cried easily, fat, slow tears that encouraged everyone to cuddle her. Even her recent transformation to stroppy young woman hadn't taken that away from her.

"Thanks, Mum, Dad. I love it." She passed it around for admiration.

"The other present's special," said Michael and turned to me. "Do you want to give it to her?"

I nodded and handed over the larger parcel. "I kept a journal – or a history as I called it – when I lived in the Citidome. Once we settled here, I transcribed it onto fiberstone and kept adding to it. We thought now was the right time for you to read it."

Joy's smile almost split her face in two. I relaxed; I'd hoped this acknowledgement of her maturity might end the hostilities between us.

"I want to read it now," she said.

"If you do, there'll be a lot of disappointed guests." I smiled. "And we'll have slaughtered a pig in vain."

It had been an extravagant gesture but we'd wanted her to have a party to remember. Luxuries were hard enough to get hold of. I remembered that first year in the village with nostalgia. Back then, Citidome traders regularly came to the Bakewell market. We never saw them these days; Citidome security had tightened. I could barely remember the taste of chocolate and proper coffee, not the powdered dandelion root that masqueraded for the real thing these days. Not that such fripperies were important. James, the village farmer had died of a chest infection last year. His life could have been saved by antibiotics. Helen, the health worker was now a prematurely aged woman of thirty, struggling with the increasing inadequacies of our medical resources. Her younger brother's death from a fall had cast a shadow over Christmas. The village needed something to celebrate.

"Oh, yeah." Joy grinned. "I feel so important and a little bit guilty. We can't have Bessie dying in vain, can we?" Even so, she started turning the pages of the book.

"You ready?" Daisy's voice rang from the door.

"Go on. Your public awaits," I said.

"Don't worry, I'll be the personification of Joy."

"I'll catch you up," said Michael then turned to me. "You really OK, sweetheart?" His eyes were warm with concern.

"Yeah, apart from the rotten timing. Best party in years and I'm missing out."

"Adam's worth it though, isn't he?"

"Yeah, and luckily he looks more like you than me," I said. I still scrubbed up well on a good day, but now, frizzy hair still sticking to my forehead through sweat, the days when I'd been considered beautiful seemed a distant memory.

"You're still gorgeous." Michael winked. "It's going to be OK. We've coped with more than an unplanned baby, haven't we?"

"Yeah, I guess so." I gathered Adam into my arms and

drew his forehead to mine as I had at the birth of Joy and Scott.

“Here’s to the future,” Michael said.

The future. This could be the year that sealed all of our futures.

CHAPTER 3 - JOY

"Happy birthday!" Beth gave me a parcel. "What's the baby like?"

"Cute, as babies go. But ugh, why does he have to have the same birthday as me?"

"Hey, come on. You know what it's like whenever there's a new baby. When Bridget was born, everyone forgot the rest of us existed."

I opened the present. "Thanks, it's lovely." I wasn't surprised to see a braided horsehair bracelet. Beth's mum Mary worked with horses and always made jewellery at birthdays and Christmas.

"Look what Harry got me, but it's a secret." I held out my necklace.

"Ooh, that's gorgeous," said Beth. "What did your mum and dad give you?"

"This dress, a lovely pink scarf, but best of all, Mum kept a journal when she was my age and they've given me it."

"You're kidding! Have you read any of it yet?"

"A few pages. It's amazing, all about the Citidomes. You can't imagine – Mum chose all her clothes on a DataBand and they got delivered clean every day and then taken away."

"Sounds like bliss." Beth's expression was dreamy.

"And there were loads of tall skinny people like Ryan and Daisy. They even called them BodyPerfects! They'd have said we were fat."

"Really? I can't think of a less perfect body than Ryan. He looks like a runner bean. Can you imagine what he's like with no clothes on?"

We sniggered.

"It sounded a fantastic place to live though," I said. "All that luxury."

"Hard to believe anyone escapes, isn't it? And no-one ever talks about it. Ryan clams up whenever I ask him anything."

"So do Mum and Dad. Most of what I know comes from Harry. He says they're evil; he's convinced they killed his dad."

It was the only aspect of Harry I didn't understand – his burning intensity when he talked about the Citidomes. The look in his eyes when he spoke of them excited and at the same time frightened me.

At that point Matt turned up with his brother David, their sister Dora and her family. But annoyingly, everyone asked, "How's the baby?" before remembering to say "Happy birthday." Then a whole crowd arrived.

"Ah, here's our brood," said Beth.

"Careful your dad doesn't give one of them away," David said with an ugly curl of his lip. He still hadn't forgiven Dad for being moved to Macclesfield, even though he visited often. I thought it a good swap; David had that awful carroty hair that was a hallmark of the villagers, and in return we'd got Mickey, who'd done what was expected of him, and produced a baby with Dora. Sadly, the poor kid had inherited Dora's red hair. Lucky Matt had escaped the family curse; his hair was the colour of ripe wheat. Matt was a good-looking guy, but not the one I wanted.

"Stop it. It's my birthday and you're not allowed to say anything shitty about my dad," I said. "Bloody hell, look at Elsie. Where did she get that dress?"

We turned to stare at Elsie, who at fourteen could pass for eighteen, if it wasn't for her vacant grin. No-one could put their finger on exactly what was wrong with her. People said she was slow, but in other ways she was developing way too quickly, and tonight's display of blatant womanhood had drawn every eye in the room.

"She looks older than us!" I said.

"Looks like hers are wasted though," said Beth cattily. "Who'd have her?"

"Hey, Joy," said Elsie in her slow drawl. "Great dress."

"So's yours." In truth, I couldn't believe Elsie was wearing such a clingy Citidome garment. It must have been designed for a skinny woman and Elsie's curves were bulging through the sheer fabric. You could even see her nipples. My simple cotton frock looked childish in comparison.

"Found it in the dumps, but Mum wouldn't let me cut it low," said Elsie.

Nanna had said that Elsie had inherited her mother's wanton streak. I wasn't certain what wanton meant – Elsie's mother died in childhood so I don't remember her – but it must be something to do with her absence of modesty. Even as a kid she'd been like that; she'd take her knickers down and show the boys everything she'd got in exchange for just about anything.

"Hey everyone," said Ryan, towering above the rest of the gang. "Joy, you look lovely." He bent down to kiss my cheek and gave me a present – a whole box of candies!

"Ooh, fantastic, thanks!" I flushed at his extravagance. Ryan would have had to trade plenty at the market for these. How should I react? I tried to look appreciative without being too encouraging. He was still new; perhaps he didn't know what was appropriate in terms of present giving. Then the music started.

"Come on, birthday girl," said Nanna. "No-one will dance until you do."

Oh no, I'd have to choose a partner. How could I give Matt or Ryan the wrong idea? Then I saw Craig, Beth's fourteen year-old brother, grinning at me. I took his hand.

"Come on, Craig. Let's see what you're made of."

As ever, the music made my spirits soar and I wished Mum could be here; she loved dancing. Sadly Craig couldn't dance at all, his arms and legs looking as if they didn't belong to him. The room filled up as the evening went on – there were about eighty people in the nearby villages, and a few of my friends from the Bakewell market turned up. But not the person I really wanted. I took a break to talk to Beth.

"Did you see that?" Her eyes were dulled with disappointment. "Ryan danced with Elsie! Didn't even glance in my direction! What's wrong with me? Is it my hair? My freckles?"

I didn't know what to say. Beth looked fine; her hair was more strawberry-blonde than carroty and her freckles made her look cute. "There's nothing wrong with you. Maybe he's frightened of rejection?" How could I make her feel better?

"Huh, he noticed you, all right. They've all noticed you.

And they all noticed bloody Elsie. So why are you looking so mopey? Ah, thinking about Harry, are you?"

"Yeah … I knew there was only a slim chance of him making it over here, but I couldn't help hoping."

"Best he didn't. Imagine what your folks would have said. Have they mentioned the spring visit?"

"No. Mum said that if I had any sense I'd stop rowing with Dad or he might decide to cancel it. So I've been the perfect dutiful daughter. But I'll burst if I don't see him soon. Twice a year isn't enough any more. Oh shit, Matt's coming over."

"I'll leave you two lovebirds to it." Beth grinned and left me facing the boy I'd known my entire life.

"Having a good time, Titch?" said Matt.

"My cup runneth over." I flung out my arms. "The fatted calf has been slaughtered. I'm basking in adulation. What's not to like?"

He shook his head. "Bloody daft, you are." His voice lowered. "They're going to play a slow one next. Will you dance with me?"

"Yeah, I guess …" My heart sank and my brain froze.

Matt laughed. "You, lost for words. Never thought I'd see the day. Come on, we've known each other our entire lives. I reckon we can be honest with each other. Do you like me … that way?"

I took a breath and spoke the truth. "I love you, Matt. You're like my big brother, but romantically, no."

"Thought so." Matt grinned. "Anna's been dropping hints that you had a crush on me. Don't look so guilty – I don't see you as anything other than a kid sister either. But I'm getting worried. I overheard your dad talking to Daniel about trading someone in Pontefract. What if it's me? If I don't settle down with you, what use I am around here?"

"But …" As children we'd told each other everything but not this. "I'm in love with someone else."

"Harry. I'm not stupid."

I blushed. "How do you know?"

"Any fool could work it out. I saw the two of you a year or so ago, running across the fields at Longstone Edge, hand-in-hand. Even then, you looked at each other differently to the way me and you do. Then there are those trips to the canals.

You're like a kid before Christmas for the weeks leading up to them and then, afterwards, you're as grumpy as hell."

"But it's hopeless. Mum and Dad caught us kissing last October and they went ballistic. And now I'm not sure if I'm going to see him this spring. Dad wants me to be with you."

"How about we let them all think there's something going on? Maybe you'll get to see him then?"

"Matt, you're a genius! You've got a deal."

He frowned. "How do you know when you love someone, like the way you love Harry?"

"I don't know what to tell you. Harry's always been part of me. He dominates my days and dictates my dreams." I hugged myself.

"Helpful, Titch, really helpful."

"Sorry, let me help you understand. If he was in the room now I wouldn't be able to look at anyone else. When you're in love with someone it's the most intense feeling you can imagine. You feel alive, but at the same time incredibly … vulnerable. You've given someone the power to smash your heart to pieces."

"I've definitely never felt it then," he said, thrusting his hands into his pockets. "Come on, let's make everyone happy."

And as the beautiful melody of a slow song filled the room, I took Matt's hand, led him to the dance floor, ignoring Ryan's stricken expression, and put my arms around his shoulders, all the time imagining he was Harry. I could hardly bear the smile that lit up Dad's face.

CHAPTER 4 - CATHY

I'd barely settled Adam in his crib when Michael returned.

"I knew she'd come round." Michael's voice was triumphant. "Matt and Joy danced together and walked back hand-in-hand."

"Oh good." I rolled my sleepy eyes. "Who did Ryan dance with?"

"Elsie." Michael frowned. "That girl's becoming a real worry. She was wearing an indecently tight-fitting dress – the sort that Uma used to wear in the Citidome."

"I'll have a word with Tia." Remembering how the disabled had been forbidden from entering the Citidomes when they were first constructed, I felt a compulsion to protect Elsie, but her precocious behaviour was getting out of hand.

"We can't let her reproduce." Michael's voice was nagging, insistent. "Didn't think we'd have to worry about it for a while yet, but seeing her tonight ..."

"She's fourteen. I was only thirteen when I donated stem cells in the Citidome, remember. But let's talk about it in the morning." I yawned.

Gene pools again. The next generation was Michael's constant preoccupation. The only reason communities had thrived was because of the steady influx of young people from the Citidomes, and since escapees had become such a rare occurrence, everyone's future was threatened. Our community had a shortage of under forties and, last year, kids as young as Scott had been recruited to gather the harvest. In terms of children, ours was one of the best communities in the region: ten under eighteen, but three were mine, four Mary's. If the AOC's plan didn't come to fruition, some would have to move when they became adults.

Adam began to cry.

"Damn it, I'd just got him to sleep."

"Don't get up, I'll see to him." Michael picked him up. "How's my little man?"

Adam's sobs subsided and were replaced by contented gurgles. He seemed to have taken to his father more than he'd taken to me. Perhaps he sensed my mixed feelings towards him. Michael returned him to his crib and peace was restored. But why hadn't Michael joined me? Oh, of course. I sighed. Silly of me to think he might go to bed without checking his DataBand.

"Three messages," he said. "Aidan's stripped down an entire hospital in Manchester. There'll be a massive supply of plumbing materials ready for us in a couple of weeks. Better tell Dee; we'll need the boat."

As Michael punched the air, I couldn't help smiling. Aidan had been a plumber in the Citidomes and trained people from around the country. His other talent was scouring the old cities and tearing into buildings for useful materials. For a while now, Michael had been waiting for him to take on a large project; for his plan he needed plenty of supplies. And perhaps I'd get to see Dee, one of my closest friends.

"It's really going to happen, Cathy. A farming academy, right in the middle of Ashford. If we ever get anyone to fill it."

"We will, after Outbreak-4." The farming academy excited me almost as much as it did Michael. "Of all the things that would bring down our community, I never thought it would be lack of skilled labour."

"Me neither." He sighed. "To lose James and then Paul in the space of a year. It makes you realise how vulnerable we are. And then that community near Oxford losing their entire herd of cattle…"

"Who's the other message from?"

"Dai, wishing Joy a happy birthday and wondering how you are."

"That's nice." The man had started the entire Outbreak operation. He'd escaped from Psi-1, a Citidome further south, five years ago and settled in a nearby community. From him we'd learnt about how Doodlebugs, an illegal site similar to our old beloved Truth Exchange, was spreading around all the Citidomes. I began to recall a conversation we'd had a while ago.

"Why Doodlebugs?" I'd asked.

"All the obvious names about truth, freedom and knowledge get picked up on the authority searches," Dai had explained.

"That figures. In our day, Truth Exchange was shut down. And they're well-supported?"

"We have more than a thousand members; now we need to work out how to get them out."

"That's wonderful! How did you get out?"

"I stabbed a guard with a jagged piece of metal. I wasn't proud of it, but I was desperate. Force is the only way to get out these days. In future, it'd be best to get groups of ten or more to leave at once. They could overcome guards without injuring them. But people are scared about what's out here."

Dai was an IT genius, and had linked Out There, our own web-based communications system, to Doodlebugs, enabling us to directly contact rebels inside the Citidomes. Following this breakthrough, Michael had called a meeting of the AOC. The alliance, comprising representatives from all known communities, had grown each year. Fifty regional leaders met regularly and all communicated via DataBands that had previously belonged to Citidome escapees. Each leader reported any changes in population to Michael, giving him the answer to a question that had plagued us for years. The known population of State 11 living outside the Citidomes was 19,251 and we hadn't ruled out the possibility of discovering new communities. It sounded like plenty. But with a growing shortage of reproducing females, it could die out within two generations.

And out of the meeting had come a plan. A number of outbreaks, involving a group of around twenty escaping from each Citidome, had been organised. Outbreaks 1 and 2, spaced at two-year intervals, had taken the authorities by surprise and almost everyone had escaped unscathed. That's why Michael had become over-ambitious.

Three months ago, Michael hatched his ludicrous idea after he came across one of the nearby correction camps, outdoor prisons where the Marked and so-called subversive thinkers were forced into manual labour. Over the next year, accommodation would be prepared for those we managed to liberate from the camp. Those with useful skills would be settled into a community that needed them, the others would be trained in academies around the country, each housing on average thirty people. In my view, the plan was fraught with pitfalls, not least the practicality of removing RedTags, a form of tracker, that were attached to all prisoners' ears. I knew about those tags only too well, the ragged stump that used to be my left ear was a permanent reminder of the one that had been sealed into my earlobe and hacked off with a knife.

"There's a message from Tau-2 as well. Yumi's been arrested; that's our tenth Hero in the correction camp." Michael put down the DataBand. "Can you believe we're really going to do it?" he said. "If this comes off, it'll be our greatest achievement."

"Mmm," I murmured.

"I'll send a message to Dee while I'm thinking about it – tell her about the baby and see whether she'll be able to transport the plumbing supplies."

"I'm sure she'll be asleep, like most sane people are at this time. Why don't you ask if she wants to come and visit for a few days? I don't think I can face the spring trip to the canal. And she'll be dying to see Adam."

"Good idea. But what about Harry?"

"Invite him too; you could brief him about Outbreaks 3 and 4. If Joy's chosen Matt, you've nothing to worry about. If not, well you know how strong-willed she is. It'll take more than me and you to keep them apart."

"OK." He input the message, and climbed into bed.

"You're freezing!" I drew the woollen blanket closer. "You never rest these days. Why don't you have a few weeks at home? Send Helen on a few trips. Alex could deputise for her if there's any medical emergencies."

"I might, but she's not very assertive in meetings."

"She's not very assertive full stop. I told you Daisy would be a better choice."

I liked Helen but she was such a mouse; she hung on Michael's every word and never questioned him. Perhaps that's why he chose her as the AOC representative – Daisy was too argumentative.

"We've gone through this before. We need to represent the needs of the village-born as well as Citidome escapees. And it's useful to have a health worker on the committee."

Sleep overtook the urge for a sarcastic reply.

The next morning was Sunday, and light was streaming through the curtains when I woke. Michael of course was already up. I leapt out of bed in panic – was Adam OK? – but he was beginning to stir. I lifted him to my breast and gazed out of the window. Fat snowflakes were falling and had coated the tree branches with white lace. My spirits rose. I never lost my sense of wonder at seeing the drab winter landscape transformed by snow. Then Adam started crying. Why did he feel so odd in my arms?

"Better get used to sore nipples again," I said to myself. Soon I felt the soft suckling sensation and peace descended on me. At least he was feeding normally. Funny, the young, ambitious girl I used to be would never have dreamed that her destiny was to have been a mother, but motherhood had been the greatest joy in my life. Until now. My memories of Joy and Scott as babies were among my happiest. That sweet smell of them. I leant down and took a long sniff of Adam. Yes, the same aroma was there. So the problem was me, not him.

"How's our little Adam?" Michael had entered the room with a cup of tea.

"Hungry. At this rate I'll have two empty balloons attached to my chest. What time is it?"

"Just after nine. Thought you needed the sleep."

"Oh hell. What about – "

"Everyone's had breakfast. Scott's gone out with Mary's gang to have a snowball fight, though they'll be lucky – there's barely two centimetres on the ground. But you'd better come down soon. Joy's desperate to talk to you."

"What now?" I frowned. "Why are teenage girls so much more difficult than boys?"

"You never know; Scott might turn into a monster when he hits adolescence." He winked.

"Yeah, maybe we should keep him nine forever. He's

perfect right now. Old enough to be good company, not too old to think he knows better than me. No angst, living for the moment. Joy was the same at that age; remember when all she wanted to do was climb trees?"

"Yeah, and I remember the time she fell off and we thought she'd broken her ribs. Ah well, the advantage of having kids so spread in ages means we'll always have one at a good stage. By the time Scott goes off the rails, this one'll be kicking a ball around." He kissed the top of Adam's head.

"That's one way of looking at it." I grinned and then, without warning, my eyes filled with tears. I blinked them back.

"Hey, what is it?" Michael crouched down beside me.

"Oh, I don't know. Every time I look at him I think … have I got the energy to go through it all again?"

"We'll get there. I know I haven't been around as much as I should, but we'll be careful about safe times in future."

I suppressed a sigh. That was the problem, wasn't it? One slip up, and I was the one left holding the baby while Michael went off being the great leader. I kept myself remote from the AOC, being officially dead, but was a member of the village council. And for the last twelve years I'd been the community teacher, a job I loved. But now all that was on hold. At least the Citidomes had no inequality of gender, although injustices abounded in every other sphere.

"I thought we were being careful until Scott's birthday party last year. I blame Anna's rose petal wine." I giggled at the memory. "Give me five minutes and I'll be down to see Joy."

When I came down, Adam squirming in my arms, I wondered if Michael had been mistaken. Joy was curled up on the sofa, engrossed in my journal.

"Morning, sweetheart," I said.

Joy looked up but didn't smile, instead shooting me an accusing stare.

"Why the hell did no-one tell me I had a sister?" she said.

"Suna." My voice was faint. The wrench of losing the biological daughter I never knew had lessened with each of the children I'd given birth to, but never quite left me. "What can I tell you, other than what's written there? I've put her out of my mind. Once I had you, the child I'd never known, whose father was an anonymous stem cell donor, didn't seem so important. I must admit, she haunted me for a while. She looked so like me. She must be – let's think – twenty now. But what was the point of telling you? You'd only upset yourself because you'd never met her."

"But Nanna contacted Dad after she escaped. Why couldn't we? Her full name's here – Suna 121968."

I smiled. I'd never forgotten Suna's date of birth.

"Too dangerous these days. We'd know her already if she was part of Doodlebugs and as for any other means, the last time I heard of anyone trying was around ten years ago – an escapee who tried to message his friend. Three days later, the authorities came and fingerprinted the whole village. They dragged him back to the Citidome – I guess they put him in a correction camp."

"So there's nothing we can do?"

Then Michael spoke and his words gave me a peculiar shiver. "We could, you know."

CHAPTER 5 - JOY

Dad looked at Mum with that weird expression people got when speaking of the Citidomes. "We should have thought of her before," he said. "She could be exactly what we need. You see, we're targeting women that have a chance of reproducing naturally."

"Targeting for what?" I said.

"Another Outbreak, like the one that brought Ryan," Dad said. "Sigma-2's one of the Citidomes shortlisted for the next one. Don't ever repeat that to anyone. Not Matt, not Beth. We organise them through knowledge bases that have links with rebels in the Citidomes."

"What, subversive thinkers?" I grinned. I was starting to get my head around these new Citidome terms.

"That's right," Dad said.

"But we don't know anything about her. I'd love to think that she was the sort to question the system, but so many didn't…" Mum drifted off into her own world and I knew there was no point in probing further.

"Leave it with me; I'll see what I can find out," Dad said then turned to me. "I had a message from Dee this morning. I'm going to Sheffield in a few weeks to pick up some plumbing materials. She reckons she and Harry'll have time to come here for a few days; they want to see Adam. Want to come along for the ride and see the narrowboat?"

I lowered my head. Don't blush, act casual. Oh hell. My heart was thumping so hard it was probably visible.

"Er, dunno. I'll see how busy I am."

"Is Matt going to be OK, having Harry around?" Dad's eyes were probing mine, trying to suss out my reaction.

"Yeah, he understands we're just friends. You know, what happened in October was a mistake. It's easier to be with someone who's around the whole time." I twirled my hair around my finger. "But I can't imagine not being friends with

Harry. Actually, maybe I should come to Sheffield with you, then I could ride with Harry in the cart. It'd be good to talk to him before he gets here, in case he's upset about me and Matt."

Mum and Dad nodded, their expressions soft and understanding. Finally, I'd found something for which I had a natural talent – deceit!

I spent the day engrossed in Mum's journal, my understanding growing with every page. And as I read, I realised that what Mum had loved in Dad were the same things I loved in Harry. Fervour, passion, hunger for knowledge. And I had a feeling that Harry knew more than he was letting on. The knowledge bases and outbreaks – was Harry involved?

"One day I'll destroy every Citidome in the country," Harry had said to me last October. "Then we'll recolonise the old cities, the ones with beauty and history and souls."

"Why not live in the Citidome?" I'd asked. "At least it wouldn't rain all the time."

"Because of everything they stand for." Harry had clenched his fist. "Conformity. Captivity. Superficiality."

At the time I'd thrilled at the passion in his voice, without understanding his words. Now I was beginning to. And I needed to talk to him. The thought of a society that made my beautiful mum and dad feel ugly had fired me up.

"Funny to think I'm the product of non-perfect genes," I said to Mum.

"There's nothing non-perfect about you," Mum replied. "But it's an eye-opener, isn't it? I know you romanticised the Citidomes; this was the best way of helping you understand."

"Yeah, I never realised. Mum … I need to know more."

"Get to the end, then we'll talk about it, I promise."

Really? I thrilled with anticipation. What had I known about the Citidomes before now? The obvious protection from the weather and also that people didn't give birth naturally, and didn't have relationships. What I hadn't been aware of were the restrictions on freedom. Sometimes, in the bitter chill of winter, I'd fantasised about living under the comfort of the dome. But now I began to understand. Citidome life was utopian for the chosen ones, torture for those who didn't conform. But how much freedom was there out here? Who cared that I didn't want to marry Matt or teach kids who didn't want to learn?

My reading was interrupted by the arrival of a wet boy, shaking like the sheep after they'd been dipped.

"I got Craig clean in the eye with a snowball so he rolled me down the bank," Scott said. "You should've come. Hey, what're you reading?"

"None of your business, it's for adults only," I said with a tilt of my chin.

"Stop acting uppity just 'cos you're gonna be my teacher tomorrow," Scott taunted. Ugh, he could be so annoying. "I'm not gonna call you Miss Joy, you know. In fact … Dad, can I stop school this year, rather than next?"

"Not a hope in hell," said Dad in that tone of voice that said, 'No arguments'.

I turned to Mum. Why had she chosen me to take over as the community teacher while she took leave to care for Adam? "You see, it's not going to work. They'll never take me seriously."

"Don't be silly, Joy. You'll be wonderful. Besides, it's only until June. Then after the summer break I'll be ready to take over again."

I shrugged and immersed myself once more in the journal, but became distracted by daydreams. If I lived with Harry on the boat, no-one would expect me to take on jobs I didn't want. I could spend my days reading, watching nature, listening to music, and not being interrupted by screaming babies who smelt disgusting. Lucky Harry; he had the perfect life.

***

The school day ended at three and I trudged to the stables to see the horses and dogs, the air heavy with the sweet, pungent scent of hay and manure. Mary was there as usual.

"How are your mum and the baby?" Her question was predictable.

"Oh, fine. Mum's a bit tired. Has Tinker had the puppies?" I asked.

"This morning, come and see." Mary had domesticated some dogs that she let have puppies every time a village woman had a baby. If the mother was unable to breastfeed, we used the bitch's milk.

I knelt over the tiny creatures that barely resembled dogs, eyes squeezed shut.

"They're so sweet," I whispered. "Talking of litters, I've just sent yours home."

"Bang goes my peace then." Mary grinned. "How did it go?"

I sighed. "Terrible. Ian pretended to be the village bull and charged at me."

"It takes time. You're not much older than them."

"That's the trouble. I don't know why Mum chose me."

"Because you're so brainy. Besides, who else is there? Dora's busy with her own kids, and my Beth, bless her, can hardly read herself."

"I'd be a farmer's wife with ten brats nipping at my heels if Dad has anything to do with it."

"You wait until you're ready," said Mary. "Still, I saw you with Matt last night. So are you and he…?"

"Yeah, we finally got it together," I said. Much as I'd like to, I couldn't afford to trust Mary. I gazed longingly at the two horses, both kitted out for riding, the ancient, cracked leather saddles giving off the honey aroma of beeswax. "Any chance of a ride?"

"Actually, I'm expecting Ryan any time. I'm going to give him a riding lesson. Unless you'd like to?"

"Does that mean I get to go on Blue Boy? OK, why not?"

Blue Boy was the larger of the two adult horses, a handsome chestnut gelding with a small white star on his forehead. Riding him was a rare treat.

"Of course. Ah, here he is." She turned to smile at him. "Change of plan, Ryan. I'm leaving you in Joy's hands."

Of course, the downside of this was being alone with Ryan. The smile that crept over his smooth face was an attractive one, but it left me feeling uncomfortable, though judging by Ryan's wide eyes, not as uncomfortable as he was with horses.

"OK, Ryan," I said. "First, you need to show Bramble

you're not scared of her."

"But I am scared." He grinned. "Terrified would be nearer the mark."

"Hang on." I took a carrot from a nearby sack. "Put your hand out, flat."

He extended a hand, rigid apart from a slight tremor.

"Now hold still." I placed the carrot on his palm and led the horse to the hand, from where it took the treat.

"Hmm, soft mouth," Ryan said.

"And your hand's intact. You're so tall, you won't even need a leg up. Put one foot in the stirrup and swing the other over. That's it."

"It's a long way from the ground." He screwed up his smooth face.

"So don't look down. Sit square and look ahead. That's it. Now pick up the reins."

I mounted Blue Boy without thinking – I'd been riding horses since I was five – and together we trotted around the yard. The stiffness began to fall from Ryan's posture, and after ten minutes we ventured out to the bridle path.

"You're doing fine," I said.

"You're a good teacher."

"I've always loved horses. I'd love to be in charge of them but Mary has the monopoly on that job."

"Matt told me she used to … trade herself. Is that right?"

"Yeah, but don't say so in front of Beth; she doesn't know. It was around the time I was born, apparently. But after that the Citidome trader stopped coming and she discovered she was pregnant with Beth."

"I don't get it. Mary's so –"

"Nice? Respectable? Mary's one of the loveliest people I know. You have to remember, out here sometimes you don't always do what you want. You do what's for the greater good." I scowled.

"Are you talking about yourself there?" Ryan's gaze penetrated, as if he could see right inside me. Damn, mustn't give anything away.

"Well I didn't choose to be a teacher. Today I tried to teach arithmetic to my brother and his friends, but all they did was make fun of me and didn't do a single sum I set. But there's no-one else available until Mum's less tied up with Adam. That's just the way it is around here. I don't suppose Mary wanted to go with the trader every week, but she got medicines for the village, that screen we have the movies on, all sorts of extras."

"So Beth's father was the trader?"

"Yes, that's why she doesn't look like her brothers and sisters. Vincent married Mary later."

"Shame for Beth," he commented. "Vincent brought the good looks, didn't he?"

My shoulders slumped. As I suspected, Ryan didn't find Beth attractive. Damn.

"Life out here's hard to get my head around," he continued. "There's a whole different philosophy, isn't there?"

"Yeah, and sometimes not an easy one. Take Bramble. She's getting old and lame. Soon we'll shoot her and eat her."

"You're joking?"

"I'm not. Not bad meat, horse, though she'll be stringy by now. Frank will have to mince her. Don't look at me like that, I hate it as much as you do, but why not eat a horse if we eat a pig? Equality for all animals."

"In that case, why not eat a human? Must've been good meat on that guy who died soon after I arrived, Paul, wasn't it?"

"Ah, this is one of my favourite subjects." I smiled. "Me and Harry, my friend on the canal, have had endless arguments about this. You're right, of course. The theory goes that animals don't have the same rights as humans because they lack intelligence. But does that make Elsie's life inherently less valuable because she isn't intelligent? And what about a human who was so mentally incapacitated that he had no intelligence whatsoever. Would you eat him?"

"Good point. But you could argue that sometimes we treat animals better than humans."

"Oh yeah? Give me one example."

"If Bramble was sick, and you knew she wouldn't recover, what would you do?"

"Shoot her, put her out of her misery."

"But that young guy, Paul. Everyone knew he couldn't

survive, but did anyone do anything to put him out of his misery? I heard he died slowly and painfully."

"Good point yourself!" I grinned.

Ryan had more about him than I'd imagined. I couldn't have this sort of conversation with Beth and Matt; they'd raise their eyebrows and tell me to lighten up. We continued debating until I said, "Time to turn round or you won't be able to walk in the morning."

"So we have to agree that we'll always discriminate on the basis of species," Ryan said.

"Absolutely. I have to say I prefer animals. Look how gentle Bramble's been. She understands your fear. Twice the intelligence of Elsie."

"Thought I was hiding the fear."

"Your knuckles are white." I grinned.

"What's actually wrong with Elsie?"

"No-one's sure, but they say the umbilical cord wrapped around her when she was born. She didn't get enough oxygen to her brain. Could be worse though. Her mother, Vanessa – she was Vincent's sister – died of an infection in childbirth. Beautiful, apparently, and never wanted to settle down and have kids, but eventually she bowed to pressure and look what happened to her." I shuddered. "That's why I'm never having children."

"Ah, that explains where Elsie gets her looks from."

"Guess you find her attractive." I smiled. I couldn't imagine someone as bright as Ryan being with Elsie, but it'd stop him looking at me in that disconcerting way.

"Yeah, she's a looker all right. But the way she is – I wouldn't go there." His expression became serious; his eyes narrowed. "What are you doing with Matt? Is your dad forcing you into being with him?"

"What do you mean?"

"I like him, but you can run cerebral rings round him. You're no more suited to him than I am to Beth. We're two of a kind; can't you see? Misfits, not belonging in this village of drudgery and routine, nor those other bubbles of conformity."

"Matt's the one I've chosen. I'm sorry."

His eyes bored in to me again; he could see my lie. Best

change the subject.

"But you're not a misfit," I said. "Why do you feel that way?"

"In the Citidome I thought I was fit but I haven't got the strength of the guys here; Matt and Mickey can lift twice what I can. So they give me all the menial jobs: fixing fences and walls, that sort of thing. I can't even help in the dairy."

"It's traditionally a girl's job. We have a softer touch." I giggled. "But you're not missing much. Pretty smelly and stuffy under a cow, y'know."

"Yeah." He wrinkled his nose, and then sadness flickered across his face.

"Are you unhappy here?" I felt compelled to ask.

"No, I'm grateful to be here, but I'd like to find something I'm good at."

"I did an experiment once. I tried to grow herbs indoors, but I didn't give them enough sunlight. They grew tall, pale and spindly, but they had no strength and died. They call it etiolated – I read it in a book. That's what BodyPerfects are like out here."

"Not much comfort." His gaze dropped to the floor.

"Sorry, I didn't mean that to come out the way it did. What I mean is, you don't have the right sort of muscles for life out here yet, but you will. Here muscles are for strength, not for beauty. The less you fit the norm there, the more you're suited to the outdoor world. Talk to Daisy; she had the same problems."

"But I didn't fit in the Citidome either. Superficially I did, but for anyone with a hint of curiosity it's a living death."

His expression was so desolate that I put my hand on his arm.

"You're not the only one who's not good at anything around here," I said. "I'm the world's worst teacher. Tomorrow, I'll produce goldenseal tincture with Daisy at the factory because that's all we do these days. No idea why we need so much. No-one tells me anything. Then we'll sterilise bottles and I'll lose concentration and make a mistake, like I did last week. Anyway, nearly back. You did well."

Ryan smiled, and mouthed something I couldn't quite catch but appeared to be "two of a kind." And it occurred to me that, if Harry had never existed and I had the choice of only two men, Matt wouldn't have been my choice.

***

"Where's Mum?" I asked.

"Taken Adam to Kate's house." Scott wrinkled his nose. "Dunno why women think he's so interesting. He doesn't do anything."

"Except scream and stink the house out with his nappies." I laughed. "Come on, let's me and you get dinner ready, then I can read."

"That old book again? You're getting boring."

But that journal was addictive, and as soon as dinner was over I immersed myself in it once more.

"Kell, Dee and Harry!" I read and succumbed to a wave of melancholia at the thought of Harry's dad. "I loved Kell. He used to let me plait his dreadlocks."

"We all loved him," said Mum. "It's so hard on Dee and Harry, not knowing whether he's dead or imprisoned."

"What happened to him?" Scott asked.

"He'd gone to help a pregnant woman; she'd been sighted huddled by the road," Mum said. "He went to investigate and no-one ever saw him again."

I remembered it vividly. Harry had been twelve, me eleven. Mum and I had spent a week with Dee on the boat to help her through it. On the first night I'd heard Harry sobbing and crept into bed beside him, intertwined with him, absorbing his grief. Mum didn't have the heart to forbid it.

I read on. "Fin was a creepy guy, wasn't he? Whatever happened to him?"

Mum's eyes darted to Dad.

"We never saw him again,' Dad said. 'We sent the word back to Hest Bank that your mum had died in childbirth, in case he ever came looking for her. That's one of the reasons she didn't join me in the AOC. When we formed the Alliance, we needed a representative from that region, but he refused to join, because one of our aims was to get more people out of the Citidomes. So they got themselves another leader. He stayed there, but refused to acknowledge the

AOC, which is just as well, because if I ever saw him I'd thump him. I heard his health isn't so good these days."

"He sounds horrendous. How dare he dictate who should be with who?" I commented, my eyes challenging Dad in what I hoped was a provocative way.

"I can't forgive him what he did to your mum. But we both had the same aims. He wanted the communities to survive as much as I did. But he went about it the wrong way. Fathering so many children himself wasn't the solution. Genetic diversity's what we need."

"But we're doing all right, aren't we?"

"Not really. Back then, we had thirteen villagers between eighteen and forty-five to work the land. Now we have eight."

"You have more children now than then."

"But four of them are Mary's, three ours." he said.

"Yeah, I guess it's not the best gene pool. But communities out here have survived for over a hundred years."

"Twenty communities have died out in the last ten years and we've had to relocate their remaining members to other places." Dad's mouth was set tight.

"Really?"

"Yeah. The Out There knowledge base helps. We're better organised than we used to be; these days people specialise in different types of farming. But some people still live on wild food. The thing that's saved us has been trading animals to mix the bloodlines."

"And people." My voice was heavy with accusation.

"What choice do I have?"

I looked at Dad, saw the strain behind his eyes, and realised with astonishment that he was treating me as an equal, an adult, for the first time.

"I understand," I said. "And I think, deep down, that Matt does, too. You had to trade David."

"It wasn't an easy decision, but we needed a husband for Dora. She's the only village woman in her twenties and look how happy she is now with Mickey and little Bridget. We don't get Citidome escapees any more. Our population's shrinking."

"You know, the more I read, the more it seems to me that

neither of the new societies – both inside and out of the Citidomes – really work. We need a new blueprint. Why did they abandon the old ways of living?"

"That, my beautiful, brilliant daughter, is what I want to restore." Dad smiled. "The Citidomes aren't intrinsically bad places but there needs to be free movement in and out of them. Our two worlds need to be integrated."

"Wow, you honestly think that's possible?"

"Maybe, maybe not in our lifetimes. But I like to dream."

"I'd certainly choose to live in a Citidome in the winter. Did you ever find the *Blueprint for a new Society*?"

"Yes. It had everything in it: Mind Values, the Domes. It was a philosophical study. They were planning to initiate it on a small scale in the USO – that's the United States of the Orient –in just one Citidome. Volunteers – students and intellectuals – were going to take part in an experiment to create the ideal society. It's based on a concept called self-actualisation. The theory is that when all your basic needs are met, you can reach your full potential as a human being. So without the threat of war and extreme weather, and the distraction of unnecessary attachment, the human race could evolve and people could realise their full intellectual potential."

"Really?" Realising your full intellectual potential. Such evocative words, and something I could never hope to achieve. "Sounds like a dream."

At that point, Adam started to cry and Mum left the room, Adam in her arms. Did I imagine it, or did she mutter something under her breath about her own potential? Poor Mum. It had surprised me to see what a high-flyer she'd been at my age: fast-tracked through her studies and with such an important job. I guess that having me had ended her potential. The thought wasn't a comfortable one.

"Yeah, well, it became a nightmare," Dad said. "When most of State 11 was wiped out by the Thebula virus, they implemented it on a large scale. But they only wanted what they saw as the superior humans so they excluded the intellectually challenged, people with disabilities and chronic diseases, and the elderly."

"So the ideals got corrupted?"

"Exactly. And no-one could do anything to change it. Anyone who challenged the system was kicked out or locked up. Citizens of the USO should be allowed the right to vote for a government, but we never had any say in how the Citidomes were run. People should have a right to opt out of that way of living."

My mind span. Harry had told me that Citidomes were governed by the USO, but it didn't seem a big deal and I'd laughed at his concern. What was the point of government anyway? The community had always had leaders but until Dad started the AOC, there had been no other organisation and everyone had muddled along. Never before had the plight of Citizens, effectively imprisoned in their giant bubbles, entered my mind.

I continued with the book, and was unable to stop until much later in the evening when I reached the end, and realised that the problems I'd brought on Mum were much, much worse than ending her career. A tight knot of guilt bound my guts.

"M-mum." I turned to her. "Your ear."

Mum smoothed back her hair. "Not a dog bite after all," she said. "We thought you were too young to know the truth."

And in that moment, the fight against the Citidomes became my fight too.

CHAPTER 6 - CATHY

"I can't believe they did that to you." Joy hugged me first, then Michael, and when she pulled away, I saw an expression I'd never seen in her before, something harder, colder. Would this be the knowledge that would allow Joy to mature? Over the last year it had saddened me to see her take her happy life for granted, become resentful of the responsibilities of adulthood, selfish even.

"It was my fault." Her voice was small.

"No it wasn't," I said. "When I first saw you, it was the greatest, most intense feeling of my whole life. Never blame yourself. Blame the people who run the Citidomes."

"I hate them, Mum. They almost killed you. They took Harry's dad away. Dad, what are you planning? I know it's more than another outbreak. You're away far more often than you were before Ryan arrived. I want to be involved. Don't say I'm too young – Harry knows way more than I do."

Michael gave me an anxious glance. I nodded – Joy should be told. Nearer the time we'd need everyone's involvement, but for now we'd tried to keep a degree of secrecy around the plans; AOC members and their close family only. We knew from bitter experience that not everyone on the outside could be trusted. But Joy at her best was bright, trustworthy and resourceful, exactly the sort of person we needed. And now, looking at the fire in her eyes, so like Michael's, I knew she deserved the truth.

"We're going to trust you with a huge secret, but remember, hardly anyone knows about it," Michael said. "The breakout we're planning from one of the Citidomes in November, is going to be small-scale, like the one that Ryan was involved in. But it's just a smokescreen. It's going to be followed by a much bigger breakout from one of the correction camps."

"But how will you do it? I thought those places hold

hundreds of people?"

"Yeah, that's why this has been almost two years in the planning. People called Heroes are getting themselves sent to the correction camps to prepare them from the inside. There'll be a team of armed rescuers outside to shoot if necessary, and we're going to blow up one of the nearby factories to account for the missing people. The escapees are going to go into underground bunkers until we're sure it's safe for them to come out."

"Underground bunkers? Where are they?"

"They're a well-kept secret. They were built centuries ago. You see, there were always threats to peace when people lived in the old ways. First it was nuclear war then biological war. Governments built enormous bunkers to make sure the population survived the aftermath of a war. But the Thebula virus attack came without warning so they were never used. They still have beds and carpets inside. Helen's located the nearest one to the correction camp."

"Helen's part of this?"

"Yeah, we need at least one health worker at the scene. We were lucky with the first and second outbreaks – we caught them off guard – but they might be better prepared now. We're gambling on the fact that they won't expect the correction camp outbreak only days after the Citidome one but people might get wounded in the struggle. The people in the camps have RedTags attached to their ears, and we'll need trained people to remove them."

"As quickly as possible." I massaged my own mutilated ear.

"Ah…that's why we've been making so much antiseptic." Joy's eyes widened.

"Exactly. We have no idea how we'll we get the tags off hundreds of people, and how the CEs will fight back. They're usually only armed with stun guns but they won't be much use against a mass riot; I can't believe they don't have other weaponry. We've instructed the people in the Citidome outbreak to bring as many medical supplies as we can, but we don't know what we'll be dealing with."

"Can I be part of the medical team? I've never been squeamish," she asked, and I shivered. Having Joy at the scene wasn't what I'd had in mind. It was bad enough that Michael was going. But right now, Joy was the loving, enthusiastic daughter I'd been so close to, and hearing the passion in her voice, I wanted to preserve this moment.

"Yes, of course you can. But it's a grisly job. We need as many trained people as we have scalpels; we have to do it so quickly, you see."

"Ugh." Joy shuddered. "Dad, the blood – you won't be able to help."

Joy understood. Since her birth, Michael had a phobia about blood. Two years ago she'd gashed her knee falling off a horse and Michael had been unable to look.

"I feel so stupid," he muttered. "But I'll be no use there. I'm going to co-ordinate the transportation."

"I'll help Helen," Joy said and my heart swelled.

"Sweetheart, that's wonderful," Michael and I said in unison.

"How many escapees will there be if it's successful?" Joy asked.

"Hard to say. About twenty from Outbreak-3, that's the Citidome one. As for the correction camp, it could be up to a thousand."

"A lot of things are slotting into place," said Joy. "Is that why Sam's working on that big old house in the village?"

"Yeah. It's going to be an academy, housing up to thirty people." He paused, then added, "We're setting up ten of them around the country, each specialising in something practical. Ours is going to be –"

"Don't tell me, farming." Joy grinned.

"Spot on. We need more expertise. James used to be a legend on Out There." I thought of the old farmer with affection.

"So there'll be thirty young men for me and Beth to choose from?" Joy said, a wicked grin creeping across her face.

"Yeah, but only for the six months they're in training. We'll keep one or two for ourselves. The rest will be allocated to other communities. And they don't have to be men; we might have some strong women, too," I said, mostly to provoke Michael.

"But most of them are likely to be men," Michael

countered.

"BodyPerfects?" Joy asked.

"No. They're strong, but not in the right way," Michael said. "We'll use them for other skilled labour; plumbing and the like."

"Ryan was telling me how useless he feels on the farm compared to Matt." Joy rubbed her chin. "Ooh, I wish I could tell Beth. Don't look at me like that. Of course I won't. But if there's going to be an army of fit young men, why are you so keen on fixing me up with Matt and Beth with Ryan? And don't look all innocent; I'm not stupid."

I grinned, relishing Michael's discomfort. How was he going to talk his way out of this one?

"Well … OK, I admit, I'd rather see you with Matt than with a Citidome escapee. The people who escape will be fine, idealistic young people but a lot of them will be Marked. I'm the last one to discriminate, but I'd hate to think of anything disfiguring your perfect skin."

"Aw, that's sweet." Joy grinned. "I have to admit, it's not a good look. This is a lot to get my head around. Dad, would it be OK if I used the DataBand sometime? I'd like to understand more."

"Yeah, I'll show you how to use it." He looked down to read a message that had come through from Doodlebugs, the lines around his eyes deepening. Then he jerked upwards and looked at me.

"You're not going to believe this. I asked my contact in Sigma-2 if he could locate Suna, and he's found her details."

I caught my breath. "H-has he made contact with her?"

"No. And he won't be able to." His voice lowered. "She's a CE."

After all these years, those two letters could still transport me back. I was sitting in the TravelPod between two CEs, hands bound together, consumed by terror as the CE told me of my fate – to give birth live on a media show called *Vile Bodies*.

"Correction Enforcer?" Joy asked.

"That's right," Michael said and turned to me. "You OK?"

I gave the briefest of nods. "I suppose it was unrealistic to think that she'd be a ministry worker who questioned the system, but I'd hoped for more for her than to become someone who enforced it."

"It's a good job." Michael shrugged. "All those privileges."

"But sometimes they escape. That guy in Hest Bank used to be a CE, didn't he?" Joy said.

"Yeah, but he's an exception." I shivered. The image of Fin telling me that Michael was dead now swirled with the other bad memories. "He had to pull out his tracker – he had a huge scar on his face. There's no way we can contact Suna: her every move's recorded. No, we'll have to accept it."

I slumped in the armchair as Michael showed Joy how to access the Out There forums. I hadn't expected to make instant contact with Suna but the fact that she was a CE seemed such a betrayal, even though there was nothing to betray. What was I to Suna other than a stem cell provider? And seeing the animation in Joy's eyes as she scanned the topics under discussion, I pushed my first-born child from my thoughts and watched with increasing discomfort as Joy gave herself to the cause that had taken Michael.

And then Adam started crying again.

It was going to be a long, hard year.

CHAPTER 7 - JOY

On Sunday, I rode to Little Longstone, my spirits soaring. Cantering across the meadow and jumping the hedge was surely the closest a human could get to flying: the rush of air, the exhilaration, my long hair blowing in my face. And the connection I felt to Bramble at these times was something I felt for no other living thing. This huge creature would blindly jump any obstacle for me, not knowing where she was going to land.

"You've got the right idea, Bramble," I said. "Where's the fun in always knowing every place you're heading for, or every move you're going to take?"

Soon I arrived at the community surgery.

"Joy, good to see you." Helen smiled in her characteristic serene way. There was something of Jane Eyre about her. She wasn't beautiful, but she had a composure I envied. Nothing rattled her. But since the death of her brother, a cloud had descended on her, the deep shadows under her eyes telling of sleepless nights.

"I wish you'd come to the party," I said, though I hadn't been surprised not to see her there. She wasn't the party type.

"I wanted to keep an eye on Bridget. She had colic," said Helen.

"Is she OK?"

"She's fine now."

"Good. But this isn't just a social call. I'm here because Dad told me all about the Outbreak plans."

"Oh ..." Helen sucked in her already thin lips. "I hope you haven't told anyone else."

"Of course not! Mum said you need an assistant on the medical side."

"Yeah." Helen sighed. "It's hard to know where to start preparing for it. I've been looking at these books."

I glanced at the tattered old twenty-first century books on

Helen's desk. One was open at a chapter headed, *Medicine in Wartime*. A drawing depicted wounded men with missing limbs on a battlefield.

"This is a bit extreme, isn't it? I thought we were only slicing off earlobes and dressing the odd wound?"

"But we have no idea of what their weapons will deliver. They're not going to have the sort of guns we have: ours are ancient. Maybe they'll have knives, lasers even. I'm going to have to learn the basics of treating war wounds, because after the day itself, everyone has to stay in a bunker for three or four weeks … until the water runs out."

"Oh yeah, guess it has no water supply."

"No, the mains water was switched off over a century ago. So we're going to have to take water butts by horse and cart. There could be three hundred people there, allow a litre a day per person …" She ran her hand through her hair. "Food, sanitation issues …"

"It must be a big bunker."

"I've seen it – it's enormous. It could hold around a thousand, but we can't stock it well enough to take that many." She closed the book. "One of the reasons we're having Outbreak-3 so close to Outbreak-4 is that one of the Citidome escapees is going to bring a supply of drugs – antibiotics, antivirals, painkillers – for us to use in the bunker. But what if they don't make it out? There are so many uncertainties. We could have cases of septicaemia. I think there'll be wounds involving blood loss so I want to try out blood transfusions."

"Blood transfusions?"

"Passing blood from one person to another. It can save lives. It could have saved Paul's life." Her face clouded.

"D'you know what caused his death?"

It had been the biggest tragedy the village had known for years. Helen's younger brother, the community dairyman and the sweetest guy in the village, had fallen off his horse. For days he suffered agonising abdominal pains before he died.

"It must have been something like a ruptured spleen. We need to advance, Joy. We need to push the boundaries, see what else is possible." The uncharacteristic vehemence in Helen's voice stirred me.

"Count me in," I said.

"You're sure?" The creases across her forehead deepened. "If you work in the bunkers, it'll be harrowing. There'll be blood, people in pain, maybe even deaths."

"You forget, I've been helping Mary with the dogs and horses since I was this big." I put my hand to the level of my knee. "I've watched animals being born, seen them die. I'm not the slightest bit squeamish. Why don't we start with the ear cutting?"

"OK, I'll show you. We'll practise on cow hide then I'll let you try on a pig."

"A pig?"

"It's the only way to try the technique on something living, unless you want to try your own earlobe."

"You haven't?" And in answer Helen pulled back her long hair to reveal two ragged ears, almost devoid of lobes. That was devotion to duty, all right.

And so, between my futile attempts at teaching, keeping the still in working order, and bottling up tinctures, I spent my free time slicing though cowhide until the action became second nature. Then came the day of the pigs.

"Sorry, Gertrude," I whispered to the sow. Before I had time to think about it, I pinched the lobe between my fingers, brought the freshly-sharpened scalpel to the flesh and sliced quickly, ignoring Gertrude's squeals. I squeezed the bleeding lobe and applied an alcohol wipe.

"Joy, that was wonderful," Helen said. "I was nowhere near as quick as that."

Glowing in the praise, I started to learn about bacteria, blood groups, and natural antiseptics, and lost myself in it. Why did I never realise that the workings of the human body were so fascinating? When I was able to drag myself away from my new passion, I continued to give Ryan riding lessons and danced with Matt at the village socials.

"I saw you riding with Ryan again yesterday." Matt frowned.

"Not jealous are you, darling?" I teased.

"Don't be daft, but your dad might think it a bit odd. The two of you looked pretty friendly."

"I like Ryan, that's all."

"And Scott says you keep going to see Helen and coming back with thick books," he said. "What're you up to?"

"I decided to learn a bit of medicine. I've always found it interesting."

"Huh, so you're studying even though you don't have to? I'll never get you, Titch."

"It's OK; you don't have to." I noticed Dad glancing in our direction and brushed a lock of hair from his brow.

Winter had released its grip and we were all happy to see the back of it. Life came back to the village, and there was plenty to enjoy: the way the new leaves on the trees broke up the sunlight into glistening shafts, the arrival of different flowers every week, nettle soup back on the menu. As for me, my life was about to begin again. Soon, I'd see Harry.

"You're looking pleased with yourself," said Dad over breakfast.

"I'm looking forward to seeing Harry. Don't look at me like that; I still want us to be friends." I turned to Mum; Dad's suspicious eyes were unnerving me. "It's OK to be friends with him, isn't it?"

"Course it is, love." Mum smiled. "Hard to imagine you and Harry not being friends. I remember when you were both crawling around the boat, talking to each other in a language you'd invented that no-one else understood. Me and Dee wondered if there was something wrong with you."

"We kept it going for years." I smiled. "When Dee stopped us, it didn't matter, because I only had to look at him to know what he was thinking."

Mum frowned and I forced my lips downwards. Damn. Nearly gave myself away.

As the horse and cart made its ponderous journey to Sheffield, I filled my head with Harry. Would the kiss have changed things between us? The quotes we exchanged through Lynn in the market now spoke of love rather than the random, jokey messages we used to send. As the canal came into sight, my pulse quickened. There was the old, familiar boat with two figures standing beside it.

"Hey Dee," I said, hugging Harry's mum, then gave a

sidelong glance in his direction. "Hey, Harry."

At that point I realised I'd have to give the acting performance of my life. I couldn't look at him without my legs shaking and – oh no – my face felt flushed. He looked the way he always looked apart from having filled out. I noticed the bulge of new muscles under his too-tight shirt and felt strange stirrings. His curls had reached the top of his shoulders; I resisted the urge to touch them. When he smiled, I saw the chip in his front tooth. I cherished his small imperfections.

"Hey, yourself. I've got a new friend on board. Want a look?"

I nodded – he was always nursing some wounded or orphaned creature – and followed him on board. I looked over my shoulder – good, Dad was deep in conversation with Dee. Once in the cabin, I turned to look at him.

"I've missed – " we both said at the same time and grinned. He grasped my hands.

"Joy of my heart," he whispered.

Our lips touched in a furtive kiss.

"I've pretended to Dad that there's nothing between us," I whispered. "Go along with it?"

He nodded, frowning.

"I'll explain it all on the way back," I said. "Where's your new friend?"

"Here." He nodded to a wooden crate filled with hay in which lay curled up – oh – a beautiful puppy.

"He's adorable," I said. The tiny creature was perfect. "Where did you find him?"

"Near Hest Bank. He was shivering and near-starving. Will it be OK to take him to yours? I need to feed him up a bit more before I release him."

"Yes, but keep him at Nanna's. They'll witter on about Adam getting diseases – honestly, that baby's all anyone thinks about. We had puppies on the farm, in case Mum couldn't breastfeed Adam, but Mary's released most of them now. Luke said she should kill them, but Mary couldn't bring herself to do it. We'll have to take this little chap well away from the village. Matt shot a feral dog last week." I shuddered.

"Farmers. All savages." He shook his head. "What's Adam like?"

"Cute but nothing compared to this." For as long as I could remember, I'd preferred animals to people.

"Animals have it right. No rules; they follow their instincts," Harry murmured.

"Like you." I pushed a strand of hair from his eyes. "Best go before Dad catches us. Thanks for my dolphin pendant. I love it. Is there no end to your talents? When did you learn to carve wood?"

"I'm still learning," he said, and held up a scarred thumb. "That's where the knife slipped. That dolphin took five attempts."

I took the thumb in my hand and kissed it. But Dad's call drew us apart. Once the supplies were fixed to the cart, Harry and I climbed on the back, the puppy nestled in my lap. Already I felt more alive.

"Brr, it's chilly; let's put a sheepskin over us," I said. The cart jerked into motion. I pressed my thigh against Harry's and reached under the sheepskin for his hand, intertwining my fingers with his. The blood ran warm in my veins. The journey was noisy and soon I heard the hum of Dee and Dad's conversation but couldn't make out any words so turned to Harry and spoke in a low voice.

"Dad thinks I'm going to tell you that I'm going out with Matt."

"You're not, are you?" Harry's thick brows drew together.

"Course not." I caressed his calloused palm with my thumb. "But we're pretending. It takes the pressure off us both."

"I don't know what your mum and dad's problem is. Neither does Mum."

"Mum thinks I'm too young, Dad wants me to stay in the village and make babies with Matt." I sighed. "What are we going to do? I think about you all the time."

"And I you. It's a good job I love your spirit as much as your body. At least I can keep that with me. Why are you smiling?"

"You. And oh – I must tell you. I read Mum's journal."

"Your mum kept a journal?"

I told him a condensed version of what I'd read. "I've been obsessed with the Citidomes every since."

"I knew some of it," Harry said.

"What?" I released his hand.

"After they took Dad, I got obsessed too. So Mum told me what they did to your mum. She said I wasn't to tell you, that it wasn't my story to tell." He placed his hand on my thigh. "Sorry, I hated keeping it from you. Hey, don't be mad at me."

"I'm not, but it's a lot to take in. You go to Hest Bank often, don't you? Do you know a guy called Fin?"

"Yeah. He nearly split the whole community up, because he loathes the AOC. He says it's because he doesn't agree with their fight against the Citidomes, that they shouldn't disturb the peace. But Mum thinks it's because your dad runs it."

"But Dad said he'd never met him."

"He hasn't. But Fin was in love with your mum. Obsessed with her; never got over losing her. He couldn't deal with the fact that she loved your dad. Oh, and he believes the official lie, that she died giving birth to you."

"Yeah, Mum and Dad told me that bit. Surprised you and your mum have never let anything slip to him."

"We don't see him often. He's not the leader any more and he's gotten reclusive. People say there's something wrong with him – some sort of neurodegenerative disorder. He's clumsy: drops things and bumps into doorways."

"Strange; he was Citidome born, wasn't he? You'd think they'd screen that out in the breeding centres."

"They do, together with dark skin, but the odd mutation slips through. Look at our mums."

I smiled. Mum was dusky-skinned and Dee was the darkest person I'd ever seen, with a face the colour of old mahogany. Kell, on the other hand, had milk-white skin, ever paler than Dad's. It had resulted in Harry's glorious skin tone. I wished I was darker – I wouldn't get so sunburnt.

"Did you read the book I lent you?" he asked.

"Yeah."

"What did you think?" The eagerness in his voice melted me. Besides, I'd been longing to talk to him about *Nineteen eighty-four*. Beth and Matt weren't great readers, and I'd worried that lending it to Ryan might be construed as encouragement.

"Brilliant." I placed my hand on his thigh. "I re-read it after reading Mum's journal. The parallels were stunning. What I had no idea of was the way the Citidomes had suppressed knowledge and rewritten history." I quoted my favourite passage from the book, about the Party stating that events hadn't happened but Harry followed it with an even longer quote. This was typical of him.

"Damn, I was trying to impress you with my superior intellect." I grinned.

"You always impress me." He winked. "But you're right. Everything about the Citidomes is screwed up, isn't it? Except, funnily enough, the principles behind it. Have you read the *Blueprint for a New Society* yet?"

"No, have you?"

"Yeah, Mum has a copy. You'll have to make the return journey with me, and then I can lend you it. It's kind of difficult to get a grasp of, particularly non-attachment. It's based on releasing desire for material goods, people, and fixed ideas, and in doing so you release yourself from suffering and become free."

"Huh, not much freedom in the Citidomes. Dad's only told me a little about it. I loved the concept of self-actualisation, when I got my head around it. If I understand it properly, it's reaching the limits of human potential."

"Yeah, how cool would that be?"

"I can see why, in theory, you'd have more chance of doing it in the Citidome. Easy to spend your life thinking about higher things when you don't have to worry where your next meal's coming from. Or having to argue with my bratty brother that spelling and grammar are useful."

"Or having to heave sacks of flour and tonnes of copper piping on and off boats. I wish I had a chance to develop my brain as much as my biceps."

"Your muscles are developing nicely." I grinned. "So's your brain, come to that. Stop feeling sorry for yourself. You get far more time to read than I do."

Harry was jealous of the fact that I grew up in a village and had other kids to play with. He'd been working since he was five and never had any proper education. But the leisurely pace of canal travel had allowed him to educate himself from the ancient books he borrowed and he knew far more than me.

"I suppose it's better than farming," he said. "But when you think what life could be like it's hard not to be bitter. Of course, there's one aspect of non-attachment I don't agree with at all."

"Non-attachment to people," we said together. Our thought patterns often coincided.

"Non-attachment to objects makes sense," Harry said. "The Blueprint initiated communal ownership of transport. Did you know that people used to become attached to vehicles and use them as status symbols?"

"Huh, weird," I said. "Although I guess I'm attached to one object. Our home."

"Yeah, me too. I can't imagine how I'd cope if anything happened to the boat. And that's why attachment causes suffering."

"I guess so. What did it say about people?"

"That people shouldn't become too attached to others because it ultimately causes pain. But the Citidomes have misinterpreted it to ban any sort of relationship between humans because that way, no-one can plot to rebel. But I think the original concept was flawed. Do you know how many animals mate for life?"

"And they get to choose their mates. I guess they don't have a dad like mine." I grinned. "Still, give me six months of suffering for a week of you."

"I want to kiss you right now," Harry murmured.

"We're breaking up, remember. Oh, and I read another book I found in the village collection: *Big Brother*."

"You're kidding? I've heard of it but never found a copy. Can I borrow it?"

It was always like this when we first met after a few months. So much to tell each other that our words tumbled out breathlessly, our conversation random and disjointed but bursting with energy, knowing that we had a limited time together and wanting to make the most of every second. I was disappointed to see the cottages of the village come into view.

"I can't believe we're almost home. I'll find an excuse for us to go out as soon as possible but there'll be the obligatory drooling over the baby first."

"I'll start practising." He grinned. "Aww. Tiny fingers. What else are you supposed to say?"

"He looks like Dad? That's what most people say, but I can't see it. He just looks like a baby. Look, the welcoming committee's out."

"Harry!" Scott was leaping up and down on the spot.

"Hey, Scotty. Looks like you've grown too big for a piggy back." Harry grinned.

"No I haven't! I want one now!"

As Harry set off down the street, Scott clinging to his back, I smiled. Of course the family would all want a piece of Harry. Scott returned and saw the puppy in my arms.

"Is that for us?" he asked.

"No, we're looking after him for a few days then releasing him," I said.

"Mum, can we keep him?" Scott pleaded.

"Just what we need, another mouth to feed," said Mum, at the same time smiling at the puppy. "OK, Scott. If you keep him supplied with rabbits to eat, he's yours." She looked at Harry with a grin. "Trust you to cause havoc the minute you get here."

Harry really was a miracle. Nothing seemed to make Mum smile these days. Even the baby gave what Harry interpreted as a smile but I suspected was wind. Then Mum got the scissors out.

"Looks like you need a haircut, Harry."

It had become a long-standing tradition that Mum cut Harry's hair when he visited us. Dee wore her hair in dreadlocks and didn't own a pair of scissors.

"I was hoping you'd say that. It's getting in my eyes."

I tried not to stare as the beautiful black curls fell to the rusty scissors, and resisted the urge to say, "Not too short." But Mum was thankfully quick. When Ryan had first come to the village, Beth and I had laughed at his perfect grooming and the evenness of his fringe. Harry's hair always looked chaotic, even now.

"I'll clear up," I said and took the dustpan and brush. If Mum was surprised at this unexpected display of thoughtfulness, she said nothing. As I took the pan of hair to the composter, I removed a thick curl and tucked it into my waistband. It was an hour before family stories had been exchanged and I was able to have Harry to myself.

"Can I take Harry to meet Matt?" I said, and felt a pang of guilt at Mum's sympathetic smile and nod.

"Where are we really going?" Harry said once we'd made our escape.

"To meet Matt, of course," I said. "Seriously, he's ploughing the fields up at Little Longstone today. But first, we're going to the top of the world. Race you!"

I ran away from the village along the patchwork of fields edged by dry stone walls that formed a steady uphill route to my favourite viewpoint, Monsal Head. Harry soon overtook me and carried on running until the stone cottages of the village had disappeared from view, at which point he stopped, turned to face me and held out his arms. I fell into them and he pressed me against him.

"What have you done to me?" he muttered into my hair.

"I cast a spell." I raised my face to his and we kissed, gorging on the taste of each other. When we pulled apart, I grinned.

"That was even better than the first time."

"I've been practising."

"Who on?"

"No girls can resist the exotic stranger who passes on the boat. It's my incredible charisma." I glared at him and saw his grin. "Fall into it every time, don't you?"

"Have you though? Got an army of female fans?" I saw the faint flush that betrayed the truth.

"Not really." He ran his hand through his hair. "You know how it is, once you turn sixteen, everyone wants to pair you off. But most girls think I'm odd. You're the only one who gets me, which is just as well, because you're the only one I want to get."

"I'm yours," I said. "And I want the world to know it."

"I'm coming round to the idea of the cover story. It's more

of an adventure this way," he said. "We can be like the star-crossed lovers of literature. Romeo and Juliet, Cathy and Heathcliff."

"But don't they always have tragic endings?"

"We've always bucked the trend."

We laced hands and continued walking and talking. As we climbed, blankets of green bracken and lush purple heather softened the contours of the hills.

"Of all the places I visit, this is one of the most beautiful," Harry murmured, starting one of my favourite topics of conversation, the places that Harry knew, that existed only in my imagination.

"You're so lucky, I hardly ever get to travel further than bloody Bakewell," I said. "But at least I'll be getting to find out what goes on in the rest of the country. Dad's letting me use the Out There knowledge base."

"That's fantastic!" Harry gripped my hands. "We'll be able to send each other messages, private ones."

"Really? Dad didn't tell me we could do that."

"He wouldn't." Harry rolled his eyes. "But I'll show you how. Make sure you close it down each time, and then your dad'll never find out. You'll love Out There; there's heaps of stuff about Outbreaks 3 and 4."

Our conversation turned to the plans for the outbreaks, and Harry's eyes flashed with the intensity I found so thrilling. We reached a bench at Monsal Head and stared at the sweeping view of the viaduct below us, the river along the valley floor and the endless hills above.

"Time for a rest." Harry sat on the bench and pulled me onto his lap. We kissed with abandon, leaving me breathless. I wanted to merge with him.

"I've been thinking…" He twisted one of his curls around his finger. "I know we're insanely young to be making long-term plans but I can't help thinking about it. I want to be with you all the time." He took my hand. "I talked to Mum – she'll be fifty in two years' time and she said she might want to settle down in a community and give up the canals. You'd be eighteen then. Maybe then you could come and run the narrowboat with me?"

My heart leapt and sank in quick succession. While the life

he suggested was idyllic, it wasn't the one I'd hoped for. In my imagination, he'd drop to one knee and ask me to marry him, like Dad had done to Mum when she found out she was pregnant with me. Of course that would never happen. Marriage was a meaningless concept, a tradition carried out only in our village, as far as I knew. But that didn't stop me imagining our wedding in exquisite detail. It was my favourite fantasy.

"Of course I want to be with you," I murmured. "But why do you have to stay on the canals? Couldn't you join our community? There's going to be plenty of new blood to take over. Maybe your mum could join us, too?"

Harry shrugged. "I dunno. I've always fancied the idea of joining a community but what would I do here? I can't see myself as a farmer. Shooting foxes? Slaughtering animals for food?"

"You don't mind eating them."

"I'm a hypocrite, I know. My philosophies are riddled with inconsistencies. Besides, you can't expect a newcomer to run a canal boat. It takes ages to learn how to work and maintain the locks, not to mention understanding the whole trading network."

"I guess so, but I can't leave Dad and the community. You know how it is. I'm this big symbol of hope, the girl from a new bloodline. I'm meant to reproduce."

"Mum said that's what you'd say. But is that what you want?"

"I don't ever want to have children. Giving birth to me nearly killed my mum." There was a new conviction in my voice.

"Maybe you won't have to. Mum says they could liberate up to a thousand people this year. Then there'd be a lot less pressure on our generation."

"Wouldn't that be amazing? We've got to find a way to be together. We've just got to! Perhaps we'd get to fulfil our potential."

A flame of hope ignited deep inside me. But then it flickered and ebbed. Children or not, could I ever imagine myself living apart from my family and friends?

"Not possible. Our potential's limitless." Harry pulled me

closer to him. "Seems wrong that women here are no more than breeding animals. You're worth so much more than that. But a combination of you and me. It'd be stunning."

"Harry, you're the vainest person I ever met!"

"No I'm not, I'm realistic. I'm above average looking; you're staggeringly beautiful. We're both well above average intelligence. Don't you hate false modesty? All the girls I meet in the other communities drive me mad, tossing their hair and whinging that they can't do anything with it."

"Stop trying to make me jealous again." I swiped a punch at him. "But you're right. Beth's always complaining that her hair curls too much, not noticing that mine curls even more. Curly hair's frowned upon in the Citidomes too. OK, I admit it. I'm above average looking. And you're infinitely above. I stole one of your curls, look."

"I want one of yours. I'm going to choose." His hands explored my hair. "This one."

"I'll cut it off for you later. Now we'd better look in on Matt for the sake of the story."

We wandered down to the fields below Little Longstone where a field was being ploughed with the help of a horse and an ancient metal implement.

"Right, hands to yourself. There's Matt, talking to Luke. Luke's friends with Dad. I'll have to act."

"Hey Luke, hey Matt." I gave Matt a chaste kiss on the lips. "You remember Harry, don't you?"

"Hey, Harry, hey sweetheart," Matt said.

I glanced at Harry and saw the flash of anger in his eyes.

"Not working today?" Luke frowned.

"Special concession because Harry and Dee are here. I'm working extra hours next week."

"Why don't we take our break now?" asked Luke. "I'll tell the others."

"Great," said Matt. "You two want a coffee?"

We walked to a nearby barn and sat on haystacks while Matt poured dandelion coffee from a pot. Harry's expression was thunderous.

"Sorry about the sweetheart thing. Best Luke doesn't know the truth," Matt grinned.

Harry managed a faint smile in reply. "Yeah, I suppose so.

Thanks for helping us with the lie."

"Helps me, too," Matt said.

Harry frowned.

"Otherwise Matt'll be traded round the country like a prize bull to impregnate the village virgin," I explained, giving Harry's hand a reassuring squeeze.

Luke joined us, along with Beth, Ryan, Craig and Elsie. I released Harry's hand.

"Hey, who are you?" Elsie gave Harry a lascivious smile. Was that girl capable of talking to any man without flirting? Did she even realise what she was doing?

"You've met before. It's Harry, my friend from the canals." I looked to Harry. "I think you've met everyone except Ryan."

"Hey, Ryan," Harry said.

Soon the barn rang with the sounds of chatting. I sat next to Matt and couldn't help but contrast the banality of our conversation with my precious hours with Harry. I was pleased to see that Harry no longer seemed annoyed and was in animated conversation with Ryan. When we stood up to go, the fine drizzle that shrouded the valley had turned to persistent rain. Matt, the last to leave, turned to us with a wink.

"You two are welcome to shelter here until the rain eases off. There shouldn't be anyone in here again this afternoon. But don't get up to anything I wouldn't."

Oh, why did he have to say that? I could hardly look at Harry. Kissing was one thing, but any further? Dare I? But when he spoke, it wasn't of dark deeds in the barn.

"You didn't tell me Matt was so good-looking," he muttered. "Last time I saw him he was covered in spots."

"He grew out of them. You forget, he's twenty now. Anyway, what does it matter what he looks like?" My voice had a hard edge. "We're star-crossed lovers, remember. If you don't trust me, what's the point?"

He pulled me towards him, "I do trust you. But it shocked me to see … I can't bear to think of anyone else being near you."

"Matt's like a brother to me. And he doesn't quote obscure poets or argue about philosophy or read books. He only comes to movie showings when it's a comedy."

"What about that other one, Ryan? Seems an interesting guy."

"He's intended for Beth, but, well, I think he likes me. Like you said, I'm irresistible." I tossed my hair. "Seriously though, I've never given him any encouragement. And he's so skinny. What's that BodyPerfect cult about?"

"Control. If they desexualise the human body, they have a race of clones, not driven by any other urges, people that co-exist harmoniously. Imagine if they let people who looked like you in there. The men would all be fighting over you."

I blushed. The mention of sex had made me uncomfortable but at the same time the air fizzed with possibility. Then I became aware of the silence that had fallen between us.

"The same could be said for you," I said. "A charismatic stranger with a body to drive women wild."

"You wanton hussy." He grinned.

"That's what people call Elsie. I've never been certain what it means."

"It means you're shameless, that you give yourself to men."

"No. Not men, plural. I give myself to man. You. Now." I held my breath. Did I really say that? But when would we get another opportunity like this?

He stared at me. Didn't he want to? The silence seemed infinite. I swear I could hear myself blink. Then he drew me closer to him. Our kissing intensified, as did my panic. What if it was awful? I knew it would hurt the first time but Beth said it would be better for me as I'd grown up riding horses. I did a mental calculation – it should be safe. But when we drew apart, his eyes told me that he was as frightened as I was.

"Can I look at you properly?" he whispered. I nodded and pulled my top off, ashamed at the sight of my grey, frayed bra. But his smile told me that it didn't matter at all. His hands fumbled at the hooks.

"Huh, how do these things work?" he muttered, but eventually released them. And then he was kissing me. Everywhere. Wow. A fluttering sensation spread from my stomach to my thighs, then something unexpected jolted through me, a spike of sensation that took my breath from me.

"Joy, you're exquisite," he said, and in that moment I felt a sense of power I'd never felt before, combined with a strange longing.

"Take yours off," I whispered and soon his beautiful brown chest was revealed to me. I explored his body with my hands and mouth and felt his taut muscles under his skin. His breathing quickened.

"We don't have to go any further," he said.

"I want to."

My hands lowered to unbutton his trousers, and then his zipper stuck. And that's what our first time was like – more awkward fumbling than the ecstatic union of bodies I'd read about. But I discovered what all the fuss was about. Lying in the hay afterwards, I smiled.

"What are you thinking?" he whispered into my hair.

"That we always owned each other's soul, and now we own each other's body too."

"We always will."

CHAPTER 8 - CATHY

I woke with a groan. Ten past nine. I'd overslept because I'd been up in the night with Adam. Again. I used to be an early riser, relishing those morning hours, the silence punctuated only by birdsong, all my loved ones asleep. Adam was easier to love that way.

When I reached the kitchen, everyone had left. A mountain of washing awaited me, including a pile of nappies. The back garden was covered in dog excrement. I fed the chickens and collected three eggs, then noticed with a frown that the fencing around their enclosure was rickety. Damn, I'd have to fix that now or I'd come down to a scene of feathered carnage one morning. Bloody dog. I'd been gambling on the fact that it'd soon find its own way in the world but it insisted on returning every night. Didn't I have enough to do? I set myself to my tasks and as soon as I stopped to rest, Scott came in, carrying two rabbits and a basket of greenery.

"Big 'uns this morning." He grinned. "Can you save the innards for Milo?"

"Course I can. Mmm, they are big, aren't they? Ooh, and is that wood sorrel? Lovely. Well done, sweetheart." I ruffled his hair, trying to show more enthusiasm than I felt. I'd be delighted if I never had to skin another animal or pluck another bird. "What are you up to next?"

"Me and Ian are off up Sheldon way to pick gorse flowers for Nanna's wine." With that he was gone.

"Why don't you hurry up and turn into a boy?" I said to Adam. Scott was permanently cheerful and why shouldn't he be? He lived a life free of responsibility: playing, foraging for wild food, and two hours' schooling a day. I started preparing a rabbit casserole and by the time the family returned for the evening, all buoyed by the first pleasant spring day after a rainy month, I was exhausted. April, the month when the village rose to greet the world once more. The season of rebirth. So why did I feel so dead inside?

"It's warm enough to sit outside if we wrap up," said Michael after dinner. "Let's go for a stroll by the river and sit by the water's edge."

Half an hour later we were sitting on a bench by the river, admiring the riot of yellow primroses competing for attention with the pink willowherb. It was that sort of transient warmth that gave false hope that summer had arrived but it raised my spirits.

"Joy's in a better mood these days," Michael said. "She's never away from the DataBand and keeps asking me questions about the Citidomes. It's good to see her taking her role in the AOC seriously. I always thought that Matt would ground her. She and Harry are too alike."

So were you and I. I bit back the words. Harry and Dee's visit had unsettled me. Was I the only one who'd noticed the way Joy's eyes shone with unshed tears when she returned from saying goodbye to Harry?

"Joy being with Matt is going to break Harry's heart," Dee had said. "He adores her, you know. I thought that our kids had a special bond, one that distance couldn't break. Guess I overestimated her."

Her coldness had made me shiver. I'd felt that Dee and I had a special bond too and the accusation in her voice tore at me. And on occasions, Harry and Joy had exchanged looks of such yearning that it had been painful to see. Later, I'd spoken to Joy alone.

"How did it go with Harry?" I'd asked. "Still think you made the right decision?"

"Yeah, it was lovely to see Harry; it always is. But he took it well. I need someone who's here, someone I can dance with at the socials and chat to after work."

Something didn't add up. The disparity between her words and Dee's had disconcerted me, and I couldn't shake the feeling that Joy had given up on something precious for the sake of convenience.

I looked at Michael with only a hint of a smile. Had he not picked up on any of my doubts? Couldn't he see that Matt wasn't the right one for our daughter? Did he even care?

"I don't see Joy and Matt as kindred spirits," I said.

"He curbs her silly flights of fancy. He's perfect."

I swallowed my annoyance. I remembered Michael telling me what the expression 'kindred spirit' meant, all those years ago in the Citidome. Michael and I used to see the world through the same eyes. When had his vision clouded over? But I was too tired to argue. "At least she seems happy," I said. "Scott said she went a whole day without swearing at them in class."

"That's something. Perhaps she's too young for the job. She doesn't seem to be a natural teacher like you."

"She was far and away the brightest child I taught." I smiled. "Perhaps that's the problem. She's so quick that she doesn't understand why other people can't keep up."

Adam's cry interrupted our talk. He'd cut his first tooth last week and was in the process of being weaned onto solids. I'd cut down the breast-feeding with relief. It lessened his total dependence on me, a dependence that I was finding increasingly irritating, and along with the irritation came the guilt. I wasn't supposed to feel like this, was I? Breast-feeding Joy and Scott had been blissful. I'd savoured every second of this unique bond I shared with my children. But with Adam I felt frustrated, willing him to finish quickly. He must have tasted the resentment in me because he hadn't taken to it as well as the other two. He'd even started teething earlier than his brother and sister did.

"Can I come out with you tomorrow and help with whatever it is you're doing? I'll scream if I don't get out of here soon."

"Er, yeah." Michael tilted his head as if trying to read my mind but afraid what he might find in there. "But what about Adam?"

"I'm sure Anna won't mind looking after him for the day. Please, Michael."

"Hey, what is it?"

"Nothing, I just need a change of scenery." I knew my words were tense, clipped. How could I explain to him that I felt trapped by my own baby?

"You look peaky. Perhaps you should go to see Helen."

"I'm bored, not ill." My jaw tightened.

"OK, no need to bite my head off. Perhaps we could have a

ride to the quarry tomorrow? Vincent brought me a package he found there; looks like it might be full of explosive devices. If they work, they might be better than anything we could make in the factory."

"Sure, what are they?"

He went to the bottom of the garden and brought out a bundle of slim cylindrical objects, partly wrapped in polyfilm.

"They look like candles." I frowned.

"But they were wrapped in layers of plastic in one of the caves, with orange tape marked, 'Danger: Explosives.' My guess is that they were used for blasting rock."

"Use by 2035." I read the small inscription and grinned. "They're a little out of date."

"I know. But the last so-called explosives Daisy made gave a cough and a splutter then fizzled out. We've got to try."

And so, the following day, I found myself on a horse for the first time in almost a year. I gazed out onto my favourite season. The hedgerows were thick with leaves and flowers, giving the landscape an exuberance to cheer even the weariest soul. I loved hawthorn blossom. It had a comforting solidity, as if it was planning to stick to the bushes forever, not like the transient fragility of the other spring blossoms. Chestnut trees were beginning to bear flowers, rising proudly like candles. I gave a deep sigh of pleasure.

"It was the anniversary of our escape from the Citidome, last week," I commented.

"Seventeen years," he murmured, and turned to me. "You really doing OK? You seemed tense yesterday. All we talk about is the kids or the AOC, and I never ask how you are."

I gave him an 'I'm-doing-fine' grin, but my eyes refused to co-operate in the smile.

"I know I'm not pulling my weight with Adam as much I did with the other two," he said inadequately.

That was an understatement. Then I realised my knuckles were white from gripping the horse's reins. "It'll get easier," I muttered, but on seeing him clenching and unclenching his grip on the reins, let out a long, heavy breath. "Sorry, I know I'm being miserable. It's so good to be out again, but I'm tired already. I'm tired all the bloody time."

"If you want to head back, I'll understand."

"No." The word came out more violently than I intended. "I'll go mad if I stay in another day. Seriously, Michael. This is going to be the most exciting thing to happen around here in our lifetimes. I'm still not sure whether it's a good thing or bad, but I hate not being involved."

"I wish you could be involved too, but what can we do? Adam has to come first."

We reached the vast expanse of exposed rock that scarred the landscape. Michael took the fiberstone-coated stick in his hand.

"I need you to watch from here, see how far the blast extends. I'll throw it as far as I can then run to you."

"You do realise it'll probably do nothing."

But my stomach knotted as Michael produced a flame and lit the wick. His throw was strong; at least thirty metres, and as soon as he'd released the stick he turned and ran towards me. Nothing happened for five … ten … fifteen seconds. Then came a roar unlike anything I'd ever heard. Instinctively, I dropped to the ground. When I looked up, dust and rubble were still falling to the ground, and Michael was lying face down. My blood chilled but the panic was momentary. He eased himself to his feet, brushing the dust from his hair.

"Think it's fair to say that exceeded expectations," he said. "I'm going to have to get some people on throwing practice."

"You can't use them! Are you mad? Imagine a blast like that in a building full of flammable liquid! You'll roast everybody within a kilometre!"

He sighed. "It has to be the biggest, the most spectacular explosion in history. Three hundred people are going to disappear into a bunker. How else do we account for the loss of bodies? We need the authorities to believe that everyone perished in the fire or they'll hound us forever. There are going to be casualties but it's for the greater good."

"But everyone *will* perish in the fire. You're going to slaughter innocent people?"

"That's an extreme way of putting it. We're taking every precaution we can. And every single one of the AOC members, as well as the Heroes, know the risks, and are willing to do it anyway."

"But who's going to throw the sticks?"

"The people who can throw the furthest and run the fastest. The blast extended, what, about twenty metres? There was a delay of fifteen seconds. Most people could run ninety metres in that time, plus a throwing distance of thirty metres –"

"But the quarry wasn't full of explosive chemicals."

"It should be safe for the younger, fitter ones. Everyone volunteers for these missions knowing that there are risks involved."

"So you'll choose Harry? He's the youngest."

"Almost certainly. I can't afford favouritism."

"Huh. You may end up killing the boy you see as your own successor. And what about those prisoners in the correction camps who have no idea what's going on? I thought the idea was they started a riot, opened the doors from the inside and then we created a diversion. Instead they're going to walk out into a furnace."

"They don't live; they exist. We're offering the chance of a better world for those who survive it."

"And do you even know how many people live in those correction camps?"

"No." He narrowed his mouth. "Five, six hundred at least, judging by the number of trucks that come and go."

"So you only have the bunker capacity to save around half of them?"

"It's all that's possible. Helen and I have gone over the figures no end of times. Some will make it to communities on their own. Most villages have safe houses."

I sucked in my breath through my teeth. The thought of him poring over data with mousy little Helen annoyed me. "What you're talking about here is war."

"Some causes demand sacrifice."

"It doesn't bother you that hundreds of innocent people could die?"

"Of course it bothers me." His voice hardened; he couldn't take the uncomfortable truth. "We're going to try and save as many as we can."

"Is it too late to talk you out of this? There has to be

another way, surely? Merging communities, like we've been doing. Things aren't ideal here, but it's a good life, isn't it?"

"But it's not just about us, is it?" He gripped my hands. "It's the whole system. We have to destroy it."

"Why?"

He shook his head. "You're forgetting what it was like in the Citidomes. We have a responsibility."

"I'll never forget," I snapped. "Not as long as I live. But what about your responsibility to Scott, Adam, Joy, and me? While you're making a better world for the anonymous millions, remember you're a husband and father."

We returned home in silence, the sinking feeling in the pit of my stomach growing stronger with every step. In all the time I'd known Michael, he'd only ever had one lapse in judgement, and that had resulted in me having to run away from the village, live in hiding for three months and then fake my own death. Surely this second lapse could only end in disaster?

Two days later, I answered the door to find Helen facing me.

"Hey, Helen. What are you doing here?"

"Michael asked me to give you a check up." Her eyes looked anywhere but at me.

I led her inside, resisting the urge to tell her what she could do with her check up. "So Michael's been talking about me behind my back, has he? What did he tell you?"

"He says you haven't been yourself since having the baby and he's worried."

"Course I haven't been myself! I'm stuck in the house all day with a bloody baby while everyone else is preparing for the most exciting event in the history of the AOC. Even Joy's more involved than I am. And when I dare to suggest that some of Michael's ideas are misguided, that he might end up slaughtering some of the AOC's most committed members, he talks about his great responsibility, and then sends for the sodding health worker. How do you expect me to feel?" Her eyes had doubled in size; I softened my voice. "Sorry, Helen. I didn't mean to take it out on you. But … the truth is, I'm scared."

"Outbreak-4 scares me too," Helen said. "I don't think I'll

be equipped to handle the casualties. But Michael's convinced it's the only way forward, and I believe him."

Typical. Helen always agreed with every word Michael said, which was why Daisy would have made a better AOC representative.

"I get the impression that maybe you're scared of more than that." Helen spoke tentatively.

Could I confide in her? Helen had been a shy thirteen year-old when I came to the village. I'd always liked her but seen her as a kid sister. The unfamiliar change of role to advisor unnerved me.

"I did a little reading," Helen continued. "And it's not unusual for women to get a sort of depression a few months after they've given birth."

"I'm not sad," I protested.

"Then how are you?"

"This doesn't get back to Michael, right?"

"Of course not!"

"Angry, irritable, resentful." I cupped my face in my hands then continued. "Look at Daisy. She goes around the country, setting up new manufacturing plants. She's famous. All those technical advances; it should have been me. I was the top student in my academic centre; Michael and I were the two young high-flyers at the ministry and now look at him – the revered leader. And what do I get? Village council member, mother and teacher."

"But you're so valuable on the village council. And you're a brilliant teacher," Helen said.

"Thanks," I attempted to smile. "But let's face it, you're the only one who had a useful education and that was the medical one you got from Alex. The educational needs of children destined to be farmers aren't exactly far-reaching. You read the *Blueprint for a New Society*, didn't you? 'A world where humans can become self-actualised, can achieve their ultimate potential.'" I sighed. "That's partly it. I can't shake the feeling that I haven't achieved my ultimate potential and I never will."

"You have a man that loves you and three children. Don't underestimate the importance of that." Her eyes dropped.

"I don't." Guilt flooded me. As far as I knew, Helen had

never had a relationship with a man. “And I wouldn’t swap them for anything. But now … we had a few difficulties with Joy at the end of last year. And Adam…” To my horror, my eyes filled with tears.

“What is it, Cathy? You can trust me.”

“I don’t feel the same for him as I did for the other two. With them it was an overwhelming, unconditional love, but with Adam … I don’t love him the way I should.” There. The words were out.

And while Helen struggled to form the words for a situation that was far beyond her understanding, I acknowledged the painful truth. I could no longer cope with the role that life had cast me in.

CHAPTER 9 - JOY

I reached into the drawer for my favourite object in the whole world – the DataBand, and opened the Messenger.

> Hey, Joy of my life. We're going to Langley Mill the day after tomorrow. Should arrive at 9ish. Any chance of you coming over for a few hours? Take the horse out for the day? I'm cherishing your soul but pining for your body; if I don't see you soon I might waste away.
>
> H xxxxxxx

My heart did a backflip. That would be Thursday and it was one of my allocated market days. Perfect – I could be gone for six hours or so without being missed.

> Hey, charismatic stranger. Try keeping me away! I'll be there by 10
>
> Your Joy xxxxx

"Nanna, can I have my beer allowance all at once?" I said. "This might be my last trip to the market for a few weeks; Helen's keen to try some medical experiments on my days off."

"Course you can, sweetheart. Medicine, eh? You're really throwing yourself into this, aren't you?"

"I love it."

My mind had already leapt into the future. Maybe this was my ticket out of the village. A travelling health worker, specialising in trauma, might be useful. And what better means of transport than a canal boat? Nanna took four bottles of beer from the cupboard. Every week she gave me one; they were my best trading commodities at the market. But this week I wasn't trading them.

I woke early on Thursday morning and was saddling Bramble by nine; to leave any earlier would look suspicious.

"Where are you going?" asked Mary.

"I haven't decided yet. It's such a glorious day, I might take her for a long ride up on Longstone Edge." I grinned. This was almost too easy.

I rode towards the moors but soon changed direction and headed south. Within the hour I'd arrived at Langley Mill. The village was quiet – most people had gone to the market – but an elderly man directed me to the canal. Harry was standing on the deck as I arrived, his grin almost splitting his face in two. He leapt onto the bank, helped me tether Bramble and lifted me into his arms, swinging me onto the boat. Once on the deck, I pressed myself into his chest. We stayed that way for a long time.

Dee emerged from the cabin. "Hey, sweetheart," she said.

"Hey, Dee," I said. "I've brought you some of our bacon; I know you love it. And some cheese. Sorry, it's not the best. Vincent didn't put enough rennet in and it's too soft to trade at market, but it still tastes good."

"Mmm, thanks. You're an absolute star," Dee said.

"And these are for you." I handed the bottles to Harry. "Happy birthday for next week."

"You know the way to my heart. Tell me this is Anna's beer." He grinned.

"Of course."

"Fabulous. So what's happening at home? Did you keep the puppy?" Harry asked.

"Scott's besotted; he's named him Milo. We've built him a shelter in the back garden. At first Scott caught rabbits for him but Mum said he couldn't keep feeding him so he fends for himself during the day but always comes back at night."

"Talking of besotted." He drew me closer to him.

"Can't you wait? I said I was going." Dee grinned and then gave me a stern adult look. "I don't approve of deceiving your mum and dad but I have to live with this lovesick boy."

"I'm not keen on all the secrecy myself," I said. "But they're not being reasonable."

"I thought your dad seemed more stressed than usual. Guess it's all this Outbreak business. And keep an eye on your mum. I think she's struggling with young Adam more than she's letting on. But I reckon she's less convinced by your so-called romance with the farmer than your dad is. My advice to you both is to keep your heads down and be patient. Don't you roll your eyes like that, young man. I know patience isn't something you have much of when you're sixteen. But things might look very different when there's a gang of new young people on the scene. There'll be less pressure on you." She winked at me. "Now, one of my friends in the village has promised me a ride to the market. Harry wants rid of me for some reason."

"You have the coolest mum ever." I leapt into his arms. We went into his cabin, and the world disappeared around us.

"I think we're getting the hang of this," I said as I lay in his arms. My head moulded into his chest.

"If we lived together, we'd be able to practise every day," he murmured.

"We'd never get out of bed again." Then came a knocking at the cabin door. We stiffened.

"Who's there?" shouted Harry.

"Caroline." A reedy voice.

"Hey, Caroline." Harry rolled his eyes. "I'm with my girlfriend. Maybe I'll see you this evening."

"Oh, OK." The voice was smaller.

"Who's Caroline?" I tried to keep the accusatory tone from my voice.

"A local girl, or should I say older woman – she's nearly nineteen. Feel a bit sorry for her, there's no-one her age in the village, so she always comes to say hi."

"Huh, what does she look like?"

"Pale and insipid." His fingertips traced the line of my jaw and wound a path around the nape of my neck. "She's a friend, nothing more. You'd like her. She's bright; she's training to be a health worker."

"I hate her already."

"Hey, jealousy doesn't suit you. Your name's engraved on

my heart; can't you feel it?"

I put my hand to his chest. "Oh yeah, so it is. Talking of engraving" – I reached for an object in my pocket – "I got you a second present. Bit cheesy, I know."

"A love token." He smiled, cradling the polished stone in his hand. On it, I'd scratched the intertwined initials H and J in an ornate script. "I'll keep it with me, always."

"When we die of grief from not being able to see each other, they'll find it on your body."

"Enough of the melodrama. I want a day of Joy, not grief."

"You're not meant to be doing anything today?"

"No. A few deliveries to the village, overnight here then off to see the bunker tomorrow. We're kitting it out with blankets and boxes of out-of-date nutribars we get from the dumps."

"You lucky thing. Wish I could see it. Looks like I'm going there with Helen to treat the casualties. What's a nutribar?"

"Rather you than me. A whole month without daylight? And as for nutribars – here, taste one." He passed me an unappetising looking green bar with a bite taken out. "I had to check it was still edible but I couldn't finish it."

"Ugh." I shuddered. It tasted as bad as it looked, like spinach that had been boiled too long. "What are you doing on Outbreak Day?"

"Taking the first of the escapees away on the boat. We should be able to take about twenty-five up to Berwick, which is as far away as we can get. We'll deposit them in a safe house, come back, patrol the area for strays and pick up more people when they leave the bunker." He ran a hand through his hair. "And I'm going to be throwing explosives at an agrochemicals factory. I had a message from your dad last night. He wants me to practise throwing sticks a long distance then turning and running as fast as I can. To tell you the truth, I'm scared. How big will the explosion be?"

"Do you have to do that?" I pressed myself closer against him. "Can't you tell him you can't throw well?"

"But I can so it's only fair."

"Dad thinks a lot of you. It's just the two of us being together he's not keen on. He wouldn't risk your life. I'll talk to him."

"And how do you do that without letting on we've been in contact?"

"But you can't – "

He placed a finger on my lips. "We all agreed that we go into this realising that it's a dangerous mission and lives might be lost."

I felt a lurching in my stomach. "We'll have to make sure you're the fastest runner with the best throw of the whole of State eleven then."

"I'll try." He grinned. "I've got to admit, I'm having second thoughts about Outbreak-4. The bunker only has the capacity to hold a few hundred. What happens to the rest?"

"It worries me, too. How many injuries can we treat? Will the Sigma-2 escapees bring enough drugs? Ah, but I haven't told you my latest scientific breakthrough. Honey."

"Honey?"

"Bacteria can't grow in it. It's a perfect wound dressing and good food to store in the bunker. A guy at Chatsworth makes it so we're busy trading as much as we can."

"That's awesome. I think someone near Oxford makes it. I'll try and get you some more."

"Then you'll have to deliver it to me." I grinned.

"You're getting sneaky, aren't you? I think I should open my birthday present early. Want to share a beer with me?"

"Sounds like heaven. I'd better take a look at Bramble first."

"Here, take her a carrot."

I dressed and went outside, then looked around in disbelief.

"She's not here!"

"What?" Harry joined me, still half-dressed. "I tied that knot really well."

"Oh no." Panic rose in me. "Someone must have stolen her. How the hell am I going to explain that?"

"No way. I trust everyone around here. You go left, I'll go right."

I scurried down the towpath, my heart thumping. I had to find her. Bramble would be an enormous loss to the village; it would take me hours to walk home and as for what Dad would say, I couldn't bear to think of it. But after five minutes I heard Harry calling my name. I turned around and exhaled in a huge rush. He was leading Bramble.

"She was eating grass. Reckon someone untied her."

We looked at each other.

"Caroline," we said together.

"Bloody idiot," Harry muttered. "Thought she had more sense." He put his arm around my shoulder. "She's not in love with me, just wants to snare a man. There's pressure on her in the village. You know how it is."

"Oh yeah, I know how it is. Where does she live? I want to put her straight. You're taken."

"No, let's not waste the time we have. We can't prove it was her. But I'm not going to speak to her at the social tonight." He drew me closer. "Hey, you're trembling. Let's get a blanket, sit on the deck and have that beer."

We settled under the blanket and drank the beer under the spring sunshine, but I couldn't stop shaking. Deception didn't suit me after all and a million 'what if' scenarios swirled in my head.

"If I'd lost Bramble…"

"But you didn't. We're star-crossed lovers, remember? We're not supposed to have it easy at first."

"I think I'll settle for a dull, easy romance."

He leant in and kissed me, a long, luxurious kiss.

"You taste fantastic. All beery," I mumbled. "Perhaps I'll bring Ryan down here. Introduce him to Caroline and get them both off our backs."

"Has he been bothering you?" His face twisted in what I was coming to recognise as his jealous expression.

"No. We've become good friends. But every time he sees Matt and me together, he shakes his head. Says that me and him would be a better match."

"He's right. Good job I claimed you first."

The day went too quickly. We ate ham and cheese on the deck, talking endlessly, cramming several weeks' worth of togetherness into a few hours.

"I'll have to go now. If I'm not home by four, Mary might worry about Bramble." My voice faltered.

"Hey, you can't cry. Joy and tears don't mix. Besides, if you do, I might join you."

"I hate goodbyes; I'll message you tonight." I turned and

left him, my chest tight with the pleasure and pain of the day.

***

Spring turned to summer, and the long, warm days fell into a pattern. I'd spend two hours a day teaching, two hours with Daisy in the factory and an hour with Helen, which allowed me to exercise Bramble and give Ryan the occasional riding lesson. On non-teaching days, I did my farm and dairy duties. And each evening there was a message from Harry.

"You're getting hooked on that," Mum commented.

"It's addictive," I said. "Every day there's something new on the forum. Someone at Norton's trying a new herbal antiseptic." Thank goodness I'd scanned the new topics. I tried not to smile at Harry's words.

> I'm lying in bed, in a glow of Joy. We're heading south for a few weeks. I'm reading, knowing you're probably doing the same. It makes me feel closer to you. The book I'm obsessed with at the moment is by André Gide – now what sort of a name is that? Male or female? He/she tells me that joy is rarer, more difficult, and more beautiful than sadness and that I have to embrace joy as a moral obligation. So who am I to argue? Mum reckons it's a French name. That's where we should head, my Joyous girl. There's a tunnel, you know, that goes under the sea, all the way to France. We should walk right through that tunnel and see what's at the other side. Ah well, I can dream.
>
> What wonders of medical science did you discover today?
>
> Love H xxxxxxxxxxxxxxxxxxxxxxx

As soon as Mum left to feed Adam, I replied.

Hey, star-crossed lover.

Outstanding medical advance of the day: after school finishes, I'm going to see Helen. We've discovered that my blood group is the same as hers – O positive – so we can try the Blood Transfusion experiment. Did you know about blood groups? It's fascinating. There used to be four main groups and something called positives and negatives (way too complicated to explain), but they bred out the B group and the negatives so all Citidome people are A or O positive. O can give to A but not vice-versa. That could make life tricky in the bunkers. Important Citidome people like Ministry workers had it recorded on their DataBands – Mum and Dad are the same as me – but not everyone knows. Not as much call for blood there, historically it was used for road traffic accidents, childbirth and gunshot wounds. So I have something positive to say about Citidomes – they're pretty safe places. I'll end up with about 100 ml of Helen's blood; she'll end up with 100 ml of mine. Let's hope I'm not transformed into a mousy dried-up little health worker. Oh, that was cruel; Helen's a sweetheart. But she's no siren.

Lead me to that tunnel! If I have to drill multiplication into my stupid brother one more time I'll commit fratricide. That's my word of the day: good one, eh? It would be amazing though, wouldn't it? My entire knowledge of France comes from the Illustrated Children's Atlas we use in class. Its spine finally crumbled last week, and France is almost wiped out by grubby fingerprints. According to the atlas, André Gide wears a stripy top, a beret, and inexplicably, has a string of onions around his neck.

Tomorrow I truly will be Joyful – no more school for three months. But with Joy comes pain, as I hope you'll never find out. I'm on farm duty next week – picking flax. And this is the summer that Beth has decided to Do It with Ryan. It's so sad; she's so half-hearted about the challenge, as if she feels she has to lose her virginity, to keep up with me. Before you panic, I trust her not to blab. And I don't want to disillusion her, but I don't think she'll succeed. Ryan's not interested. And they're not exactly a match made in heaven. Much as I love Beth, I have to admit that Ryan has twice her intellect. I've half a mind to tell her to save herself, knowing that she might have a collection of lusty young trainee farmers to choose from in a matter of months. But how can I? Besides, they'll all look like Ryan, won't they? Poor Beth. How will she ever find her soul mate from such slim pickings? I feel blessed to have found you, man of my dreams.

We have to find a way of meeting. That lock of hair I kept is getting thinner.

With love and Joy xxxxxxxxxxxxxxxxx

After school, I visited Helen with less confidence than I'd had when I wrote the message. Although logic told me that there couldn't be much of a risk in exchanging such a small quantity of blood, my imagination had come up with a million horrific scenarios. Suppose one of us had a latent virus that activated itself in the other? And another worry had entered my mind. Did Helen have the Mark? It wasn't always on the face. Would I get it?

Helen had a row of needles ready when she arrived.

"Where do you get all this stuff?" I whistled.

"Mickey finds them at the dump sealed in plastic bins. They only use them once and throw them away; can you believe it? Don't worry. I sterilised them."

"Uh, Helen, have you ever had the TJB virus?"

"No I haven't. I've never been with a man, so you can rest assured on that score." Helen's mouth was a tight line. "But it's a good point. Other viruses can be sexually transmitted, you know. Have you ever – "

"Um, yeah." I felt the heat in my face. "But it was the first time for both of us, so I guess we're OK. Please don't say anything to Mum and Dad. They might say I'm too young." I held my breath.

"You're sixteen." Helen's smile held a hint of longing. Funny, it had never occurred to me that behind that façade of practicality was a woman with feelings. "And Matt's a lovely boy. It's good to see you happy."

Helen located my vein, inserted the needle – a pricking sensation but not the pain I'd expected – then raised my arm. I blinked. There was my blood, flowing down a polymer tube until it dripped from the needle at the other end.

"Hey, don't waste it." I laughed.

"I need to calculate the flow … raise your arm a little more … that should do it. OK, here goes." With impressive dexterity, Helen inserted the needle into her own arm.

"It's working!"

We watched, open-mouthed, as my blood flowed into Helen.

"This is the most surreal thing I've ever done," I said. "Can you feel anything?"

"Only the needle." We waited for a few minutes. "That should be 100 ml. Let's stop." Helen took out both needles and gave me a sterile pad to hold to her elbow.

"Just a tiny little bruise. Amazing," I breathed. "How much can we give in an emergency?"

"A maximum of 10 ml per kilo body weight. I guess you weigh about the same as me – around 50 kilos – so that's 500 ml."

"And how much blood could someone lose if they were shot and still survive?"

"A few litres at most," Helen said.

This sobering thought swirled in my head as I returned home. Were our efforts going to be any use whatsoever? But a message from Harry sent my spirits soaring.

Joy of my heart, do you still exist, or have you been fatally infected with sensible blood? I've had a wonderful idea. We've been sorting out our schedule for the next month, and we're on our way up the Lancashire canal soon. We'll be passing Macclesfield on the morning of the 15th July. I've managed to talk Mum into staying there for a few hours. Can you make it over? I know the timing's not ideal, but the farm will survive without you for one day. I'll spontaneously combust if I don't see you soon, and burn the boat. You can't be responsible for Mum losing a son and a livelihood. The horses still need exercising don't they? Get yourself on the stable rota; I know you'll work something out. Love you forever H xxx

I fired off an immediate response.

I survived intact – the transfusion was a stunning success! Though whether it's going to be any use in a practical situation is another matter entirely. I can't help thinking all our silly little experiments are just spitting in the wind and we'll never be able to carry them out on a large scale. But I guess we have to try.

But you, my genius boy, have made my heart sing. I'll check the rota tomorrow; I get stable duty at least once a week. But I'll be there, even if I have to walk every step. Usually we exercise the horses early so I'll be there waiting for you.

I discovered Helen has never been with a man – I wanted to scream at her: get out of this room now, get out there and LIVE! Three weeks, then I can live again too.

With love and Joy xxxxxxx

I closed his message and hugged myself. Living like this wasn't too bad. Working with Helen had given me a renewed sense of purpose. Daily messages from Harry, and illicit meetings every time he was within a twenty-five kilometre radius. Oh yes, it would do for now.

CHAPTER 10 - CATHY

As heat ravaged hope of a good night's sleep, I wished I could join in the backbreaking labour that was summer on the farm. I'd always adored the camaraderie and the fact that Michael didn't travel during these months, the demands of the land taking over. Even Scott was part of the grand effort, busy in the soft fruit plantation where the children, faces pink from the sun and furtive strawberry-eating, fingers red and sticky, filled baskets of strawberries, raspberries and gooseberries.

I looked at Adam with the now familiar mixture of resentment and guilt. Although almost weaned from the breast, he still cried often, no doubt yearning for the love that I wasn't providing. Why had I thought that telling Helen would help? All I'd done was confirm the awful truth I'd been unable to voice. And now Helen came to see me every few weeks and I was running out of things to say to her.

"We've got to get past this, sweetheart, haven't we? Maybe I'll take you to see Nanna," I said to Adam.

I wandered over to Anna's where she and two other older residents were busy preserving fruit and vegetables, and breathed in the spicy, acid aroma. I loved the smell of pickling vinegar.

"Hey, everyone. Can I help?" I said.

"You could sterilise some jars," Anna suggested. "How's my little Adam?"

"He's fine." I suppressed my irritation as everyone fussed over the baby. But soon I found myself enjoying the industrious atmosphere. While Anna pickled asparagus, Kate, perched on a chair because her joints were playing her up, filled jars with strawberries and then placed them in a pan of boiling water. Even her husband Jack, his eyes milk-tinged and almost sightless due to cataracts, was able to shell peas and place them on a tray for oven drying. My spirits rose. I'd always enjoyed Kate and Anna's company. Then Adam started crying.

"Sorry, I'd better take him out," I said.

Anna picked him up and he stopped crying. I shot him a look of hurt and anger.

"Why don't you leave him with us for a while?" Anna suggested. "Take yourself off for a walk to the farm; it's too nice a day for you to be stuck indoors with us old farts."

I wandered up to the fields and surveyed the scene with a mixture of satisfaction and anxiety. As cows chewed indifferently in the sun, their ears and tails flicking away the flies, the humans laboured like frantic drones, pausing only to wipe the sweat from their faces. There was no time to rest; any delay in bringing in the barley harvest could lead to spoilt crops and that would mean food shortages in the winter. And every year, our gang of workers became more depleted. The first person I saw was Daisy.

"Hey, lucky you to miss this," she said. "I've had to stop for a rest. My back's killing me."

"Huh, I'm bored stupid, to be honest. I'd give anything to be working with the rest of you. Honestly, Daisy, what's happened to me?"

"Still not bonding with him?" Daisy asked. I'd confided in her. She was the only one apart from Helen I dare tell; perfect earth mother Mary wouldn't understand. I loved Mary, but she'd always sailed through pregnancies and motherhood with sickening ease. Scott and her third child Ian had been born within months of each other but while my labour had lasted twelve hours, hers had only been four.

"Not really. Poor thing; it's not his fault."

"You ought to talk to Michael," Daisy said.

"Huh. All he's good for these days is having a beer when he gets home then spending the rest of the evening on his DataBand."

"This big plan you can't talk about. I know." Daisy's words were heavy with resentment.

"Sorry, I wish I could, but you know how he is. He doesn't even want to be at home at the moment, I can tell. He feels trapped; he wants to be working on The Plan."

"Tell you what, come and do a morning on the fields

tomorrow," Daisy suggested. "I'll take Adam and Scott to the market."

"Oh, would you? I never thought a morning's backbreaking work could be so appealing."

"Time with the kids. You know I love it. Seriously, Cathy, let me share the burden more." Daisy's eyes held a wistful expression and I became consumed with guilt. Daisy had so much to offer, but her slim frame, so desired in the Citidome, wasn't considered attractive on the outside, and her choice of men was, of course, limited.

"You're wonderful. Joy and the boys are so lucky to have a second mum." I hugged her. "But look at us. We're all getting older. Daniel shouldn't be working so hard at his age." We glanced at the village leader, hefting heaps of cut stems. He was approaching sixty and his face was a worrying shade of pink that spoke of something more serious than sunburn.

"Who's winning the contest?"

"Matt, of course, but he's got his fan club egging him on."

I smiled. The competition to cut the most barley in a day was a longstanding village tradition and Scott and Ian's vocal support was helping Matt. This year the competition seemed more one-sided than ever. Matt had formed a mountain of stems.

"Boys are so much more straightforward than girls aren't they?" I commented to Daisy. "Scott idolises Matt. All he aspires to is being as good a farmer as him."

"But Joy's changed, hasn't she?" said Daisy. "She's more focussed in the lab and seems happier all round. Never thought she'd settle down with Matt but they make a lovely couple."

"Yeah, they seem inseparable these days. She's out with him every evening, that's when we can prise her away from the DataBand."

"What's she doing with that?"

"Exchanging medical knowledge on Out There. She's really taken to helping Helen."

"Seems odd; Helen's a bit young to be needing an apprentice. Or is she going into the AOC full-time? I heard that yes-men go a long way."

My eyes darted to the ground; the secrecy was becoming increasingly difficult. And Daisy had always resented the fact that Helen was in the AOC and not herself.

"No, Joy's doing this in her own time so I'm not discouraging it. Typical Joy, she doesn't just study the useful things, but tries to cram the history of medicine into her brain. But it's calmed her down. And Matt's a good influence."

"Poor old Ryan," Daisy commented. "He's still hung up on her, you know. And he's not doing very well in the competition. Even young Craig's done more than him. I feel for him; he tries hard, you know, but he hates farming."

"Yeah, he seems a bright kid, wasted out here. I often wonder why Joy didn't choose him; they seem to get on so well. I think she's leaving him free for Beth but that relationship's never going to happen."

"No, he told me the same. He feels pressured to ask Beth out but he finds her boring."

"Weird, isn't it? Michael and I were both considered ugly in the Citidomes, and yet we managed to produce this girl that three young men are in love with."

"The third being Harry, I take it?"

"Yes. Dee doesn't say much when I ask how he is; I guess he took it badly."

"You never could accept how stunning you wer – are, could you?" Daisy corrected herself hastily. "Anyway, I'd better get back to work."

I trudged home, feeling even more dispirited. Yes, perhaps I was stunning once, by village standards, at least. But now look at me. I placed my hand on the loose flesh of my stomach. No, mustn't be negative. Seeing Joy happy and settled was the best thing to happen in our household for a long time. And as for Adam, maybe I would talk to Michael. Maybe it was time to bind our family closer together.

***

I'd barely finished washing up after dinner when I heard the bang. It sounded like Michael had thrown something against the wall. Then came a thundering down the steps. He slammed the DataBand on the kitchen table.

"Where's Joy?" he growled. His face was crimson, a vein twitching in his temple. What was it? For an awful moment I thought he was about to have a seizure.

"Down by the river. What's up?"

"Shouldn't have trusted her. She didn't log out last night. One thing I thought I'd drilled into her was to log out at the end of every session. Imagine what would've happened if anyone had got hold of the DataBand. She could've ruined everything. Then I noticed her private messenger flashing, which was odd. I never showed her how to use it. And guess what I found? He shoved the DataBand over to me. The virtual screen was filled with a list of messages, all from someone listed as H. I opened one at random.

I'm feeling Joyless today.

I smiled. Ah, it must be Harry. So they'd remained friends. I was pleased.

But your msg helped. Have you swallowed that medical dictionary or what? I've never heard of half of those conditions. The cancer epidemic always fascinated me. I heard of one case of it, in Hest Bank, but it's rare. Interesting that they can't screen it out in the Citidomes, isn't it? But if I was forced there, I think my cells would rebel and become one huge tumour. And yes, I suspect that Fin might have multiple sclerosis. The symptoms seem to fit. So he'll end up unable to walk? Poor guy; I don't like him but he doesn't deserve that.

"What's your problem with this?" I said to Michael. Joy was obsessed with learning about twenty-first century disease at the moment, and had told me her theory of Fin, not that it comforted me. I wouldn't wish that sort of illness on anyone. "They're only exchanging ideas. She can't have this sort of

conversation with Matt, can she?"
"Read on," Michael said.

> We went to Oxford, remember me telling you, that city with the ancient colleges? It gave me a curious sense of melancholy, a nostalgia for a life I've never experienced. They call it the city of dreaming spires you know, and sitting here, my imagination runs free. I wonder if we'll ever be able to use the cities again? This place should be top of the list for recolonisation. It has everything – fabulous architecture, canal and road links. The college buildings could accommodate hundreds, thousands even. You and I should settle there and enjoy lives of idle content, realising our potential.
>
> But now I'm back on the boat with a ton of electrical cable. Why does the mundane always interrupt our dreams? Talking of which, say hey to Matt for me and don't dance too close to him at the social. And don't spend too much time with Ryan. I'm getting jealous of all these cosy chats you tell me about. You should only ever be cosy with me. Yours with love and jealousy H xxx

Oh no. Not just a friendly message. I could feel the anger emanating from Michael, a pot about to boil over. I tried to keep my voice even. "I'm disappointed in her; didn't think she'd do that to Matt. How many of these have you read?"

"Only one at first, pretty much like that. But I had to see when it started, so I read the first one." I scrolled down and noticed that the messages had started on the day Harry last visited in the spring.

> Hey, my Joy. Let me know as soon as possible whether you got this. I won't sleep until I hear from you. It killed me to say goodbye to you today. You were on the verge of tears, weren't

you? So was I, but life will be so much better if I can at least speak to you most days. Don't msg me every day if your dad's around; he'll get suspicious.

We're spending the night outside Leeds. I'm reliving yesterday, how I discovered Joy, and wondering why the hell we didn't do it sooner. In my head I'd been building the First Time into something so epic that it could only disappoint. How wrong I was! All those wasted years of virginity. We have to meet again. When's your dad next away? Maybe you could go out on the horse for the day? I have to see you again soon. Sexual frustration is bad for a man's health.

Say hey to Matt for me. I liked him – he's a good sport to go along with this. And now I've met him, I'm not threatened at all. I know you'd never settle for someone who wasn't intellectually curious. Glad it's not Ryan your dad wanted you to be with. He strikes me as more of a threat; he has more about him but not the body of a charismatic stranger, obviously. Now I'm thinking about your body ... Anyway, enough of my jealousy; I'll erase the image of you dancing with Matt from my memory. One day we'll dance together like that.

Love you, H xxx

A rush of nostalgia seized me, remembering when Michael and I used to exchange passionate messages of longing. But now wasn't the time to say this. I'd started to read another when Michael's arm twitched and he thumped the table.

"Looks like all three of them have been laughing at me behind my back for the last few months. Well it stops now."

He marched out of the house, slamming the door behind him. I followed, terrified what he might do in this mood, and at the same time cursing my own stupidity. Why hadn't I questioned Joy's sudden change of heart about Harry? But those messages had stirred me. When did Michael and I last have any sort of amorous exchange of words? And what sort of mother was I if my daughter was prepared to concoct such an elaborate deception?

The group of laughing young people, all enjoying the long evenings and Anna's cider, dispersed at Michael's bellow.

"Joy, Matt, here. Now."

"Let's go indoors," I urged. "We don't want to entertain the whole village."

"You two follow me," Michael said to Joy and Matt. They slunk behind him in silence, heads hung, until they reached the house. He turned to Joy first. "You're not going on Out There any more," he said. "As if it wasn't bad enough you not logging out, I saw your messages to Harry."

Her hands shot to her hips. "You had no right to read my private things," she snapped.

"Yes I did, and I'm not surprised you're blushing. And you've got no right to go behind my back. In case you've forgotten, I'm your father, and as long as you live here you'll do as I say."

"Then I won't live here any more," Joy said. "You don't own me. I'll run away, go to Harry."

"Run away and you'll never set foot in this house again."

I opened my mouth to speak but before I had a chance, Michael had started on to Matt. "And what the hell have you been playing at, making fools of everyone?"

"S-sorry," Matt stammered. "It was my idea."

"But why?"

"I love living here. I want to take over the farm one day. Please don't trade me the way you did David."

Michael let out a heavy sigh. "I never planned to trade you, Matt. You're doing a brilliant job on the farm. Go back out and join the others; I need to talk to Joy on her own."

Matt made his escape and Michael dropped to his seat. Joy's expression was mutinous.

"You can't stop me seeing him," she hissed.

"You're only sixteen. You're too young to know who you want to be with."

"And if I said I wanted to be with Matt, my age would be

irrelevant. Besides, I've known Harry my entire life. What about you and Mum? You were almost as young as us when you got together."

"That's not the point. I introduced you to Out There because I thought you were interested in what we were trying to achieve, but all you've done is use it to deceive me. And leaving yourself logged in? What would have happened if someone had found it? You could have ruined everything."

"I'd have been honest with you if you'd been reasonable," Joy yelled. "What's wrong with me loving Harry? Don't you want me to be happy?"

"Course I do, but I'm not convinced Harry's the one for you. He's never going to leave Dec, you know. And you have a duty to this village; don't forget that."

"Huh, I have a duty to be happy. We've got it all worked out. When I'm eighteen I'm going to take over from Dee." Her mouth was set tight.

"But –" I started but Michael interrupted.

"And does Dee know this?"

"Yeah. Can I go now?" Joy stood up.

"Hang on, don't I get a chance to say –" I began but once more Michael cut me short.

"Get out, I can't bear to look at you," he muttered, and Joy marched out of the door, slamming it.

"Think you could've handled that better," I said.

"Does everyone have it in for me at the moment?" He slammed his fist on the chair arm. "Are you going to join the rest of them – Joy, Matt, Harry, Dee, all plotting behind my back?"

"No, I just wanted the chance to get a word in edgeways. What's the high-handed father routine about? In case you hadn't noticed, I'm her parent too."

"The soft-and-friendly approach doesn't seem to have done much good," he growled.

"But if she's so determined to be with Harry, surely we should at least talk to her. You read those messages. They're more than lovestruck kids fooling about."

"I've done all the talking I need. I'm putting a stop to this." He left the room.

I slumped in my seat, dropping my head into my hands.

Adam started screaming, as usual. At that point, Scott slunk indoors.

"Why was Dad shouting?"

"Don't worry, sweetheart. Joy's been cheeky again, that's all. Look, your baby brother's upset. Shall we see if we can cheer him up?"

I looked into the frightened eyes of my son and blinked back my own tears. It tore at me to upset the one uncomplicated member of my family. How had we come to this? And how could I stop my family falling apart?

CHAPTER 11 - JOY

I stormed back to the river, the happiness of the balmy evening ruined. I returned to a collection of gawking eyes, everyone itching to hear all about it.

"Have another cider," said Matt. "How bad was it?"

"Bad with a capital B."

"What's happened?" asked Ryan.

"I've been sending messages to Harry with Dad's DataBand. Intimate ones." My eyes dropped to my feet. "Dad found out."

Ryan frowned. "You mean that you two…"

"Have been leading everybody on. Yeah," said Matt.

"A courtship of mutual convenience," I added.

Elsie started laughing. "You're terrible," she said.

I clenched my jaw. Elsie had managed to become part of our group rather than hanging around with the younger kids and I found her presence increasingly intrusive. But since everyone was working together on the fields we couldn't ignore her. Not only was she irritating, but also she was useless. She'd been pulling the flax with me last week and hadn't listened to a single one of the instructions, meaning I'd had to work twice as hard as usual.

"Why don't you wait until your dad's calmer, and talk to him about how you feel about Harry? Make him see how real it is," said Beth.

"I guess so," I said without conviction. I'd never seen Dad as mad as that before. He'd have to be a hell of a lot calmer before I could even mention Harry's name. In six more days I'd see Harry anyway. Getting myself on the stables rota had been easy; Luke had always been easy to manipulate. Beth was on the nearby dairy and would cover for me while I was out.

I returned home to find Mum on the sofa, Adam and Scott both curled up on her lap. Mum gave me a half-apologetic look. I didn't meet her gaze; if she was on my side, why hadn't she said so? Dad was using the DataBand. Was he going to give me another mouthful? But when he looked up, his expression had changed: sad and defeated.

"You've blown your chances of using this from now on," he muttered. "To think I thought you mature enough to handle it. And you're grounded apart from when you're working. No movies, socials or market day for a month. Or working with Helen when you're supposed to be out on the land. I'll have to rethink whether I want you involved in Outbreak day at all."

I shrank from him. His disappointment was almost harder to bear than his anger.

It took two days to get the house to myself. The Sunday movie was a family one – E.T. – so Mum had taken Scott. Of all the annoyances of being grounded, I missed the movies more than anything, but the same ones came around every year. Once upstairs I ran to the drawer and wasn't surprised to find it empty. Dad wasn't that stupid. But after a frantic hour, I still hadn't found the DataBand. That made my mind up. If Dad was going to treat me like a child, I'd act like one. I was getting on that boat with Harry and never getting off. I'd message Helen from Dee's DataBand; I wouldn't let her down on Outbreak day whether Dad wanted me involved or not. But I wasn't going to live here any more.

Mum and I didn't get any time on our own until Monday. "Why didn't you feel you could tell me?" she said.

Oh no. Why was everyone trying this hurt, despondent approach? But it made a change to hear soft words from Mum, whose default setting these days was irritable. "You've got Adam to think about," I said.

"Be patient, sweetheart. Your dad'll soften in time. He was more upset about you not logging out than messaging Harry."

"I have to be with him, Mum." I sobbed. "I can't live without him."

"Sometimes the timing's wrong. Think of your dad and me in the Citidomes. We had to wait. Everything's going to be different after Outbreak day. It's only four months. Can't you wait until then?"

Four months? She may as well have said four years. On

Wednesday I cornered Beth.

"If I don't come back tomorrow," I whispered, "I'll leave Bramble tethered by the canal in Macclesfield. Mum and Dad will know where."

"You're not! You can't!"

"I can and I will." I looked at Beth's stricken expression and softened. "I'll come back and visit sometime, but I can't live here any more."

"You'll never get away with it! They'll drag you back then you'll never be able to see Harry again."

"They can't stop me. We have no laws. I'm free to live with whoever I like."

Deep down I suspected Beth was right. I knew it was a crazy thing to do and that I wouldn't get away with it. But crazy and desperate were how I was feeling. It had been the worst summer I could remember. The heat was oppressive, the field work tougher than ever, and when I left early one afternoon to see Helen, you'd have thought I'd single-handedly caused the crop to fail. Every move I made seemed to confirm my status as Difficult Daughter. Nothing felt right these days except messaging Harry and talking about medicine with Helen. And now Dad had taken both from me.

On Thursday morning I set off at dawn. Dad was already up.

"Starting early, aren't you?" he said.

"Bramble didn't seem quite herself yesterday," I said. "I wanted to make sure she was OK."

"It's nice to see you caring so much," Dad said.

By eight o clock I'd fed, groomed and exercised all the horses, mounted Bramble and was galloping across the hills in the direction of Macclesfield, a knot of anxiety tightening in my stomach. What would Harry have made of the sudden silence? What if he'd changed his plans at the last minute and hadn't been able to tell me? By the time I arrived there was no sign of the boat. The stomach knot tightened but my rational voice took over. I'd waited here for hours in the past; it was impossible for him to give accurate times.

I tethered Bramble, made a daisy chain and fastened it round my neck. He'd like that; he was the one who'd shown me how to make them. I looked at my watch; he couldn't be long now. He was coming from the south, wasn't he? Perhaps I'd intercept him early. I mounted Bramble, trotted southwards down the canal, and after twenty minutes saw a young girl gathering wild herbs.

"Have you seen any canal boats here today?" I asked.

"Yeah, a while ago. The one with the lady with dreadlocks and her son with the curly hair. They're nice," the girl said.

"D-did he say anything about meeting anyone?"

"No, I asked if they were stopping, but they weren't."

I ripped the daisy chain from my neck.

He hadn't stopped? Why not? How far up the canal would they be by now? Could I catch them up? I changed direction, but the towpath northwards became so overgrown with nettles that it was impossible. I made the long journey home, my heart calcifying with every kilometre. It was mid-afternoon by the time I reached the stables and Bramble was panting. Once I'd settled her, I ran to the dairy.

"What happened?" whispered Beth.

"He wasn't there. He'd passed through without stopping. How am I ever going to find him?"

"Forget it. You know it was a daft idea."

"But why did he do it?" I was whimpering by now.

"I don't know; maybe he got the date wrong. He'll send you a message at the market; he always does. Bloody hell, calm down. You're in deep shit, you know. Everyone's been asking where you are."

It took ten minutes of Beth calming me before I was able to face the army of disapproving adults.

"Why have you been out so long? You know Bramble shouldn't overdo it on a hot day." Mary was the first to start on me. "And weren't you meant to be picking salad greens today?"

"I fancied an early morning ride but Bramble started limping. I had to walk her back."

"Hmm, I'll have a look at her." Mary's face said that she didn't believe me.

Then I saw Dad. "Do you want to be grounded forever?" But there was a lack of conviction in his voice.

And then cold, clammy realisation dawned. If he'd read all my messages, he would have known about our planned meeting today. But what could he have done to stop it? Harry wouldn't have been deterred by a message forbidding him to see me. At the very least, he'd have left a message with the girl on the canal bank. Nothing made sense.

As my status in the family reached an all-time low, I tried and failed to understand what had happened to Harry.

"You've got to move past this," Mum said. "Luke told me that you didn't show up for work the other day. I haven't told your dad, but if he gets to hear he's going to ground you for life."

"I don't have to live here, under his tyranny."

"Actually, you do. If you have family here, you live with them until you get married. You know the village rules."

"I'll run away."

"Where to? And how? Mary's banned you from riding the horses. Grow up, Joy. I know what Harry means to you but you've got to earn our trust again. Prove you're not the selfish kid your dad thinks you are."

As Mum's sympathy ebbed away, my despair grew. My only hope of contacting Harry was Lynn at the market stall. The boat only passed through Langley Mill every few months. But Dad wouldn't relent on his market veto until the middle of August. I prepared a message but by the time I next saw Lynn, it was too late.

"I saw Harry this week," she said. "What's happened between you two?"

I stiffened. What had he said? "Dad's stopped me from contacting him. Did he have a message for me?"

"No. When I asked him, he said he had nothing to say to you. I assumed you'd fallen out. He stayed at our village for two nights. And he had – sorry, there's no good way to tell you this – he had his arm round Caroline, my niece. She's had her eye on him for years. They've always been friends, but it's turned into something more."

In that moment, my world came to an end. And nothing mattered any more.

***

"You've got to eat something, sweetheart," Mum urged.

"You're going to make yourself ill."

"Why don't you go join the others by the river tonight?" Dad said. "It's a beautiful evening."

"No, I want to be on my own. But if I'm not grounded any more, I'll go for a walk."

I marched up towards Monsal Head, setting a ferocious pace, but the pounding of my feet against the dry, cracked earth couldn't block the roaring in my brain. It hadn't stopped since Lynn told me. Once I reached the top, I sat on the bench where I'd sat with Harry, five months ago. Where he'd asked me to live on the canals with him. My thoughts turned to Mum's friend in the Citidome, the man who killed himself. I'd found it impossible to imagine despair so all-consuming that would cause someone to end his life. But at that time I couldn't imagine Harry ever leaving me for someone else. I looked towards the viaduct. If I jumped from the top … could I? I was so lost in thought that I didn't realise that someone had sat down next to me.

"Daisy!"

"Your mum asked me to look for you. She's out of her mind with worry and thought that since you wouldn't talk to her, maybe you'd talk to me."

I don't know what it was about her voice but something snapped in me. I hadn't cried, not once, and normally it didn't take much to make me cry. But now it felt like I'd never be able to stop.

"Looks like you needed that." Daisy handed me a square of cloth and I blew my nose. "Come on then, tell all."

"It's a secret," I muttered.

"Thought it might be."

It had always been the same. I told Daisy everything. I'd always adored her, not in the same way as I did Mum and Dad, but it was easier to talk to someone who didn't take my every failing so personally. Someone older who treated me as a friend, not a disappointment. And so I spilled out the whole story.

"I can't tell anyone. If they find out I tried to run away … But Harry – I don't get it. Surely he must have guessed that Dad had stopped me using the DataBand? How could he replace me so quickly?" Fresh tears escaped my eyes.

"I don't know." Daisy sighed. "But has it occurred to you that Harry might have rigged up the scenario with this girl deliberately, knowing it'd get back to you? To punish you for not keeping in touch?"

"B-but, why would he be so childish? He's not like that."

"People don't think rationally when they're in love. You're the living proof. Honestly, Joy. Running away? What were you thinking?"

"I guess it wasn't my smartest move. But Harry must have guessed the reason why I stopped messaging. I suppose he couldn't resist the temptation any longer. They all throw themselves at him you know – the young women in the communities he visits. He has this exoticism about him."

"You're not going to settle until you contact him, are you? I've had an idea. Let's go and see Helen. She's the only other one with a working DataBand. Say you need to use it on AOC business and your Dad's not around."

"Daisy, you're a genius." I hugged her. Helen would be on my side.

I was wrong.

"I can't allow it unless it's approved by your dad," Helen said, her lips thinned to the point of invisibility. "He told me about your deceit. I have to say, I'm disappointed in you. Now, if you'll excuse me, I'm busy." She closed the door in our faces.

"I don't believe it!" I said. "Is everyone against me? Helen's one of the few people that doesn't treat me like a kid."

"Huh, prissy bitch," Daisy said. "She needs a good shagging; that's her problem."

"Daisy!" I giggled despite everything.

"It's not natural, you know, living on your own like she does."

"But you don't – "

"Have anyone. No, but I meet guys in Bakewell from time to time. Better than nothing, you know. Talking of better than nothing, I had a visit from Ryan last night."

"You like him, don't you?" I said. "You're always talking at socials. Shame he's too young for you."

"I wouldn't say no to a younger man. But I think he's kind

of adopted me as a mother figure. Us BodyImperfects have to stick together." She laughed. "Last night, he'd come to talk to me about something else. He's thinking of moving on after the harvest ends because he knows he's never going to win your heart."

"Oh no. Pile on the guilt, why don't you? What am I meant to do? I can't force myself to love someone else. I can't imagine being with anyone but Harry."

"I know this is going to seem like the most inane comment ever, but time and perspective changes things." Daisy put a hand on my shoulder.

"It sounds like the sort of thing an adult says to a child." But until that point, she'd treated me like an adult and I was grateful. "Daisy, have you ever been in love?"

"No. There was that guy from Chatsworth a few years ago but he wanted me to move there and I couldn't leave my family, could I? Some people just aren't hardwired for passion and I'm one of them."

"I always wondered – did you love my dad?"

"Hell, no." Daisy smiled. "Forgot you've been reading your mum's journal. It took her a long time to trust me. I liked your dad – we were good mates from the start. Don't get me wrong – and I know this is weird to hear about your dad – but he was sex on legs."

"Daisy!"

"Sorry, couldn't resist." She grinned. "But even if he hadn't been taken, you could tell he was one of those intense types. Ambitious. Wasn't what I wanted."

"Not sure it's what Mum wants any more." My eyes lowered. "I haven't told anyone this, but they're always rowing these days."

"What about?"

"Everything. Me – Mum's on my side about Harry, and –" I cut myself off in mid-sentence. Daisy didn't yet know about Outbreak. "About him being away so much. And there was a time when I used to hear them at night – y'know – pretty icky to hear your mum and dad doing the deed. But there was something kind of comforting about it. If nothing else, I knew they really, really loved each other. But they don't any more. And Adam cries, and Scott plays up to get attention.

Everything's falling apart."

"All relationships have bad patches. If anyone can get through this, your mum and dad can. It'll be AOC business taking up all his energy. What you have to remember about your dad, is that he's motivated by hatred. No-one hated the Citidomes more than him."

"Except maybe Harry; they're so alike in that way. Why couldn't Dad see that?"

"Maybe he could. Maybe that's why he wanted to save you."

"I didn't want to be saved." I took a long, weary breath. "Come on, let's go home."

As we approached the village, we saw David talking with Matt and their sister Dora. Strange, he didn't usually visit midweek.

"What are you doing here, carrots?" I swallowed my words. Their eyes were rimmed with red. "What's the matter?"

"It's Gran. She d-died this afternoon."

I rushed to hug them. We'd all been worried about Kate when she said she had abdominal pains. It must have been appendicitis after all. The more I read, the more the inadequacies of our medical facilities frustrated me. A Citidome surgeon could have operated and saved her. Even worse, for the last few years, Kate had been in constant pain from a condition called osteoarthritis, something that ran in her family along with red hair and freckles, and her husband had an eye condition called cataracts that meant he could barely see.

"I'm so sorry. Your gran was lovely. I'll come and pay my respects later. Is Beth OK?" Beth was Kate's great-granddaughter but since Kate was more like a mother than a grandmother to Mary – her own mum died in childbirth – Beth also called Kate gran.

"Yeah, she's there at the moment, with Mary," David said. "I'm going to ride over to Hathersage, to tell Uncle Peter."

I felt Daisy stiffen. Of course. Peter was Kate's son. Daisy's ex-partner. And, I thought with a sinking feeling, of the person whose betrayal had almost killed Mum. Could life get any worse?

CHAPTER 12 - CATHY

The clear, sharp-shadowed days seemed endless. The once brilliant green fields faded to parched yellow and glowed salmon pink in the evening light. Even I had found my mood mellowing with the colours around me. But losing Kate had cast a cloud over the community.

"I never had a friend as good as her." Anna could barely speak for crying.

I consoled her as much as I could but words couldn't bring Kate back. I knew how Anna felt – I valued my friendships with Daisy and Mary as much as my own family. As Daisy approached, my tension loosened. Joy was with her.

"Nanna, we just heard." Joy flung her arms around Anna.

Daisy beckoned me away from the others. "We saw Matt and David," she muttered. "Peter's going to have to come back."

"Ugh, of course. Let's hope it's a short visit. Oh – that won't be easy for you, either."

My heart lurched. Over the years I'd witnessed many deaths in the community but Kate's had touched me more than most. I remembered talking to her on my first visit here; her self-deprecating charm had been one of the reasons I felt I'd be able to start a new life here. Now the presence at her funeral of the man I despised with every cell of my body, would intrude on my grief. I swallowed the thought, along with the rising acidity. Of course Peter had the right to mourn his mother's death. But Peter had been the only scourge in my happy first months of village life, first groping me in the dairy, then telling the Citidome authorities my hiding place when my pregnancy had made me the most wanted woman in the state. The price for his betrayal was a jar of coffee. I tried to force thoughts of him out of my mind, and return to the most important problem: my beautiful daughter, who didn't eat or talk to me any more.

"Don't worry about me; I'm long over that slime," Daisy said. "It's you I'm worried about. So's Joy. What's going on with you and Michael?"

"Oh, I don't know. He took such a hard line over Joy; we always used to agree on parenting. Now, it seems, we don't agree on anything. Did she say much to you?"

"Yeah. She's in bad shape, all right. I'm not supposed to tell you, but she used to exchange messages with Harry through Lynn at the market. But he's gone off with someone else."

"Oh no. That's the last thing I imagined. There has to be some mistake."

"That's what I told her."

"I'll send a message to Dee and try to get to the bottom of this."

Our conversation was interrupted by a stream of expletives from Anna. Joy must have told her about Peter.

"Huh, the hypocrisy of it," Anna raged. "Kate hasn't seen Peter for years. There was no love lost there; she never forgave him for what he did to you. But I guess he has to come; he's still close to Margaret. Funerals aren't for the dead; they're for the living."

"Don't expect me to be civil to him," Joy said. "I think he should be banned from here forever."

I smiled at the vehemence in Joy's words, pleased to see some of her spirit intact. But if Harry had found someone else, how was I going to get her through this? I'd become tired with fending off complaints that she wasn't pulling her weight in the harvesting and seemed distracted half the time. Her silent treatment of us had lasted all summer. All she did each evening was go to her room with those damned medical books. Typical Joy. Of course I understood why she couldn't settle to full-time farm work, like Beth or Matt. She needed intellectual stimulation. I'd spent the last year trying to find her a role she might feel passionate about. Mentally challenging jobs were hard to find, and the chemical plant and teaching had failed to inflame her. But medicine? After Outbreak day, we'd have no need for a second health worker in the community; it was too much of a luxury. Michael, of course, didn't see it that way, and said she should be encouraged. And he'd refused to relent on letting her contact Harry.

"She's my daughter too. Don't I get a say in what she can and can't do?" I'd protested. "It's killing me to see her this unhappy."

"And it's making me proud to see her growing up and settling down to her studies."

Would this latest crisis bring Joy and us closer or draw us further apart? The gathering around the bridge began to disperse. Adam stirred in his buggy. "I'd better get this little one home. Coming, Joy?"

"No, I'll stay outside a little longer."

I shrugged. Could Joy not bear to spend even a few moments in my company? These days Daisy was doing a better job of parenting my kids than I was. When I returned, Michael was slumped in the armchair.

"Hey sweetheart," he said. "I dozed off. You have a nice time by the river?"

"Yeah." Which piece of bad news should I give him first? "But I've got some sad news. Kate – she didn't make it."

"Oh no. How's Mum taking it?"

"Not well. And Daisy found Joy. Turns out she found out from Lynn in the market that Harry's found someone else. But we're not meant to know that, so don't say anything to her."

"Well, it was bound to happen eventually."

"I suppose so – but Michael, do you want her to be so miserable? Why don't we send Dee a message, see whether it's serious? It might just be a rebound thing – revenge because Joy cut off communications so abruptly."

"No. Leave it. I'll be seeing them tomorrow anyway. I'll find out what's going on."

I'd forgotten that Michael was due to visit them. AOC business, of course. But I didn't trust him to come back with an unbiased version of events. "I'd rather contact Dee myself. Where are you hiding the DataBand, anyway?"

"I'd rather no-one used it except me. Joy's already wasted enough time on it."

"So you're telling me what I can and can't do now?"

The resulting argument exhausted me so much that I

couldn't face telling him about the prospect of Peter's visit. Why was he being so high-handed? Unless … were there some messages on there he didn't want me to see? But Scott came back, then Joy, and Adam started crying. Again. I put him to bed, and when I returned downstairs, Michael had dozed off. The next day he left for a three-day visit to the canal.

Daniel visited me the following morning. The village leader had aged in the last few years and had lost some of the vigour that had made him well respected.

"Cathy, I have two things to ask you." He swallowed. "I don't know if you've heard, but Peter came back yesterday."

"I heard he was on his way." My voice was leaden.

"He and Margaret came to see me last night. He wants to rejoin the community. He says his dad needs him."

"Hell, no." I wanted to scream, to stamp my feet and shout, "Keep that man away from me." But Daniel hadn't come to me to hear a childish tantrum. I tried to focus. Jack's eyesight was too poor for him to live alone; someone needed to look after him. "Can't Margaret and Frank look after Jack?"

"He needs someone in the house with him, and with Matt still at home, there's barely enough room for him to move in with them. And there's another thing." Daniel hesitated, and then continued. "Peter's only forty-three and still fit and strong. He used to be a damn fine dairyman, you know. Since Paul died, we've struggled in the dairy. Vincent does his best but we could use Peter's help."

I said nothing. Daniel wanted me to give him my blessing to bring Peter back and I couldn't give it. The worst thing was, he was right. We desperately needed an experienced dairyman. I'd lost count of how many failed batches of cheese we'd had in the last year. It had been one of our best trading commodities at the Bakewell market.

"I said we'd put it to the vote at the council." Daniel's eyes didn't meet mine. "There'll be a meeting this evening. But I wanted to see you in private first. If it'll be too difficult for you, we'll have to take that into account."

"How do we know that Peter hasn't been kicked out of the Hathersage community?" I said.

"The thought crossed my mind. I sent a message to the

village leader. She said that Peter had been a hard-working, valued member of the community and had a long-term relationship with a woman there but they'd recently split up."

"So that's the real reason he wants to come back," I muttered. "He wants a new woman."

"Probably." Daniel sighed. "Truth is, I don't want him back any more than you do. But I can't find any reason to turn him away. There's one other way ... it's something I've been wondering about for a while. I'm going to stand down as village leader, and carry on as a council member. I haven't told anyone but I've been getting chest pains and my blood pressure's high. Helen thinks I should rest more. Traditionally a retiring leader proposes someone new and the council votes. I'd like to propose you, if you'd agree."

"Me?" I gasped. "Surely Michael or someone older? Margaret? Frank? Virginia? They've been on the council far longer than me. Or someone new? What about Daisy?"

"Michael's too busy with the AOC. Virginia's no leader. Margaret's related to so many of the villagers; she and Frank wouldn't be impartial. And Daisy – I'm not sure she takes things as seriously as you do. You're a natural leader, Cathy, the perfect choice. If I propose you as leader first, it'd give you a chance to veto any decisions made."

I blinked away the traitorous tears that would belie the faith Daniel had placed in me. Me, a natural leader? Was I up to it? For so long, I'd felt incapable of being anything other than a mother and I wasn't doing a brilliant job of that, these days. Maybe this was my time. Time to fulfil my potential. A thrill passed through me.

"I'd be honoured," I said. "But I haven't a clue how to handle this. I haven't been on good terms with Margaret since the trouble with Peter all those years ago. Trading David didn't help. And since things didn't work out between Matt and Joy, the snide comments have started again. If I refuse to let Peter back, things will get worse, and surely a leader's meant to keep the peace?"

"You'll work out the appropriate thing to do." Daniel's words failed to reassure.

Where was Michael when I needed him? What would he do? Huh, I knew that, all right. He hated Peter even more than I did. But what was the mantra he endlessly preached? For the greater good. And Peter had been an excellent dairyman. I looked to the sky as if it held the answers. Instead the gathering black clouds glowered at me. It had been a hot, oppressive day, the type that needed a thunderstorm to break the humidity.

"Joy, can you stay in and look after Adam this evening? Council meeting." The question was unnecessary. Joy rarely went anywhere these days.

"Yeah, sure. You're not due a meeting, are you?"

"Can you keep a secret?"

She nodded.

"Daniel wants to step down as leader and guess who he wants to replace him?"

"You? That's great." But her voice lacked animation. The old Joy would have never used a word as banal as great. The colour had gone from her language, as well as her face.

My appointment as village leader proved as straightforward as Daniel had predicted. Margaret and Frank exchanged a sour look, but voted yes, along with the others. I made my way to the front of the hall with trembling legs. Why did my first duty have to be so difficult? I took a few measured breaths.

"Peter Baxter, who was banished from the community sixteen years ago for betrayal, has asked to return. He's volunteered to look after his father as well as resume his duties on the dairy and farm. If you feel he should be allowed to rejoin the community, raise your hand."

The hands of Margaret and Frank shot into the air, together with one other, while those of the other three council members remained down. Six pairs of eyes bored into me. The casting vote was mine. And I still hadn't decided what to do. Surely a strong leader didn't allow personal feelings to cloud their judgement?

"I think …" I swallowed. "Peter should be allowed a one-month trial. I'll make a final decision at the end of that time."

"Good compromise," Daniel whispered.

But as we left the building, the clouds burst, lashing rain against the pavement. The crashes of thunder felt like portents of doom.

***

"You're a bloody fool. He'll cause trouble." Michael exploded.

"Thanks for the vote of confidence. I was pleased with my compromise, pleased I'd been made leader. Just for once, I had to make a decision on my own. Is it too much for you to admit it might be the right one? Have a look at the dairy; he started on it straightway. According to Daisy, it's gleaming. And apart from the usual undressing women with his eyes, he's behaved himself."

Michael grasped my hands. "Sorry, sweetheart, I didn't want to belittle you. I couldn't be happier about you being leader. It's just … I hate that bloody guy. And there's another thing." He rubbed his forehead, as if trying to erase his thoughts. "I had a message from Doodlebugs. A young woman escaped from Tau-2 by killing a guard; that's why I stayed an extra day. Dee and I searched up and down the canal. The CEs probably won't search as far as here, but it's the last thing I need right now, with Outbreak so close. How am I going to stock the bunker with CEs sniffing around? And we haven't even started searching the correction camp area to find the factory. And now we've got that traitorous bastard back … I wish you'd talked to me first."

"Believe it or not, as village leader there'll be times when I have to make decisions for myself, and the great Michael Heath won't be here to advise me; he'll be too focussed on his higher cause."

I regretted the comment as soon as it had left my lips. Something had changed in Michael, the lines of strain across his forehead deeper, the shadows under his eyes darker. Luckily Joy came in, taking away his chance to reply.

"How's Harry?" she murmured.

Michael looked away. "He's fine. He said to give you these." He reached for his backpack and extracted ten jars of honey.

"What aren't you telling me? He's got someone else, hasn't he?"

Michael couldn't meet her eyes. "Sorry, sweetheart. There was a girl with him."

"What … what was her name?"
"Caroline."
But rather than flying into a rage, Joy slumped to the sofa in silence, a steady stream of tears rolling down her cheeks, and it was the saddest sight I'd ever seen.

***

You didn't persuade Joy to come?" Michael said, as we made our way to the movie showing, Anna once more looking after Adam. I swallowed my guilt. Daisy, Joy and Anna's regular babysitting was lifting the burden of Adam from me. I shouldn't still be thinking of him as a burden, should I?
"No, she's getting worse. She's hardly spoken since you told her. So what else did you find out? This girl, Caroline – do you think Harry was serious about her?"
"He seemed quiet, not his usual self, but I think the stress of Outbreak is getting to him, too. He showed me his throwing and running skills. The boy's bloody brilliant; I knew he would be. As for the girl, she seemed to be a permanent fixture. She's set herself up as a travelling health worker. She was nothing compared to our Joy, but she hung on Harry's every word. He seemed pretty demonstrative with her. I hate to say it, but maybe he's outgrown Joy."
"But surely you spoke to Dee in private and found out what happened?"
"Didn't get the chance but the three of them seemed quite the family unit."
I bit back a number of recriminations then drew in my breath. "It's Peter and he's coming this way."
Peter had changed little, his red hair faded and interspersed with speckles of white, his serpentine smile now further marred by gaps in his teeth.
"Hey, Michael," he said then directed his gaze towards me in a way that made me uncomfortable. "Congratulations, hear you're the new leader. And … thanks."
"Welcome back," I said, my voice monotone.
With that, he passed on to greet the other villagers.
"Looks like he's not out to cause trouble," Michael muttered. "But could you have a word with Luke? Try to

keep Joy off the dairy rota."

"Yes, I think he'll understand." I shivered. All I wanted was for Joy to smile again, and something about Peter's smile told me that he was the last person she should be near.

***

The trial month was almost over and it appeared that my decision to let Peter stay was vindicated, which was lucky as Michael was rarely around. As the rich green summer leaves shrivelled and prepared for their final glorious display of yellow, russet and brown, productivity in the dairy increased. Luke reported that Peter's behaviour couldn't be faulted. Meanwhile, preparations for Outbreak Day intensified. It was time to start stocking the underground bunker. The still was working overtime and several litres of alcohol taken to store. Michael took the horse and cart with the first of many water butts, bottled fruit, ham, vegetables and cheese, the whole effort hampered by the knowledge that the escapee was still on the loose and CEs may be out in pursuit. Michael no longer travelled alone, taking Helen with him as a lookout. Joy was deputising as village health worker in her absences.

"I'm so proud of you, sweetheart," I said.

"Don't be," said Joy. "It's only dishing out advice for outbreaks of diarrhoea. Anything serious, I'd have to ask Alex."

I sighed. Nothing could lift Joy from her misery. Then early one morning, a pounding on the door woke me up. It was Tia, Elsie's adoptive mother.

"I need you and Joy. It's Elsie. She's got the Mark."

"You're kidding? Who from?" I said, shuddering with the memory of it.

The Mark, the deliberately introduced virus that shamed any Citidome individuals who indulged in illegal sexual activity, hadn't struck the village for years. The last cases had been more than ten years ago. Most of the older villagers, of course, were Marked. So who had given it to Elsie? The girl wasn't yet fifteen. Admittedly, her precocious behaviour encouraged men but Elsie had mental deficiencies that were obvious to anyone. Someone had taken advantage and it couldn't go unpunished.

"She says ..." Tia sucked in her lips. "Well, I can't say it. I need her to say it to you. B-but, you might not want Joy to hear it."

"Why? It can't be Matt; he doesn't have the Mark. Besides, he and Joy aren't together any more. Ryan doesn't have it, as far as I know. So it must have been someone older, or someone from the market. I'll let Joy examine her then I'll talk to her. Give us half an hour. I'll leave the boys with Anna."

I knocked on Joy's door. "Wake up, sweetheart. We're needed. What do you know about the TJB virus, the one that causes the Mark? Elsie's got it."

"I've read about it. But euww, that's gross," she said. "Who'd stoop so low?"

"I wondered if you'd have any clue. You hear more gossip than me."

"Not so much these days."

I gave her a sympathetic look. Joy seemed to have withdrawn from all her friends, even Beth.

"It could be anyone," Joy said. "We all know she's not choosy. She comes onto any man like a bitch on heat. She's tried with Matt and Ryan, you know. But they wouldn't."

"I always wondered." I seized the opportunity to capture Joy's confidence. "Did you and Harry ever –"

"Yeah, twice." She smiled and her voice took on a wistful tone. "Don't worry, we were careful. But oh, Mum. It was lovely."

The thought comforted me. I needed to know that Joy had known some happiness this year. We made our way to Tia's house where Elsie sat, rocking herself, shivering from the sickness that accompanied the Mark, her breasts half showing. The poor girl appeared to have a Mark on her breast as well as one covering her cheek. I'd never seen Marks so disfiguring. We left Joy to examine her. While I was trying to formulate tactful words, Tia spoke.

"Before you say anything, I know what everyone says. I try to keep Elsie decent, you know. I find her things with high necklines but she always cuts them lower. But whoever did this to her; I'll kill them myself."

Joy returned to the kitchen.

"As far as I can see, it's a classic case of TJB," she said. "There's not a lot I can do for her without antivirals so she's going to be pretty sick for the next few weeks. Keep her in bed and give her plenty of fluids. She might not be able to keep solid food down; chicken or rabbit soup will be best."

"Thanks," said Tia. "Did she tell you who did it to her?"

"No, but she kept giving me a weird smile, as if she was enjoying a private joke at my expense. Well, I'll be off now."

"Can you stay, Cathy?" The groove had increased between Tia's brows.

"Of course," I said as Joy left. "So what aren't you telling me? Who did it?"

"I can't say it." Tia's hand covered her mouth.

Let me talk to her," I suggested. We returned to the living room. "Hey, Elsie, your mum tells me you're not well."

"I'm dizzy and look at my face," said Elsie. "I'm not pretty any more."

"It'll take more than a Mark to stop you being pretty," I said. "Did you understand what Joy told you?"

Elsie shook her head.

"You've got a sickness. It's not serious, and you'll feel better again in about a week. But this sickness, it's something that a man gives to a woman when he's done certain things with her. Do you know what I mean?"

"You mean when they're nice to me?" Elsie asked.

"That's right. Who's been nice to you, Elsie?"

"M-Michael."

The absolute silence was deafening. I waited for the girl to laugh, to say she was joking, but no-one spoke. I let out a long, unsteady breath. Why was Elsie lying? It couldn't be true, could it? When was the last time Michael and I had made love? Weeks, no, months. Since Adam had been sleeping in our room I felt inhibited. Could a sexually frustrated man resist someone as attractive as Elsie throwing herself at them?

"You see, I had to let you hear it for yourself." Tia carried on talking but her words washed over me. Nothing could shock me any more. Nothing could be worse than what I'd just heard. Then I took a grip of myself. It was impossible.

Michael wouldn't. He just wouldn't.

"You're sure you mean Michael? My husband, Michael?" My eyes bored into Elsie's.

"Yeah, Michael gave me the Mark." Elsie parroted the words. I frowned. Where did she hear the expression "The Mark?" None of us had said it in her earshot. It sounded rehearsed.

"So you're saying that Michael was nice to you. When and where?"

"Umm, last week, in the cowshed."

"Which day?"

"Tuesday. No, Wednesday."

I let out the breath I'd been holding and turned to Tia. "She's lying. Michael was away from the village on AOC business last week with Helen. Ask Helen if you don't believe me."

"I do believe you," Tia sighed. "I knew from the start it couldn't be him. But who could it be?"

"Someone who hates me and Michael enough to want to destroy us." Of course. Why hadn't I thought of it straightaway? My head sank to my hands.

"Who?"

"Peter Baxter." My voice was small and dense.

"I'll kill him!" Tia clenched her fists.

"No, wait. We don't have any proof. We need Elsie to admit it." I turned to the girl. "Elsie, do you like Peter, the new dairyman?"

"Yeah …" The smile that Elsie couldn't suppress gave her away instantly.

"What ? The filthy – " Tia's face burnt crimson.

I put my fingers to my lips. Anger wouldn't get us the admission we needed.

"Has Peter ever been nice to you?" I persisted.

"No. Michael gave me the Mark." Elsie clamped her lips together.

"But Peter's nice too, isn't he?"

"Michael gave me the Mark."

I sighed. This was hopeless.

"Tia, can you keep her indoors? I need to find some proof."

"Who needs proof? It's bloody obvious, isn't it? Let's face

up to that bastard now."

"That's not the way things work, and you know it. Leave it with me."

I trudged home, and gave way to self-loathing and tears. How could I have been so stupid as to trust that Peter had changed? How could I deal with this? I couldn't tackle a man that frightened me, that may even attack me. I was even more unfit to be leader than I was a mother. I stayed home all day, alleviating my sense of hopelessness by spending quality time with Adam and Scott. Adam was now becoming more mobile and inquisitive, and I passed a happy afternoon playing with the tattered toys and wooden blocks that had passed down all the village children.

"He's getting more interesting," said Scott.

"He is, isn't he?" I agreed. "And look, his eyes are starting to look just like yours."

"But he's light skinned, like Dad. And his hair's like Dad's." As Scott started his favourite game of comparing facial features, my stomach loosened. Why wasn't parenting always this enjoyable? Perhaps everything would be OK. I'd swallow my pride and admit to Michael that I couldn't handle this alone. He could come with me while I told Peter that he was no longer welcome in the village. No-one would believe Elsie's ridiculous allegations and it was easy to prove that Michael and Helen had been away. By the time Michael returned, I felt optimistic that this would be resolved without any harm being done. Peter had played right into my hands. Now I'd be rid of him for good.

"How was your day?" My face fell as soon as Michael lumbered in, his expression desolate.

"Useless," he muttered. "We got the stuff to the bunker, then went to the camp, but there's too many people outside. We're nowhere near as organised as we should be at this stage. Cheer me up. Tell me something good."

But that was the one thing I couldn't do.

CHAPTER 13 - JOY

It had been a mild, dry autumn, the sort that the villagers inexplicably described as an Indian summer. My black despair had passed but, without Harry, time continued its dismal trudge. I performed my tasks dutifully and without enthusiasm, and that evening sat in a secluded place by the river that trapped the evening sun and the silence. Settling myself on a springy bed of clover, I opened one of my medical books. I'd already memorised every detail that would be useful in every warfare scenario Helen had envisioned – she had a pretty vivid imagination – and had progressed to reading other chapters. But filling my head with new knowledge couldn't fill the aching void that Harry had left. I hadn't known pain like this before and time refused to heal it.

For a while Mum and Dad had been concerned, almost penitent, but it hadn't lasted, and yet again I'd been pushed into the background, both of them too busy with their separate preoccupations. Adam didn't help either. Why, after seven months, did my baby brother's presence in our family still feel like an intrusion? Things were getting worse between Mum and Dad too, the rows almost daily. I'd refused to take sides on the latest fight – the Peter Question. Trouble was, I could see both sides. I thought Mum had reached a fair compromise. She had to be seen as a leader untarnished by emotion. But my jaw tightened every time I saw that vile man, which luckily wasn't often.

But that night came the mother of all rows. At the sound of sobbing, I tiptoed to Scott's room.

"What's up, Scotty?"

"Mum and Dad. They're going to split up, aren't they?"

"Hey, don't be silly. Dad's got a lot on his mind at the moment. You know he gets grumpy when he's busy."

"But they never stop arguing these days. I'm scared."

It sounded like the usual subject, Peter. But there was something new, something I couldn't catch. Elsie's name was mentioned and then Dad roared, "You got us into this mess, you get us out of it. Prove he bloody well did it. If I see him I'll kill him, and then everything's ruined. I'm leaving first thing tomorrow, and I'm not coming back until this is fixed."

My mind struggled to process this information. Had Peter given Elsie the Mark? Euww, that was disgusting. But who else could it be? Elsie had been hanging about the dairy a lot lately. So was Dad running away from it? Leaving Mum to handle it on her own – that wasn't like him at all.

The following morning, on my way to collect our loaf of bread, I heard Margaret's whiney voice inside the bakery. At the sound of Mum's name I paused to listen – Matt's mum was always moaning about something. I knew something that could get rid of that sanctimonious sneer. Then I caught the end of what she was saying.

" – thinks she's better than the rest of us. Why on earth did Daniel choose her as leader? Well she can wipe that smug smile off her face now. I always said there was something suspect about that man. I'd heard that their marriage was in trouble. Thought it was young Helen he was sniffing after – they go out together every day, you know – but to stoop that low."

She stopped talking the minute I walked through the door. The others in the shop gave me a look of what could only be described as pity. Even worse, when I left the bakery, Beth crossed the road a few metres ahead and continued in the direction of the farm without acknowledging me. What was she playing at? I knew I hadn't been out as much as I used to, but she'd seen me; I was sure of it.

"Hey, Beth!" I ran to catch her up.

"Oh, hey, didn't see you." Beth looked everywhere but at me.

"Is there some new piece of village gossip I don't know?"

"You mean your mum and dad haven't said anything?"

"No. They were rowing last night but that's nothing new these days."

"Well, Elsie's got the Mark, and it was your dad that gave it to her."

I was going to be sick. To be sick and then die. I leant against the wall and took a deep breath, trying to make sense of it, but the words refused to sink in. I sprinted home, to find Mum in the kitchen.

"M-mum, why didn't you tell me?" I stammered.

"Tell you what?" Mum was never a good liar.

"About Dad and Elsie. It's not true, is it?"

"What have you heard?" Mum gripped my wrists with such savagery that I flinched.

"Beth said that Dad gave her the Mark. I think everyone knows."

"That bloody woman! I told her not to let Elsie out. I have to get that idiot girl to tell the truth." With that, Mum stormed out of the house.

"I don't get it, Joy," Scott said.

"Neither do I, Scotty. The world's gone mad. You've been picking tomatoes up by the dairy, haven't you? What's Elsie been up to?"

Scott giggled and made the noise of a grunting pig.

"What's that?"

"Peter and Elsie."

"You mean you saw them together and he was making a noise like that?"

"Yeah. He had his trousers down and was doing this." Scott thrusted his hips forwards and back. "It was really funny."

"Who else knows about this?

"Just Ian."

I sighed. It made perfect sense. Peter would try and pin it on someone else, and what better way than to settle old scores with Dad? But I didn't exactly have reliable witnesses. Two children, one my brother, the other Peter's great-nephew, who would no doubt change his story as soon as he was questioned. Think, Joy, think. How could I confront that ape of a man? Then I smiled. I had something he didn't: the weapon of intellect. I strode to the dairy, an idea unfolding in my brain. Walking past the field, I waved at Matt, but he didn't appear to have seen me. A sob caught in my throat. Matt too? Were people so willing to believe this of Dad? I heard footsteps approaching behind me but remained focussed on the path ahead. I wouldn't speak to anyone. The whole lot of them could rot in hell. But then the pace slowed to match mine and a warm voice said, “Hey, Joy. I never see you these days.”

“Ryan.” I gave him half a smile. “Heard the rumours about my dad?”

“Yeah, I wanted to check you were OK. What surprises me is that anyone believes it. Elsie tries to go with every man she meets and there’s plenty with the Mark.”

My voice lowered. “I know who did this. Peter.”

“Huh, yeah, that figures. I can’t stand him. But you’ll have a hard time proving it. He’s related to half the village, isn’t he?”

“I’ve got a plan; I’m about to confront him.” I told Ryan what I intended to do.

“Clever, that could work. But you shouldn’t be on your own with him. Your dad said you mustn’t go near – ”

“Even Peter wouldn’t be stupid enough to try anything with me.”

“It’s too risky. What if he threatens you physically? He’s a big guy. I’ll come with you.”

I was about to comment that Ryan wouldn’t be much help in a fight with Peter – he must be about half his weight – but it might be tactless to point this out. “Thanks, Ryan, but the only way my plan can work is if he thinks our conversation is confidential. Anyway, what’s he going to do in the dairy, when anyone could walk in or out? Remember, he’s still on trial. One complaint and he’s out of the community.”

“I’m not sure his mind works so logically. I’m about to start fixing the fence by the pigpen. If he frightens you, scream. I’ll hear.” Ryan drew himself up to his full two-metre height, but still looked as though a gust of wind would blow him over.

I strode into the dairy where Craig was stirring a vat of curds.

“Craig, your mum needs you at home now,” I said.

Craig frowned and left.

Peter leered. “Well, if it isn’t the little princess. I’m honoured.”

I took a deep breath. “I’ve been talking to my friend, Elsie.”

"Oh yeah?" He scratched his nose. "I've heard she's a friend of the family."

"Funny. My sides are splitting. She told me all about you and her. As did my little brother and his friend, who heard you together. Oh, don't get angry with Elsie. She's fulfilled her part of the bargain. She told everyone it was my dad. But there's another problem, one she hasn't told anyone except me. She's pregnant."

Peter's red cheeks faded to pink. "You can't believe a word that girl says."

"Yeah, that's the fatal flaw in your plan, isn't it? Her word can't be trusted. Except there's one thing that'll give you away. Wonder what colour thc baby's hair will be?"

His eyebrows shot up. Ah, I'd got him. Ice cool, Joy.

"You and my dad are so different in colouring, I don't think there'll be any need for a paternity test, though I have a contact in the Citidome that can do that if necessary."

"You're making it up."

"No, I'm not, but I want to help you. Don't look so surprised. My motivations are entirely selfish. My dad's going to kill you when he hears about this, and I don't want him to be a murderer, so I've got a proposition for you. See Elsie and tell her to take back her lies about my dad. Then leave the village, now. Go back to where you've been for the last sixteen years, and I'll arrange for Elsie to have an abortion. I know how; I've been studying medicine with Helen. There'll be no scandal, no disgrace. No-one will ever know the truth."

For a moment, Peter didn't speak, his hand cradling his chin as if considering his options. When he did speak, it was with a movement so fast that it took me unawares.

"You little bitch." He darted forwards and with his foot, took my legs from under me. Before I was able to scream, he was on top of me. He clamped his filthy great paw of a hand over my mouth, the other tore my top in two, revealing my bra. "Let's see if you'll give me what your bloody mother wouldn't."

He pinned me to the ground, his foul breath warm against me. His weight was suffocating me. His lips came down on mine. I squeezed them shut, terrified to move, breathe, even exist in this moment. My stomach was rising, stuffing itself into my throat. Then I heard a voice.

"Let her go, you bastard." Ryan appeared, brandishing a hammer.

"Huh, and what are you going to do about it, Citidome boy? Think you can take me on, do you? One move and your girlfriend's dead."

He placed his other huge hand around my throat, his fingers rough against my skin. My mind flailed. If I could free one of my arms … it was trapped under Peter's weight. I wriggled under him, freed the arm and clawed at his face. He yelped, tightened his grip, squeezing, constricting, crushing my windpipe. I couldn't breathe! My terrified eyes met his pale blue ones. He was bluffing, surely. He wouldn't risk harming me. Oh, who was I kidding? That had been the weakness in my plan, hadn't it? Believing that this monster was capable of reason.

"Right, boy. Turn round and get your skinny Citidome ass out of my sight, or you're next," said Peter.

For what seemed an infinite time but could only have been thirty seconds, none of us moved, as if a scene in a movie had been paused. I closed my eyes. Think, Joy, think! My thoughts were taken away by a sickening crunch. The pressure released around my throat and Peter's body relaxed on top of mine. Then the weight was gone and I sat upright, taking great gulps of air, clutching at my throat. Ryan pulled me to my feet and into his arms. I placed my arms around his back, feeling the sharp angles of his shoulder blades through his woollen sweater. When we pulled apart, Peter lay motionless, a pool of dark blood oozing from his head.

"What have we done?" I was the first to speak.

"Come on, we have to get out of here."

"B-but." The floor was tilting. I staggered. Ryan lifted me into his arms.

"Let's find a place to think."

He carried me outside and I drank in the air, desperate to free my lungs of the stench of curdled milk and Peter's breath. We continued to the summit of the wild meadows at Longstone Edge, where the wind grumbled across the exposed ridge. Here a patchwork of purple clumps of heather and grasses stretched away on either side.

"Sorry, I'm not perfectly cast in the hero role," Ryan said. "I can't carry you any further."

He set me to my feet. Realising with horror that my top was gaping open, I crossed my arms around my chest. But he appeared not to have noticed. He crouched on his heels and buried his face in his hands.

"What have I done?" he said.

"Saved me." I knelt beside him and put an arm on his shoulder. "Hey, you're shaking." This was an understatement. Ryan's body was convulsing. "We're in this together, Ryan."

His eyes met mine then he crouched lower, allowing his head to lean on my shoulder. I stroked his hair – so fine and straight – until his shaking subsided, and only at that point did I realise that I was trembling too. Then a familiar dog bounded up to me, the remains of a rabbit in his mouth. It was almost as if Harry had seen us together and sent Milo to part us. No, Harry's with Caroline, I reminded myself.

"Hey, Milo," I said. "This is Scott's pet, or semi-pet. He takes off every morning but comes back to his shelter every night."

"Hey, boy," Ryan said, and scratched Milo behind the ear.

"He likes you. You're privileged."

We smiled at each other, the tension momentarily diffused.

"Let's keep walking away from the village until we decide what to do." I stood up.

"You should go back. It's me who's the m-murderer."

"We don't know he was dead."

"Whatever, I don't think I'll be flavour of the month, do you?"

"I hope he is dead," I growled. "He's evil. But they don't know it was us."

"How long do you think they'll take to work it out? Besides, I didn't pick up the hammer. It's still lying next to his body."

"Oh shit."

"Exactly."

"I started the whole thing. We stand together on this."

"No, I can't go back. And I've been thinking for a while; I

don't fit in the village. I know what's planned for me. Beth's a nice girl, but marrying her and having a houseful of brats in a few years' time? That's not how I envisaged my life."

"Can't say I blame you. I love Beth, but a houseful of brats is the limit of her ambition." I smiled. "But how did you envisage your life? I know you once told me you didn't fit in the Citidomes but surely it wasn't that bad?"

"Most people want to escape for one of four reasons: attachment, because they've got the Mark, the search for the truth, and the fear of oppression. For me it was the last two. Can you imagine what it's like to live in constant fear of being arrested for saying the wrong thing? I'd started studying at an academic centre, met some guys who introduced me to Doodlebugs, and that was it. I knew I had to get out."

"I understand." I told him about Mum's journal.

"It's worse than that now. Your dad wouldn't have got away with any of the things he said. Citizens get arrested at the slightest suspicion of subversive thinking." He sighed. "I'll try and find a different community. One full of girls who find me attractive." He gave a weak smile.

"It's not that easy to move to a different community these days. They'll want to know where you came from. Then they'll probably contact Mum to find out why you've left."

"Think your mum's going to understand what I did, don't you? It's the others, Peter's family, that worry me." He grabbed my hand. "Come with me, Joy. It's obvious that you're not happy there either."

"I can't," I muttered, then my thoughts turned to Beth crossing the road and Matt ignoring me. When was the last time I was happy there? I couldn't remember. "But I have to get away from there for a few days. I feel like I'll burst if I don't."

I took in our surroundings then changed direction, striding with new purpose.

"Come on; I know where we'll go," I said.

"Where?"

"We'll head west to Macclesfield. There's a lot of empty houses there, and it's the most used stretch of canal. Then we can wait for the next boat."

"To see your forbidden lover?" His lip curled. "Why would I do that?"

"You can visit a few communities with him; see which one takes your fancy. Besides, we're not together any more, but I need to talk to him. He's seeing someone else and I need to know why. She'll be there on the boat."

"Are you sure that's a good idea?" His voice softened. "What if they're besotted with each other? Do you really want to see that?"

"I've been thinking for a while of confronting him but I'm scared to. But with you … sorry, Ryan, it's a terrible idea. I'd be using you."

"No, let's do it, if it's that important to you." His Adam's apple bobbed up and down in his skinny neck. "I have to admit, I liked Harry. You and him seemed well-matched."

"Why are you so good to me?" My top caught in the wind and blew off my shoulders. I tightened my grip around it. "Maybe I should go to the Citidome dump and find something else to wear."

"Bit of a risk in the daylight. Besides, you always look good to me." That smile again. It transformed his face.

"Why me? I'm hardly your physical type. I'm the shortest adult in the village and you're the tallest."

"It's the way you talk. It's hard to believe you're only sixteen; you don't talk like any sixteen year-old in the Citidome. I've never met anyone like you. Matt and Beth are fun but they never have anything memorable or original to say. You're unique, Joy. And your face – it's perfect. It's the sort of face you want to see every day, to remind yourself that there's beauty and goodness in the world. As for the other side of it … to be honest, sexual attraction isn't a driving force in my life." He grinned. "Matt talks about it all the time, but I guess I was in the Citidome too long. Not that I wouldn't mind trying it out some time. But if I did, the only person I can imagine being with is you."

His words gave me a shiver; his blue eyes softened with the love in them. Pull yourself together, Joy. I changed the subject.

"We're nearly at the main road. If we keep walking that way we'll reach Macclesfield by sundown. Tell me more about yourself. Why do you never talk about your escape? I heard it was a big success."

"Yeah, that's how it was reported, wasn't it? Only one casualty but no-one remembers what happened to that one, like he's unimportant. I remember, all right. We hit the guard on the head then ran to where a few people were waiting with TravelPods and horses. Me and my friend Han were the last to get away. A guy was helping us mount the horse when a CE came running out of the Dome. They shot at us and Han yelled. We got away, Han with his hand pressed against his left side. And all the time we were riding, Han was howling like an animal."

He paused and took a deep breath.

"When we stopped, well, I've never seen anything like it. The shot had taken about ten centimetres of his skin and flesh away. His guts were hanging out of his body cavity, spilling into his hands. When he saw it, the guy on the horse, the one who was meant to be rescuing us, shot him. Afterwards he told me it was the kindest thing; he would never have recovered. Great success, huh?"

I shivered.

He stopped and turned to face me.

"Is it worth it, Joy? Is human life so cheap? After that, I wanted to make my life exceptional, to vindicate Han's death, but what use am I out here? I'm no use on the farm. And now look at me. I've taken a life myself."

"Your life can still be exceptional. It's more than the work you do; it's the impact you have on people's lives. You've been a good friend to me, to Beth, to Matt. You've been a surrogate son to Daisy. And what you did to Peter – it was the bravest thing I ever saw. You saved me from being –" I stopped, unable to say the word.

"You're an incredible person, Joy. Harry's a bloody fool."

He lowered his face to mine, and I gave way to impulse. At this moment someone loved me, someone wanted me and was in need of comfort. And if his lips felt wrong on mine, if my body didn't soften in his arms the way it had with Harry, I pushed the thought to the back of my mind.

And that was why neither of us heard the silent approach of the TravelPod.

Then a jolt made my knees go loose and the next thing I saw was the steely eyes of what could only be a CE.

CHAPTER 14 - CATHY

I returned from Tia's house feeling more weighed down than ever. Elsie seemed to have retreated into her own private world. Tia had kept to her promise to confine the girl to the house, so Peter must have started the rumours. But surely no-one believed him?

A pounding at the door shook me from my thoughts.

"I want a word with your bitch daughter." Margaret, her face crimson and wet from tears.

"She isn't here. Why?"

"Beth found Peter in the dairy, d-dead. He'd been hit with a hammer and just before it happened, Joy came in and told Craig a lie to get rid of him.

I staggered to a chair. Peter, dead? I felt nothing but relief. But relief was soon replaced by horror. Joy ... surely she didn't?

"Joy? Where is she?"

"That's what I want to know."

I sprang to my feet and ran to the dairy, where a number of people had gathered outside. When I approached, the group parted. Daisy stepped forward and took my hand, leading me away, but not in time to prevent me seeing Alex covering a body with a sheet, blood already soaking through. Craig was sluicing away the scarlet puddle with a bucket of water.

"S-so it's true," I stammered. "Where's Joy?"

"No-one's seen her." Daisy squeezed my hand. "And there's something else. Ryan's gone missing too. The hammer that was used was the one he was using to fix the fence."

"So it could have been Ryan?" Hope flooded me.

Then the sound of hooves sent us outside. Mary dismounted from a horse.

"What's going on?" she said.

I told her, and the expression on her face told me that she

had more bad news.

"What is it?"

"I was exercising Bramble on the moor and I saw a tall young man carrying a girl. Her top was gaping open. I wasn't close enough to be sure but it could … it could have been Ryan and Joy."

The pain that shot through me was physical and I staggered backwards with the intensity of it.

Luke laid his hand on my arm. "I'll get the other horse. We'll find them. In the meantime, I think everyone had better stop working for the day. Cathy, why don't you call a village meeting? Or would it be better to hand over to Daniel for now?"

"No, I'll do it." Luke was right. Professional, must be professional.

"You unlock the village hall; I'll knock on every door," Daisy said. "Anna's going to stay indoors with the boys."

"Don't tell anyone what's happened, I don't want them all coming in whispering."

As people trickled in, I stood at the front of the hall, forcing my breathing to steady, but the looks and murmurs told me that the news was already spreading. I barely gave people the chance to sit down before I started speaking.

"There'll be a lot of rumours flying round so I want to set the record straight. This morning, Peter Baxter was found dead in the dairy, killed by a hammer blow." I looked at Elsie as I spoke. Elsie let out a high-pitched wail, causing everyone to swivel and stare. But I quenched the immediate outbreak of muttering. "My daughter, Joy, and Ryan have also gone missing, last seen at Longstone Edge. We have evidence that they were involved in the incident at the dairy and that Joy may have been physically assaulted. Mary and Luke are searching for them now. If anyone hears anything, please come and see me at once." I directed my gaze at Margaret. "I'd also like to address some rumours concerning my husband. He was out of the village on the night that the alleged incident took place, and under the circumstances, I'd like no-one to refer to it again." I paused and looked around the room. "Does anyone have anything to say?"

The silence was broken only by Elsie's weeping.

As everyone filed out, I staggered to the nearest chair.

"And you said you weren't up to being leader? That was bloody wonderful," Daisy said.

At her grin, my composure crumbled and my knees turned to rubber. "He r-raped her, didn't he?" I whispered.

"We don't know that. Don't torture yourself thinking about it. Someone'll find them."

But no-one found them. By the time darkness fell, Mary and Luke called off the search for the night. Then it occurred to me where Joy might be. I walked by torchlight to the next village to see Helen.

"Helen, can I borrow your DataBand for the evening? It's an emergency."

"Course you can." I was touched to see that Helen, too, had been crying. "She'll be back. But what's happened to Michael? We were supposed to be meeting today but he didn't show up."

I was on the verge of telling Helen the truth, but something in her face when she spoke Michael's name stopped me. Perhaps this was the last person to whom I should confide that my husband had walked out on me last night and said he wouldn't return until the mess I'd created had been put right. I walked home in a daze, collected a fractious Scott and Adam from Anna and flopped onto the sofa, exhausted. But first I needed to look at Helen's messages. Was something going on? Was this why Michael had hidden the DataBand from me? I held my breath. There were messages from Michael. Plenty of them. But all brief and to the point, related to AOC business. Anxiety must be making me paranoid.

I input a message to Harry.

> Harry, have you heard anything from Joy? She and Ryan have disappeared and I wondered whether they might have gone in search of you?

Harry's reply was swift and terse.

Haven't heard a word from her in months. Not since she got together with Ryan.

I frowned. Surely there hadn't been anything between Joy and Ryan?

How long have she and Ryan been together?

The reply was even shorter.

You tell me. I thought I knew Joy but it turned out I never did.

Huh? What other secrets had Joy kept from me? Then the door opened, and Michael came through. His tormented face told me that he'd heard the news. I took a step forward, willing him to open his arms, so I could throw myself against his chest and feel that something was right in the world. But his arms remained folded, his eyes heavy with censure. He poured a glass of water and drained it in a gulp.

"What's the latest?"

"Mary and Luke gave up an hour ago. They'll start again tomorrow."

"That bastard. What was she doing in the dairy? I told her never to – "

"She heard the rumours about you. Seems the whole village has."

"That's all I bloody need. I'm not even going to start on I told you so."

"Good, because I'm in no mood to hear it. Don't you think I've been torturing myself enough as it is? I even contacted Harry, thought she might have gone looking for him, but it turns out he thinks she's been with Ryan for months.

Michael rubbed his nose. "That's because I told him she was."

"*What*?"

"When I confiscated the DataBand from Joy, I didn't trust her not to find some other sneaky way to keep in contact with him. So I sent Dee a message about Outbreak and dropped in the fact that Joy had split with Matt and had fallen for Ryan." He sighed. "Last week, Dee asked about her and I concocted a story about the two of them being inseparable. But – huh – it didn't take Harry long to get over her by the way he and that Caroline girl were all over each other. I told you they were too young to know their own minds."

I turned from him. "Go away. I can't bear to look at you," I muttered.

He walked upstairs, his tread slow and heavy.

"Joy'll be in a strop, as usual. She'll be back tomorrow." Scott's voice raised at the end, making the statement more of a question.

"Course she will, love. Hey don't look so sad. Come and sit by me."

I sat with Adam perched on my lap, Scott snuggled up by my side and tried to focus on my two beautiful sons, one wanted, one not, but now the only constants in my life. But the inner voice wouldn't be silenced. I'd lost the girl who had first shown me the miracle of a mother's love for a child. And maybe, as a result, I'd lose the only man I'd ever loved.

CHAPTER 15 - JOY

Another shock from the CE's weapon dulled the pain of my hands being bound behind my back. The whole action had been so swift that neither Ryan nor I had time to struggle. Although the day was warm, a cold wave of disbelief and terror made me shiver.

"Try anything funny and I'll increase the strength and fry your brain," growled the CE, then pressed a pad against my finger.

"You're not a Citizen." He frowned.

"N-no." I released my breath. Of course. He couldn't do anything to me. How could they explain me away in the Citidomes – a healthy girl that was born on the outside? But poor Ryan, what had I done to him? His face was a tight mask of pain.

"Padi 031029, part of the breakaway gang in Phi-1, eh?" the CE sneered. You're far more interesting. You're coming with me." He bundled Ryan into the TravelPod.

"No!" I screamed. "Leave him alone." I ran in front of the TravelPod and lay on the road.

The CE turned to me, put his foot on my breast, exposed except for my bra, and spat on me. "Wanna stay with your boyfriend, eh? Well why not? Sight of you might wipe any ideas out of anyone else who thinks it's so wonderful out here."

I looked up, as if expecting a rescuer to fall out of the clouds. Then a sharper jolt made my whole body jump into the air.

"Open that mouth again and you'll get more," the CE growled. He grabbed my arm, hoisted me to my feet and tossed me into the TravelPod, next to Ryan.

"Veez, you're filthy," muttered the CE, spraying sanitiser onto his hands.

I pressed myself against Ryan's side, mouthing the word,

"sorry" but the terror in his eyes chilled me. His eyes appeared to be staring but not seeing me. His breath was no longer even, bursting in and out in pants. The TravelPod drove eastwards, passing through Bakewell, the market town, but today it was deserted. And mixed with the clenching fear was another feeling, a heavy feeling of guilt, a feeling that I just cheated on Harry. I closed my eyes in an attempt to make it all stop, to rewind my life to a point before Harry and Caroline.

The TravelPod accelerated and we travelled in silence for several minutes. As the imposing Citidome – much bigger than I imagined from my distant sightings – came into view, I felt Ryan's muscles tense. I rubbed my foot against his leg in an attempt at reassurance but the structure loomed increasingly large ahead of us. The TravelPod stopped at a gate, which opened. We drove inside.

"Get out, creevs," the CE said.

I staggered out of the TravelPod and the gate closed behind us. I peered down a straight road, dazzled by the gleaming rectangular buildings. All was clean lines and symmetry. The whole scene was beautiful in a perverse way. I looked to where the sky should be and saw only the semi-translucent material of the Dome.

"Surreal," I whispered to Ryan.

I assumed we'd be immediately confined, but no. The man barked the order, "Keep walking."

Silently, fear stiffening my body, my leaden legs propelled me forwards and curiosity temporarily stilled the terror. People wearing skin-tight clothes were walking around, apparently happy. But it was a muted happiness; these people could be synthetic clones of humans. The clothes weren't unusual to me; I'd seen plenty in the Citidome dumps. But I couldn't take my eyes from their hair. Beth and I had laughed at Ryan's sleek, flat hair when he'd first arrived, but it had been unkempt compared to the gleaming crowns that clung to the skulls of each of the Citizens. Even those with long hair scooped it back into severe pony tails. In the village, I'd be able to identify every individual by hair alone but here people were all so alike that they could have been manufactured in a factory. The only expressions that animated the clones' faces were the looks of disgust that assaulted us from every direction.

"Veez, must be a runaway – she looks like a savage," one Citizen said to his companion.

Better a savage than a robot. I bit the words back. A number of people had stopped and were pointing at me, their mouths gaping. I shuddered, understanding how Mum had felt. I was a freak here, my tanned skin and dark brown curls an anachronism among these gaunt, ghostly figures, their stark white skin almost transparent. I took in a marble square lined by raised beds of flowers, all identical. The square contained geometric sculptures, as well as chairs and tables, where people were eating, drinking and chatting. I saw squares of grass so uniform and short I wondered if it was real, smart entertainment malls advertising movies, as well as DanceZones, GameZones, ChillZones and all manner of other Zones that meant nothing to me. The other buildings must be work centres and Residence blocks. But the beauty here was sterile. Every building was white and steel, every surface smooth and glossy.

"I never imagined it would be so unnatural," I muttered, glancing at Ryan.

"Escaped dissidents on their way to correction camp," declared the voice behind. Correction camp! Of course! Hope flooded me. Which Citidome were we in? Tau-2, surely. How many camps were there around here? Would we be going to the one targeted for Outbreak day? Then fear twisted my guts as I remembered one of Mum and Dad's rows. There was going to be an explosion; Mum believed no-one would survive it. And Harry would be there, throwing the explosives. Perhaps this was destined to be the ending to our star-crossed romance, to perish together on Outbreak day.

The rapid breathing of the tall figure next to me drew my attention back to the present. I'd kissed Ryan. Actually kissed him, and not just a peck on the cheek. What had I been thinking? But at this moment I would have grasped his hand if mine weren't bound together. He was my only friend in this hostile, alien world and he looked so young, so vulnerable. Then a woman lunged forward and spat at me. It landed on my face, but I had no way of wiping it off. Her companion laughed and did the same. Soon disgusting globs of saliva were flying at us from all directions. My stomach heaved. And they called us savages!

Thankfully, it didn't take long to walk from one entrance of the Citidome to the other, at which stage the CE placed his finger to a pad on a white, windowless building and a door slid open.

"Found these two outside," he said. "This one's one of the Phi-1 breakaway gang, she's a savage."

"I'm not a savage! Aaargh!" Another pulse from the weapon made my head throb.

"Let's get 'em cleaned and tagged," said a hard-faced woman.

Of course. This was what Helen had trained me to remove. I winced at the sight of a metal implement being clamped to Ryan's ear. At a loud clicking sound, Ryan sucked in his breath through clenched teeth. The RedTag was bigger than I'd imagined. I could see why Mum had so little flesh on her ear. Before I had time to consider the mechanics, the woman reached me in one stride, and crushed my lobe between her fingers. The pressure of this alone brought tears to my eyes and when white-hot heat shot through my lobe, I was unable to suppress a yelp. Next she hauled me into another room.

"Sit on that chair," the woman said.

I perched on the edge of the plastic seat, which was covered in buttons and levers. The woman snipped the cord that bound my hands and pushed me into the seat, which moulded to my shape. I raised my hand to lash out but straps appeared from nowhere, fastening me down so I was unable to move. A man appeared, jerked my head to one side and – I gasped – hacked my hair off with scissors. Then he ran an electrical device, which buzzed and stung, over my scalp. The remaining clumps joined the pile of luxurious curls on the ground. I fought the urge to cry; I loved my hair. The straps released. I put my hand to my bald head. Ugh, I could feel every bone of my skull. It felt as though it no longer belonged to me. Then I heard a sound that chilled me even more – howls from the other room. Ryan's howls. What were they doing to him?

"Cleaning next," a voice said.

I followed mechanically, wondering what fresh hell awaited me. Ah, this must be a shower. I'd never had one. At home we had baths – most of the showers had packed up years ago and we couldn't get replacement parts. I'd imagined them to be like warm summer rain. But this was hot, blisteringly hot. A woman handed me what looked like a scrubbing brush and a tube of paste.

"Scrub yourself all over, or I'll be forced to do it, and I won't be gentle."

The bristles were hard, the paste excoriating, but I brushed it against my skin, trying not to give her the satisfaction of seeing my pain.

"Harder," said the woman.

By the time the water was turned off, every scrap of flesh burnt, leaving my skin scarlet. The woman led me into a tiny room, bare except for a folded blue bodysuit on the floor. I put it on – much too long in the leg. Then she locked me in. I curled up on the floor, hugging myself into a foetal position and craving oblivion. Tentatively, I touched my ear. A convex disc protruded from the front of my lobe, around two centimetres in diameter; at the back was a smaller, flatter disc. By running my nail under the back I estimated that the two halves were attached by a bar maybe 5 mm thick. I pulled at it. Mum had been right. There was no way it would come out any other way; I'd have to cut off half my ear to remove it.

In the first hour, my mind concocted all sorts of worst-case scenarios, a torture worse than the shower. So instead of looking forward, I looked back. When I was a kid, I once asked Mum where birds went at night. She said they went deep into a hidden place in the sky. I loved the idea of it; a hidden place full of birds, where no-one could shoot at them. Now in this world with neither sky nor birds, I retreated there once more.

***

"On your feet!"

The voice roused me. Had I really managed to sleep? I put my hand to my ear – yes, the tag was still there. I raised myself, winced at the pain of moving – my skin was still pink – and saw another CE. My bladder was full.

"I need to, uh, urinate," I said.

"You'll have to wait. This way," she said.

I followed her to the entrance and my heart leapt to see Ryan, though a barely recognisable Ryan, the bumps of his gleaming skull visible – and his nose swollen and red. A wave of affection enveloped me.

"You've got a nice shaped head," I whispered to him.

"Have to admit, I preferred you with hair." Oh, he was still able to smile.

"Quiet, you two," the woman barked.

A man of around Mum and Dad's age, slim but not BodyPerfect, stood next to Ryan, his tag marking him as another prisoner. His eyes, rimmed with dark shadows, looked kind, and he nodded in my direction. But, not being able to face another electrical jolt in my head, I remained silent, fearful of even smiling.

Soon we reached the outside and I shivered at the sight of the black sky. What time was it? I looked at my wrist but my watch had been taken. I'd loved that watch. It was over two hundred years old and had been given to me on my thirteenth birthday. How curious that there was no distinction in lighting and temperature between night and day inside the Citidome. An open truck stood opposite the gates and someone shoved us into the back of it. On either side of the truck were bare metal benches, seemingly designed to inflict back pain. At first the cold air was balm to my still-burning skin, but soon I shivered.

Ryan's hand reached for mine. I interlaced my fingers with his long, bony ones. His skin was smooth, baby-soft. All the adult hands I'd ever known – Harry's, Matt's, mine, come to that – were roughened and hard. How could the feel of his hand be so different, like holding a different limb entirely? As if reading my mind, he released my hand but then placed his arm around me, drawing my body against his, and this time I didn't think of Harry, just of the comfort of human contact. The lorry started moving along a rutted road, each jolt stretching my bladder to its limits. Should I urinate in my bodysuit? No, not in front of Ryan. It was too humiliating.

"I think it's safe to talk now." An unfamiliar voice, presumably the older man. "I'm Aki."

"Hey, I'm Ryan."

"I'm Joy," I said. "Don't these things pick up our speech?"

"No, they're trackers, that's all. So many of us, no-one would have the time to listen." Aki laughed mirthlessly. "Only the CEs get voice trackers."

"Ryan, what did they do to you?" I said.

"They've got some new electric devices to get information out of people. I won't tell you where they put them, but the nose was the least painful."

"Euww." I swallowed. "Are you in pain?"

"A bit sore. Could've been worse."

"What information?" Aki said.

"I escaped from Phi-1 almost a year ago, along with a gang. They wanted to know where they'd all gone. So I made up the name of a village and said it was south of here, near to Phi-1. Seemed safer."

"Ah, so you were part of Outbreak-2," said Aki in a knowing way that caught my attention. He knew about the Outbreak missions? Was he part of Doodlebugs?

"I wonder which correction camp we're headed for?" I said.

"What does it matter?" Ryan said. "You don't get out of them, you know."

"Not unless … Doodle?" Aki whispered.

"Bugs!" I said.

"Why have I never seen you before? Are you one of the Heroes too?" Aki asked.

"No," I said. "I've come from the outside."

"The outside –" Aki began.

"Will someone make some sense around here?" asked Ryan.

"Keep your voice down." I hissed. "There's going to be a mass outbreak from a correction camp. But I have no way of knowing if we're heading for the right one."

I heard Ryan's intake of breath and the pressure of his arm around me increased.

"We are; I'm certain of it," said Aki. "That's why I'm on my way there, to help with Outbreak-4."

I shivered. When was it planned – the end of November? Could I survive here for five weeks?

"Help how?" I asked.

"You see, I'm a Hero. For the last six months I've been working as an electrician, servicing the Citidome gates and getting to understand them. Then I got myself Marked so they'd throw me out. No doubt you've heard of Michael Heath, the leader of the AOC. He reckons that everyone from Sigma 2, Tau-2, Upsilon-2, Pi-2 and Rho-2 gets sent to the same one."

"Michael Heath's my dad," I said with a swell of pride.

"You're joking! Surely he hasn't sent you here?"

"He doesn't know I'm here. I was with Ryan and got arrested by accident."

"Michael Heath's daughter. It's an honour to meet you, young lady."

"But how do you know the gates in the camp are the same?"

"I don't, but I've gotten pretty good at disconnecting the circuitry."

"B-but I'm worried about the explosives. Mum reckons the blast might be too big. Might incinerate the whole lot of us."

Aki sighed. "There's so many potential pitfalls in this plan we can't think of them. But we have to try."

"Forgive me if I don't get too enthusiastic," Ryan muttered.

The rest of the trip passed in an exchange of stories. Aki and I told Ryan the full details of Outbreak Day.

"So Harry's going to commit suicide and then the rest of us step out into an inferno? Huh, I'm with your mum on this," Ryan said.

The word suicide lodged like a pebble in my stomach but I ignored it. Blind optimism was all I had now. Meanwhile, Aki drank in my description of our community with the excitement of a child experiencing their first Christmas.

"Sounds like everything I dreamed of," he said.

"Hopefully you'll get to see it. How many Heroes are there at the camp?"

"I should be the tenth."

My face fell. I'd expected more.

The vehicle juddered to a halt. The journey had taken no

more than half an hour.

"That didn't take long; must be the right place," Aki muttered.

"Out," a voice barked.

I jumped out of the lorry, shivering in the chill night air. I wrinkled my nose; a bad smell pervaded the air, like the toilets back home. At our approach, a bank of lights activated and illuminated the path to a huge metal gate. Damn. Intruders would be spotted from some distance away. The CE pressed his finger to the pad and the gate opened. I glanced towards Aki, taking mental notes of every detail, and read the anxiety in his expression. We followed him some distancc along a gravel path, my panic mounting at the sight of a walled enclosure whose entrance again was a metal gate. And we weren't even in the complex yet. How could such a high level of security be overcome?

"Oh Dad," I silently cried. "You'll never get me out of here. I'm trapped."

CHAPTER 16 - CATHY

"From now on I'm going out every day until I find Joy." I discreetly took a deep breath, not wanting it to be interpreted as a confrontational sigh. "I'll take Bramble. I'll go south – no-one's tried that direction yet – and stop in every uninhabited village. Anna can look after the boys."

For once, Michael had no argument. "Good idea." But he didn't smile. "I've sent their descriptions to everyone in the AOC. They'll have to go to a community eventually; they'll need food."

"I heard someone say Joy was a murdering bitch," said Scott. "What does bitch mean?"

Michael gave me a look of accusation and left the house. I didn't bother asking when he'd be back.

The following day Mary travelled west on Blue Boy. I headed south on Bramble, stopping at every settlement I found. At Langley Mill, I ran into Lynn from the market.

"Oh no, not Joy," she said. "She took it badly about Harry, didn't she?"

"Hasn't been the same since," I murmured. "What did you exchange for them?"

"Presents, daft messages, all sorts. Had a language all of their own, those two did."

The now permanent mass of guilt I carried inside expanded. As Lynn continued to talk fondly about Joy, I realised that so many people knew her better than I did. But no-one seemed to be able to shed any light on Joy's relationship with Ryan. Beth seemed resentful that Joy had 'stolen' the boy intended for her. She told me that Ryan had rejected all her advances, and that she suspected that Joy and Ryan had been seeing each other in secret. Mary said they talked non-stop on their riding expeditions but seemed nothing more than friends. Daisy said that Ryan was in love with Joy, but Joy didn't feel the same way. I couldn't make sense of the conflicting stories.

After several hours of fruitless searching, I realised I must be close to the correction camp. Motivated more by curiosity than hope, I continued my journey southwards and soon saw the first in a series of industrial units – no more than giant concrete blocks – surrounded by gated fences. This must be the complex. I looked around and noticed a hill from which I could survey the area covertly. I spent the next few hours there, making a mental map of the scene. Apart from black dots moving around what looked and smelt like a sewage treatment plant and inside the complex of giant polytunnels – presumably the site of vegetable plantations – there was no sign of human activity.

As the sun cast its last feeble shadows I turned away, not wanting to ride in the dark, when I heard a rumble. Open-topped trucks left the largest and furthest of the buildings and entered the gates of each unit. Armies of blue-clad figures climbed onto the lorries and were transported back to the large building. I shivered and turned away. So many people – how could we save them all?

By the time I returned, Michael was frantic.

"Where have you been? I thought you'd be home hours ago."

"I checked every village directly south of here. Any word from Mary?"

He shook his head. "Daniel drove to Bakewell and then to Buxton, but nothing. He drove on to Macclesfield to see if they might be there, waiting for a canal boat. Dee and Harry have been searching too."

"With Caroline?" I spat the name with contempt.

Michael's head dropped. "I didn't ask."

"I spent some time watching the correction camp." I related my observations, which brought a faint smile from him.

"Do you think you could go there early in the morning and track the morning movements? We need to target the explosion site, too. Before Aki, the latest Hero, left, I asked him to leave stones by the gate of any unit that uses flammable chemicals. If you could start checking that, it'd be a big help."

"Yeah, no problem." I forced the corners of my mouth

upwards, recognising the request as a peace offering. "What did you do today?"

"We tried the permanganate bomb. Not bad, but not as good as the sticks."

We spoke to each other as acquaintances, workmates even. We ate. I played a game with Scott, while Michael spent his time with his DataBand. And this set a pattern for the following empty days. I searched villages and observed the correction camps. Being there took my focus from the village I was meant to be leading and yet seemed to be turning on me. Needless to say, the Baxters would hardly look at me. My usual friends, with the exception of Daisy and Mary, distanced themselves from me, as if by coming too close they'd be sucked into the vortex of catastrophe that had attached itself to my family.

That weekend, Mary looked after all the children, enabling me to go to the village social, but my reception was as cool as the air outside. Thankfully, Helen had made a rare appearance. As she approached me I smiled, glad that someone seemed to be on my side.

"Helen, great to see you," I said. "You should come down more often."

"That's what Michael said so I thought I'd give it a go." I frowned. Michael, encouraging her to come to the social? Odd. And I wasn't the only one to have noticed, it seemed. Margaret was standing in a corner, talking to Joanne, someone I considered a friend, and nodding in my direction. "No news of Joy, I guess?"

I shook my head.

"I was hoping to have her with me in the bunker," Helen said. "She was a natural, you know. She located my vein in no time."

"She's an exceptional person." My voice cracked in my throat. Already, everyone except me referred to Joy in the past tense. "But so are you. You'll be wonderful in there."

Michael joined us. "Keep telling her that," he said. "She's having a crisis of confidence."

Helen gave Michael a smile of – what? Gratitude? Adoration? I shivered. As the three of us chatted, I noticed Margaret and Joanne's growing interest. As soon as I could, I found Daisy.

"Can you find out from Joanne what Margaret's been gossiping about?" I asked.

When Daisy returned, it was with a glass of one of Anna's strongest spirits.

"Bloody hell. Do I need to be drunk to hear this?" I said.

"Margaret's a one-woman rumour mill these days," Daisy muttered. "I guess it's to detract from the fact that Elsie's stomach's looking a bit swollen."

"Ugh, I hope not." I shuddered. "That's all we need. But it's horrible around here these days, isn't it? Everyone talking about everyone else. We used to be such a close-knit community. Go on. Put me out of my misery."

"She reckons there's something going on between Helen and Michael."

I rolled my eyes then took a hefty swig of my drink.

"You don't seem that surprised," Daisy continued. "Hey, you don't believe it, do you? She's just throwing every piece of shit she can find at Michael at the moment in the hope that some sticks."

"I suspected that's what she was talking about; just wanted to be sure. The funny thing is ... I'm starting to wonder if she's right this time. I've noticed something odd in Helen lately, a way she looks at him. What's wrong with me, Daisy? I thought I'd got this sort of stupid jealousy out of my system years ago."

We glanced across to where Helen and Michael were still talking. Helen was laughing, her face alight at whatever Michael was saying.

"If they were carrying on, they wouldn't flaunt it so publicly, would they?" Daisy said. "But I think Helen might have a bit of a crush on him. I suppose I ought to confess something. When Joy was desperate to contact Harry, I thought Michael was being too hard on her, so I took her to see Helen, hoping she'd let Joy use her DataBand. But when she heard that that Michael had forbidden it, she went really weird. At the time, I put it down to her being so bloody prim and proper, but perhaps there was more to it ... Don't worry, even if she has the hots for him, he's never going to look at her, is he?"

"Probably not. Huh, I'm almost past caring. He doesn't look at me that way any more. He doesn't look at anyone or anything except his DataBand."

That was the point that I realised that something had died inside me.

CHAPTER 17 - JOY

"That's your bed. When you hear the bell, it's time to get up," an unsmiling woman said.

I screwed up my eyes and saw row upon row of identical beds, each almost touching the other. The entire room must sleep around fifty people. How was I expected to sleep in such close proximity to others? Even worse; the room wasn't completely dark, low intensity lighting emanating from the ceiling. My bladder was by now bursting.

"Where's the toilet?" I asked.

"Turn left outside; first on the right. Hang on; you need authorisation." She scanned my fingerprint onto something that looked like Dad's DataBand.

I located the room and pressed my finger to the black pad by the door. So only certain doors would open? Once inside I gasped. A gleaming white tiled bathroom lay in front of me. I'd never seen such a clean, shiny room. Then I glanced at a long passageway, one wall of which was studded with showerheads, nothing dividing them. Ugh. Not only would I have to sleep with strangers but it appeared I'd have to shower in front of them too. At least the toilet cubicles had doors. I entered one that contained a toilet, but it was like no toilet I'd ever seen before. It contained water! It was odourless! Once I got up, I jumped. Water was flushing through the ceramic bowl.

I returned to the room of beds and saw Aki and Ryan already lying down.

"You OK, Ryan?" I whispered.

He turned to face me, and proffered his hand. I took it.

"Bet you liked the toilet." He grinned.

"Amazing! But you could have warned me about the water flushing through. Scared me half to death."

He laughed. "We'll get through this," he whispered.

The door opened, and the woman returned.

"No talking," she said. Her hard stare told me that the consequences of disobeying would be dire, so I sat on the empty bed. A white top and pants were folded on the pillow. Scrambling out of my bodysuit, I put them on. Hmm, nice soft fabric. I lay down. There were no covers, not that I needed any; the room was warm. But the mattress was so thin I could feel the metal slats of the bed beneath. Without the comforting weight of blankets and under the distraction of the light and my turbulent thoughts, I found sleep impossible. Was this my future?

A loud bell interrupted my thoughts. I rose and saw that everyone in the room was stirring, their actions mechanical. All had bald heads so prisoners must be shaved regularly. The thought was depressing.

"Hey, newcomers," said a young woman. "Follow me; I'll show you the ropes. Bathroom first."

The woman shed her pyjamas and stood naked in front of me. I winced – the woman's ribs were visible and her breasts no bigger than bee stings. To my horror, Aki and Ryan had also taken their clothes off. I cast my eyes downwards. Did no one have any shame around here? I'd only ever seen one naked man before – the memory brought a smile – and he'd been the only person to see me.

"Do I have to strip off in front of everyone?" I muttered.

"Of course you do, doofus. What's wrong with you?" she said.

"Just do it. It's normal behaviour here," Ryan whispered.

I shed the garments quickly, folding my arms across my breasts, which a glance around had confirmed were larger than any of the other women's. I cast my eyes downwards. How much more degradation could I stand?

Despite the lack of privacy, the delicious hot shower lifted my spirits, and when I returned to my bed, I was pleased to see a clean blue bodysuit, but breakfast made them sink once more. At least talking seemed to be permitted.

"What is this?" I asked Ryan, frowning at the food in front of me, which had the texture of plastic and little flavour.

"Protibacon." Ryan grimaced. "No-one eats meat in the Citidomes."

"Where exactly are you from?" asked the girl sitting

opposite me.

"Outside," Joy said. "I was born there."

"Veez, you're kidding!" she hissed. "How did you end up here?"

Several heads turned towards mine and for the rest of breakfast I was deluged with questions about my life. At least I'd be popular. Ryan put his finger to his lips. Of course, he was right. Trust no-one. I kept details to a minimum. But what happened next? As people finished their breakfast they returned their trays to a hatch then pressed their fingers to an array of pads on a wall.

"That tells you your work for the day," someone explained. "You'll then get a number; that's the number of your transportation. Woow, you're short, aren't you? Roll up the legs of your pants; you'll trip up otherwise. Come on, I'll show you."

I pressed my finger to the pad and the words Water Treatment, 12 appeared on the screen.

"Bad luck, that's a shitty job." A guy laughed as if he'd told a joke.

"What did you get?" I asked Ryan.

"Laundry, five," he said, his voice leaden.

"That's one of the worst ones: steaming and chemicleaning clothes, then packing them for redelivery. The fumes get to you; you'll have a stinking headache this evening," the guy said, and on seeing Ryan's frown, said, "Well how did you think you used to get clean clothes every day? That's what we do here: all the behind-the-scenes jobs that make the Citidomes run smoothly."

"How long have you been here?" I asked.

"Let's see, must be eleven years now."

"Eleven years?"

"Yeah. It's a life sentence you know. No-one goes back."

"How do you stand it?"

"No choice, have we? After a while you get used to it." He shrugged and I saw an expression that I soon came to recognise in the other inmates – a dullness behind the eyes, a sort of resignation. But surely these had been the rebels and so-called subversives in the Citidomes? How had their spirits been so crushed?

"I'm on unit six, whatever that is," said Aki, then lowered his voice. "Here's hoping. Maybe I'll see you later, Joy."

My frustration increased. Our only chance of a successful escape was through collaboration, but if I could only conspire with a trusted few and I was separated from these during the day, how would it be possible?

Reaching the door, a young woman said, "You'll need boots. Smaller sizes are to the left."

I goggled at the gleaming rows of pristine black boots – footwear back home was either home-made or salvaged from Citidome dumps and tended to be repaired until they fell apart. I tried on a few pairs until for the first time in my life I had perfectly fitting footwear.

"Ooh, these are blissful," I said.

The others looked at me as if I was mad.

"You haven't even fastened them properly," said a stick-thin person – I wasn't sure whether male or female.

Pressing a button to allow the boots to tighten to a perfect degree, I entered a large courtyard on which stood a fleet of lorries and scanned the numbers until I found number 12. Following the actions of the others, I queued to see a supervisor who scanned my finger. He looked up.

"You're new, I see. Suzu, show this one what to do."

Suzu, the young woman who'd shown me the boots, climbed aboard the lorry and positioned herself on the bench seat that lined the compartment. A few people nodded greetings, others chatted among themselves. How, among this group, would I find people I trusted, people whom I could recruit? A tall, pale man who appeared to be in his mid-forties dropped himself next to me with a thump, then smiled and nodded at me. I smiled back then drew in my breath, recognising a face I hadn't seen in years. Without the dreadlocks that had been his distinguishing feature, it was hard to be certain, but the shape of his face – similar to Harry's – it had to be.

"Kell?" I whispered.

He drew his brows together. "Who are – no, it can't be. Little Joy?"

When I nodded, he threw his arms around me. Happiness coursed through me, at a point when I no longer thought myself capable of it. If only I could tell Harry his dad was alive. Seeing the frowns of the others, I pulled out of his embrace.

"How long have you been here?" he said.

"Since last night. I got captured outside the Citidome."

"Aw, honey. Anyone showing you the ropes?"

"I am," said Suzu.

"I'm an old friend of Joy's. How about I take over?" said Kell.

"Suits me." Suzu shrugged.

Kell winked at me. "You ever see Dee and Harry?"

I nodded. When and where was it safe to talk to him?

"They thought you were dead," I whispered.

"Huh, no such luck. I was fixing a lock one day, saw a pregnant woman. Next thing I knew, a CE came chasing after her. Tried to help, punched the CE, wound up in here." He dropped his voice. "We can talk more when we're working."

The journey took only ten minutes and as we approached, the unpleasant odour that pervaded the outside air intensified.

"What goes on here?" I asked.

"Water treatment plant. Those fancy flush toilets; it's all got to go somewhere. They treat the waste and some goes to fuel, the rest to fertiliser. Don't look so stricken; most of it's automated. We have to clean up some of the equipment, check water levels, that sort of thing. The smell's no worse than the outdoor toilets in your village."

"But I only have to stay there for a few minutes at a time!"

"You get used to it," said Kell. "Here, you'll need some brushes."

To my relief, no-one objected to me shadowing Kell and we were soon out of earshot of the others.

"We have to clean that out?" I wrinkled my nose. "It's gross!"

"Your sense of smell deadens after a few hours."

The work was horrific, scrubbing out pipes encrusted with human excrement. I retched and my breakfast made a repeat appearance, but the noise made conversation possible without risk of being overheard.

"When is it safe to talk?" I asked.

"If you mean, when do the CEs listen, only at night when

we're in bed. Anywhere outdoors is OK, though be careful who you trust. They have a system where anyone who reports someone for being out of line gets extra privileges."

"Privileges? What sort?"

"Nothing worth having, if truth be told. Extra food, a day off work but that's not much fun. All you have for entertainment is a few games and those deadly media shows from the Citidomes. Anyway, we're safe now, so tell me all about Dee and Harry. That's the hardest part of being in here, not seeing my boy grow up to be a man."

"They're still working the canals. Dee's the same as ever and Harry became a fine man. He's about as tall as you, strong and … oh, he's gorgeous. He's incredibly bright – the brightest person I know – and funny and caring and passionate about the things he believes in. And everything he says is original and memorable. You'd be so proud of him." Tears pricked my eyes.

"Hey, what's up?"

"Me and Harry." The story tumbled out, culminating in my flight from the village.

"I'm sorry to hear that. I kinda hoped the two of you would have got it together."

"My life's a mess, Kell." I couldn't control my tears any more. "I can never go back home. Ryan and I killed a man."

"Think that's the least of your worries, honey. No-one gets out of these places. I've seen people trying to make a run for it before. They get tortured in public as a warning to the rest of us. The only time you're not in a secure complex is when you're getting on and off the bus."

"But there's a plan – a mass outbreak. We need about a hundred people but no more. If too many people know, the authorities might find out. But I don't know if we'd even get that many. Everyone here seems so passive."

"You think we haven't tried? I've been here five years, remember. There was a riot in one of the sleeping huts a few years back. Everyone involved got forced to work without a break until someone told them who organised it. It was three days before someone cracked and blabbed. The woman who organised it got stapled to the wall of the hut. Took her over a week to die."

"But this time there's outsiders helping." I scrutinised our surroundings before telling him everything I knew about Outbreak. "They want to target a factory that has flammable chemicals."

"Hmm, sounds more promising than anything I've heard of. We use chlorine here, solvents in the laundry, let me think … unit three, that makes agrochemicals, y'know, fertiliser and the like. Yeah, that might be your best bet. Those vats of ammonium nitrate, covered in safety warnings, they are. But the timing … it's the smallest unit; only around fifty people work there."

"Yeah, timing's everything. We need to be able to fight immediately before the factory blows up. That's 7:15 am on the 25th of November. And the explosion needs to be so big that it would account for the loss of bodies when people go into hiding in the bunker."

"Ah, there's your weak link. What's the date and time now?"

"It's –" I did a quick calculation – "October 16th. Start counting the days."

"Is it really?" He rubbed his chin. "I can see it's autumn, but I thought September. You lose track here. And the time?"

"Oh. I don't know." Without my trusty watch I had no way of knowing. Then inspiration struck.

"What time's sunrise in this area at the end of November, Kell?"

"Hmm, now you're asking. We never had any exact sense of time when we were on the canal."

"I reckon it's about a quarter to eight."

"Yeah, sounds about right. And when does it get light?"

"About half an hour before that?"

"And when do we all rise here?"

"As soon as it's light – ah!"

"Dad said this section of the plan was a bit of a gamble. I guess 7.15 was an estimate of when prisoners would rise. I'll check with Aki and get back to you."

"I dunno, honey. Don't raise your hopes too high. I've seen so many people killed in here I've lost count."

"If I never see Mum and Dad again, I may as well be dead."

"You've got their spark, all right. If there's a chance of seeing Dee and Harry again, you can count me in. I'd risk anything for them. For now, at least we've got each other, eh?"

"But how do we see each other? I guess these work rotas change regularly?"

"Yeah, every week. But we have evenings. For those who don't want to watch the mindless crap on the media console, there's another room where people can go to play games or chat."

"And that's OK? I read my mum's journal. Don't they split people up if they get too close?"

"Sometimes they break it up – they can get nasty if they suspect a romance or a plot – but most guards are pretty stupid. We can talk a little if we're careful. Introduce me to your friend from the village and the other guy – Aki was it? – tonight. Now, out of the way. I've loosened a huge clod of shit and it'll come flying out once I sluice it."

How could I stand even five weeks of this work? But I soon mastered the range of routine tasks. The morning, punctuated only by a short break for a hot drink, passed quickly. Kell devoured every detail of the years he'd missed with Dee and Harry, and I was happy to talk about my favourite subject. Lunch was a vile green bar but by then I had no appetite.

"Euww, this is a nutribar isn't it? Harry gave me a taste of one once. They're stocking the bunker with them."

"Yeah, get used to them."

"Don't we even get a break?"

"No, we work until it gets dark," Kell said. "Think yourself lucky the days are getting shorter."

By evening I was shattered. After dinner, another bland, mushy affair consisting of that weird meat substitute, I found Ryan and Aki who brought a woman with him. Together, they huddled around something called a VirtuGame, a game played on a virtual screen.

"This is Kell," I said, and to Ryan, "Harry's dad."

"You're on board?" said Aki.

Kell nodded.

"This is Yumi," Aki said. "She's one of the Heroes."

"And you're the famous Michael Heath's daughter?" asked Yumi.

I smiled and nodded.

"Your father's the true hero in all this," she said. "The only thing that keeps me going sometimes is the dream that I'll meet him. There's quite a team of us now. Over the next few weeks I'll introduce them to you. There's a chain of communication for spreading messages."

"We know which factory it is," I whispered to Aki.

"So does Yumi."

"Unit three," we whispered together.

"Yumi's working there this week. Each day she's going to drop a stone by the gate. That's the sign I agreed with your dad. Hopefully we'll build up a pile big enough for someone to see it."

"For now, everyone needs to collect potential weapons and hide them," Yumi said. "Things you can pick up at work, hide in your clothes and then store in the bathrooms; they're the only places that don't have cameras. Someone managed to loosen a panel behind the second cubicle from the left in the bathroom nearest the entrance. Rocks and sticks are good."

At that point, Suzu approached us. "Hey, Joy," she said. "What are you lot talking about?"

"Joy's never played a VirtuGame before," explained Kell. "We're showing her what to do."

"Of course; you've missed out on so much, Joy," said Suzu. "Never seen any media shows either? We need to civilise you."

"I've – " I was about to protest that I'd seen movies but Yumi cut in.

"Why don't you go with Suzu, see what you've been missing out on? Besides, Ryan hasn't played this for years. He needs a turn."

Strange, why did they want rid of me? I turned to join Suzu.

"What's the deal with you and those guys?" Suzu asked.

"Ryan was in my village. We went to look at the Citidomes – I'd never seen one close up – and we got caught. Aki – the older guy – was in the truck with us when we were taken here. And I know Kell from years ago. It was nice to see some friendly faces." I took a breath before continuing. "But I'd like to meet some others."

"You and Ryan. Are you?" She gave a suggestive smile.

"No." What should I say? Who could I trust?

"Hey, kitten, it's OK by me. How do you think I got this?" She pointed to the Mark.

"Were you …" I searched for the appropriate terminology. "Attached to someone?"

"I thought I was." Her voice was low. "But after I got Marked, I never saw him again. I used to dream about the outside. Tell me all about it."

I gave vague details. We watched a media show – *Vile Bodies* – that disgusted me. It was the one they'd threatened to put Mum on. I cringed at the sight of a savage crowd laughing and jeering at a woman with a larger than average nose. I was relieved to see Ryan, together with Yumi.

"Want to join us?" he said.

I followed them to a sofa.

"You didn't say anything personal to Suzu, did you?" Yumi said.

"I don't think so."

"Good. I wouldn't trust her. I have no proof, but she gets a lot of privileges."

"So how do I know who to trust? I thought that she was safe, since you encouraged me to talk to her."

"Didn't want to draw attention to us."

"Oh." As if to confirm my foolish and very young status, my eyes filled with tears.

"Don't worry," Ryan said.

"I'll leave you two to it." Yumi winked. "Only thirty minutes before lights out anyway."

"Really?" I looked at my wrist where my watch should be. It couldn't be more than around eight-thirty. Then Ryan and I were alone.

"I hate it here," I said. "The work's horrific, these people scare me, the food's shit and that media show was downright sadistic."

"It was never going to be the Pleasuredome, was it?" Ryan said. "Hey, we'll cope. I've been talking to the others. Kell's a nice guy. He's been here such a long time that he has a network of people he trusts so we don't have to worry about recruiting people. Sorry about Yumi assuming we were a couple. I didn't get the chance to correct her."

"It's OK." I looked into his hope-filled eyes. "Uh, Ryan, we should talk about that kiss. I shouldn't have done it. You see, whatever Harry's done, I'm still in love with him."

His eyes dropped. "I'm clueless when it comes to love, but I understand that much. But you like me, don't you?"

"Course I do."

"Well that's enough for me." Ryan looked so happy that I thought, what the hell? If I could make him smile in this dismal place, how could it be wrong? So when he covertly took my hand, I allowed it to rest in his.

New routines entered my life. Each week I was assigned a different work task, some more bearable than others. Picking fruit and vegetables gave me a comforting sense of familiarity, though the scale of the production here was staggering, and the technology involved in climate control mind-blowing. The food production plant, boxing up endless portions of proti mush made me nauseous. But I focussed on the task of accumulating weapons. A not-quite-empty spray can of chemicals, a jagged rock, a kitchen knife, all were added to the cache in the bathroom. I spent evenings as inconspicuously as possible, passing messages among members of the group I learnt to trust, watching media shows occasionally so as not to attract attention. But the only thing that gave me genuine enjoyment was being with Ryan.

"Sounds weird, but sometimes I'm happy here," he murmured. "The food and the work might not be up to much, but I could spend forever talking to you." He gave me that look again, that started in the eyes, crept down to his lips then lit up his face. I shifted my weight.

"I'd be happier if I had hair again. I can't believe they shave our head every week. I wonder why." I tried to steer the conversation away from the emotional.

"Hygiene. Head lice spread quickly."

"Had those at home from time to time. They're not a big deal. Home, do you ever think of it? It was Scott's eleventh birthday last week."

"It never felt a home to me like it was for you. To me, home's more than a place. It's about who you're with. Right now, I feel at home." There was that look again.

And then guards approached us from either side and a stun gun took my senses away.

When I regained consciousness, I was in the dining room, encased by a sort of cage that forced me to stand in the same position, statue-like. Opposite me was Ryan, similarly restrained. But as soon as our eyes met, my brain was once more stunned into submission. It took me a painful half hour to realise that an electric shock had been programmed to trigger every time I looked at Ryan. But I could look around him. Above his head – and presumably mine – was a sign bearing the words: "Attachment is wrong." The other thing I noticed that day was that Suzu had extra rations at dinner.

It was two days before they released us – two days in which I had to urinate and defecate in the clothes I was wearing and wonder what would kill me first – the hunger or the thirst. The only thing we were given was, judging by the horrific consequences on my bowels, a laxative. By the time they released us, I'd become used to my own stench, the humiliation pushed aside by a grim determination to survive. My mouth was like sandpaper and I could talk only in a rasp.

"Come on, creev. Let's get you cleaned up," said a guard. Once more I was subjected to an excoriating shower that left my skin peeling.

I didn't risk being alone with Ryan after that.

***

"You OK, honey?" Kell said. It was five days later and we were unpacking deliveries to a warehouse. In that time I'd plumbed new depths of misery. I'd had no real conversations with anyone and none of my so-called allies had spoken to me.

"Depends how you define OK. If you mean, am I so sore all over that I can't sleep at night, that I've got something that looks like my baby brother's nappy rash, that the torture chamber I was incarcerated in has left me with a permanent headache, and that I could cry with loneliness, then yes, I'm OK."

"Sorry, sweetheart. We're so close to the big day that we can't risk talking to you," he said. "I should have warned you off spending so much time with Ryan. But I thought you two were just friends. Thought you were in love with my son."

"There's nothing between us. I just want a bit of affection. Is it so wrong?" I asked. "Harry's with someone else back there."

"Take any comfort you need, honey. Seems to me that right and wrong don't apply in here."

As I crossed off the dates, I told myself that Outbreak had to work, that my fate couldn't be to live and die here. I'd kill myself first. And I tried to imagine a future beyond Outbreak day, a future when I returned home and Harry was there waiting for me. But even my imagination didn't stretch that far.

CHAPTER 18 - CATHY

As the rich autumn palate faded into the monochrome monotony of winter, my gloom intensified. I'd resumed my role as village teacher, the act an admission that Joy was never coming back.

"Will you stop looking at me like that?" said Michael for the hundredth time.

"Not until you stop looking at me the same way," I said. "And before you ask, yes I am going out again before dusk."

He sighed and left the house. How could it be possible? I'd believed that our relationship would last a lifetime. But neither of us could get past blaming the other for the loss of Joy and deep down I blamed myself too. I'd had the power to stop Peter's return. So much for making a decision for the greater good. The community remained as divided as ever, the rumour mill grinding furiously. Most of the gossip still concerned Peter and Elsie but the increasing efflux of water butts from the village was starting to attract attention. Margaret seemed to be engaged in her own campaign to destroy Michael's reputation and the Michael-and-Helen story seemed to be gathering momentum. I no longer had the energy or inclination to confront Michael.

My daily rides to the correction camp had become as much for myself as for the AOC, driven by a need to feel useful and to validate my position as village leader. Over the last weeks I'd observed the precise movements of the trucks, identified hiding places, but there was still no sign of which of the factories could be the chemical one. I'd narrowed it down to three units, having seen food supplies entering one of the other candidate concrete cubes.

I arrived at four thirty as the last of the convoys of trucks were leaving. Today's target was a small building, unit three. I dismounted and tied the horse up by a tree and tiptoed to the perimeter fence. Timing was everything, I'd discovered. In fifteen minutes, the motion-activated lights would be operational. And then I let out a cry of relief. A collection of around twenty stones lay to the left of the gate. That had to be it! Oh, the positioning of the factory couldn't be better. Close to the gate of the residential unit, but not so close that escaping prisoners would walk straight into the blaze. For the first time, I began to believe that Michael's plan might work. I kicked the pile over, a sign to the inmates that we'd got the message.

I scuttled towards the horse then stopped at the sounds of barking. Although Mary had domesticated some dogs in the village, most were savage, feral creatures and I wouldn't want to disturb one. Then I noticed that several dogs had gathered around an object on the ground; presumably a dead animal. Grateful for the distraction, I mounted the horse. As the horse broke into a trot, the dogs dispersed. I glanced at what they were eating. My stomach heaved. It was a human corpse, a woman with dark brown hair.

"Joy?" I whispered. I dismounted. Was this the fate of my daughter, to become food for wild dogs? As I approached the body, the carrion stench made my stomach heave, but I had to be certain. The build – it could be Joy. Then I caught sight of the face. The eyes were gaping sockets, but the face was nothing like Joy's. Tears flooded down my face, and in my distraction I didn't hear the approach of footsteps.

"Hey, you," came a hard female voice.

I swivelled around to see the uniform of a CE and froze. Michael and I were both officially dead as far as the Citidomes were concerned but we weren't sure what would happen if we were confronted and fingerprinted. Would our records have been deleted from the system? I looked into the face of my enemy. Then my hand shot to my mouth, as did that of the CE. It was like looking at my younger self.

"False alarm, just a wild dog," said the young woman, then pressed her fingers against the tracker on her cheek and coughed.

"Who are you?" she mouthed.

"If you're Suna 121968 then I'm your biological mother," I whispered.

The woman staggered backwards, leaning against a tree for

support. She was a few centimetres taller than me, her skin paler than mine though still darker than the norm, but her hazel-green eyes, black hair – straightened and flattened against her hair in Citidome style – and full pink lips made our similarity impossible to miss.

She nodded, then whispered, "But how … you can't be …"

My mind raced. This was my daughter. But my daughter upheld the rules of the Citidomes. I couldn't afford to trust her. "Will that pick up what we're saying?" I pointed at the tracker.

"Not if we whisper. But not long. Meant to be back soon. You should stay away … runaway on the loose. But you know my name?"

"I escaped from Sigma-2, seventeen years ago. I saw you twice, at kindergarten. I realised from your date of birth and your looks that you must be the child developed from my stem cell."

She stared at me with the look of a rabbit in a snare, clearly too terrified to say more.

"A CE; that's a good job," I said. "Do you enjoy it?"

Suna didn't react at first, as if formulating the answer in her mind. Then her head dropped and she shook her head. "Is it good outside?" she mouthed.

"It has its own problems but yes, I've been much happier outside than I ever was in Sigma-2." I paused; should I say more? "I've given birth naturally; you have a half-sister and two half-brothers."

Suna bit her lip, then turned away. "Have to go."

And with that she was gone. So that was the daughter I'd wondered about all these years. Why didn't I feel more? She'd piqued my curiosity – she seemed so unhappy. But I didn't feel a yearning to see her again. Maybe the part of my brain that felt emotion had just had enough. Still, I returned home feeling lighter than I had for weeks.

When I returned, Michael had prepared dinner. He acknowledged me with only a nod, evaporating my mood.

"I found it," I said. "It's this one." I pointed to a place on the map we'd constructed.

He span around. "That's fantastic."

"Glad to know I can do something right," I muttered.

"Well you have. It's the last missing part of the puzzle." His manner was one of a leader congratulating an underling. "Me and Helen got another three water butts to the bunker today and separated off a section for medical treatment."

"That's nice for the chosen few." Why was I being like this, taking any chance to snipe, to undermine? According to my counts of the arriving and departing trucks, around seven hundred people inhabited the camps. Those who were last to reach the bunker would have to take their chances. Maybe they'd have to shoot people at the entrance. Perhaps I was too soft-hearted to be a leader. I'd encountered violence, attacked people myself, but the thought sickened me. Maybe I should tell Daniel I wasn't up to the task, resign my leadership. But not yet. Not with Outbreak day so close.

"Sorry you don't think liberating hundreds of people much of an achievement." Michael's voice was tight. "Dinner's ready."

We ate in silence except for the scrape of cutlery against plates. Should I tell him about Suna? I sighed. No, I couldn't face his disapproval over how I'd handled the situation. No doubt I'd have said too much or too little and somehow compromised the safety of bloody Outbreak day.

"That was lovely, thanks," I said, although Anna's cider had failed to soften the stringiness of the rabbit in the casserole. We'd been living on rabbit and squirrel for weeks; all the AOC members were saving their meat rations for preserved meats to store in the bunkers.

"I'll wash up; you must be tired," Michael said, excruciatingly polite.

How long could we exist like this? Once the boys were in bed, the evening stretched out in front of us and I felt too tired to read. I'd have to make an effort to make conversation, but any attempt to say what I wanted to say would be futile. Any attempts to repair our relationship would have to wait until after Outbreak Day.

***

The following day was a school day, but gossip had even reached the playground.

"Miss Cathy, where's all the water going?" asked Ian. "Dad says there's something funny going on."

"We're taking it to another village; they've got a contaminated water supply."

"Told you," said Scott with a smug grin.

"And is it right that Uncle Peter got Elsie up the duff, and did the same to Joy, and that's why Ryan hit him over the head with a hammer?"

I sighed. I'd always considered myself a natural teacher but the endless questions were becoming harder to fend off. A chill settled over me. Had Joy gone into hiding because she was pregnant? But where was she? It was becoming harder to imagine that she was alive.

That evening Michael returned from his session on the DataBand, looking even more preoccupied than usual.

"I had a message from the AOC rep in West Bridgford," he said. "A CE paid them a visit. She was looking for a villager who fitted your description. And he said that she looked like a younger version of you."

"Suna." I sighed. "I saw her yesterday." I told him all about the encounter.

"Why didn't you tell me?"

"Thought you wouldn't approve of me talking to her."

"Oh, Cathy." His sigh was long and heavy. "But if she was looking for you ..."

"She was only out because she was looking for that escapee."

"Ah. In that case she won't be out again. I had another message, from Ann in Bradfield. I knew they'd been hiding the escapee. A CE came and captured her today."

"You didn't tell me you knew where the escapee was."

"No. It seems we don't tell each other anything any more." Michael scratched his head, as if searching for topics of conversation. "I had a message from Harry, asking if we'd heard anything from Joy. So he still cares."

"Shame he didn't show it earlier."

And that's how we were until the last weekend before Outbreak Day. Michael was more stressed than he'd ever been. I felt him shifting around in the bed beside me and wondered whether he slept at all. Not that I asked; we seemed to have lost the ability to communicate about anything real. Daisy and Anna had been briefed on the plan, Daisy being recruited as a driver.

"Is everything in place?" I asked.

We'd all almost forgotten Outbreak-3, the small outbreak from Sigma-2, which was scheduled three days before Outbreak-4, the big one. I hoped Michael hadn't neglected it too much. People had been injured and killed on these smaller missions, too.

"Yeah," Michael said. "We have detailed plans of where the TravelPods and horses go, as well as the route to the bunkers. Helen's going in first – we'll put any injured people from Outbreak-3 in there with her and send everyone else along the canal to the safe house in Hest Bank." At this he shot me a tender look. The 'safe house' was the house with a cellar in which I'd spent an unhappy few months. Tears filled my eyes. He still cared, of course he did.

"You haven't had second thoughts about me coming with you instead of Daisy?"

He gave the sigh that was becoming his trademark response to anything I said these days. "We've been through it time and time again. We can't risk anything happening to both of us, for Scott and Adam's sake."

"It's like no-one can say her name any more. She'll always be the lost daughter –" but the rest was lost in tears. His arms encircled me, and I could feel from his shaking shoulders that he was crying too.

"When does it stop hurting?" he whispered into my hair.

"I don't think it ever will."

We held each other and gave way to our grief, my body shuddering, but the tears refused to ease the pain. And just as I thought we'd had a breakthrough, Adam began crying. The moment was lost.

Soon there was no time for anything except intense planning. On the Tuesday, Helen came to say goodbye before installing herself in the bunker.

"I'll be thinking of you," I said. "You look pale; you OK?"

"Just been a little run down. I hope the community copes while I'm gone." Helen's pale face showed her strain. She seemed much older than her age – only thirty – and I felt a pang of guilt at my suspicions. Helen was married to her work. Surely she wasn't capable of conducting an illicit affair?

"Ah, here's Michael," I said, and drew Helen into an embrace. "Stay safe."

Michael dismounted and helped Helen up. As he did, I couldn't help notice a flush settle on Helen's cheeks.

"See you later," Michael said to me, and then to Helen, "Ready for some fun? I don't ride slowly."

As Helen gave an uncharacteristic giggle, I felt the chill again. No. It was impossible. I stood there, watching them until they'd disappeared from view, my eyes focussed on Helen's arms around Michael's waist. I returned home, fed Adam but couldn't settle.

"Scott, do you mind looking after your brother for a little while? I need to see Nanna and Daisy."

"Sure," he said.

Within minutes, I was sitting in Anna's living room, venting my fears to Anna and Daisy.

"I heard the rumour," Anna said. "It's rubbish, you know that. I know our Michael's not perfect. But infidelity? That's not his style at all."

"I thought we'd gone through this before," Daisy said. If anything's going on, it's one-sided – oh shit, excuse me." And with that, Daisy fled the room.

"She's been like this all day, vomiting from both ends," Anna explained. "I reckon she's picked up a bug. I don't think she should go tomorrow. But back to you, Daisy's right. What if Helen has feelings for Michael? He'd no sooner cheat on you than –"

"I didn't want to tell you, but things have been so awful between us …" My words were drowned in sobs.

"I could bang your heads together," Anna said. "Do you think I haven't noticed? Even if Michael hadn't told me all about it, it's obvious. Whenever you're both in the same room, the temperature goes down by a few degrees. You need to stop blaming yourselves. Whatever happened to Joy, it wasn't either of your faults. And Cathy … I know about the difficulties you're having with Adam, too. Why don't you tell me things any more?"

"It's such a dreadful thing. I couldn't admit it to anyone except Daisy and – oh no – Helen. She might have told Michael. I don't want him to know. That's why I couldn't tell you."

"I wish you had," Anna said. "Michael might be my biological child, but I love you both equally. And for what it's worth, I think Michael's in the wrong. He tells me you're snappy and he thinks you don't spent enough time with the boys but hasn't questioned why. He's focussed on this sodding outbreak so much that he can't see what's right under his nose."

"I feel so useless these days," I muttered. "I thought becoming village leader was my big chance to step out from under Michael's shadow, but I made one decision, and it led to disaster. All I seem to have done is divided the village."

"Huh, it's Margaret that's doing that. She still won't accept what Peter did to Elsie and Joy, so she's trying to turn people against you and Michael."

Daisy returned, her complexion even more washed-out than usual. Deep, dark shadows surrounded her eyes. I added selfishness to my list of failings. Why hadn't I noticed?

"Been shitting through the eye of a needle for a day now," Daisy grumbled.

"Did you sleep last night?" I said.

"Not much."

"Daisy, you need to rest – "

"I know what you're going to say, but don't. I'm still driving tomorrow."

"You can't. If nothing else, you'll be a danger to the others if you're not on top form. I'll go instead. I've wanted to go all along but Michael insists I don't."

"He's got a point. What about Scott and Adam?" Anna said.

"You could take them again tomorrow, couldn't you?" I pleaded. "There isn't anyone else."

"That's not what I meant. I don't want those boys to be orphans."

"Drivers are safe. Besides, tomorrow's the easy one. It's the next one we need to worry about." A sick feeling of dread settled on my stomach.

When Michael returned, I said nothing about Daisy. If I sprung it on him tomorrow, he'd have no choice. Instead, I said, "Was Helen OK?"

"Yeah," he said, not meeting my eyes.

"Poor thing. I wouldn't fancy being in that huge bunker on my own all night. And it'll be seven weeks before she sees daylight again."

"If anyone can cope, Helen can. She's one of the most capable people I know."

Unlike me. I bit back the words.

As I lay beside him that night, unable to sleep and suspecting he was also awake, I began to fret. After insisting that Daisy would be unfit to drive, I couldn't afford to be tired. So it was with surprise that I heard the alarm call of the DataBand. Six o clock! I'd managed to sleep at least five hours after all. Michael leapt out of bed and frowned as I followed.

"Don't flip, but Daisy's got a stomach bug. I only found out last night. I'm driving."

"Why the hell didn't you tell me?" he growled "Daniel could have driven."

"I reckon Daniel's heart's worse than he's letting on; it seemed too much of a risk. If you can't trust me to make any decisions of my own, what's the point of me being leader?"

"And what about Adam and Scott? Oh, I forgot. You're not bothered about your sons, only your lost daughter."

In reply I slapped his face, a crisp, sharp sound that gave me no satisfaction. "Anna's coming over," I muttered.

"We haven't got time for this. Let's get going."

I drove the TravelPod in silence, biting back the tears. Had I made yet another disastrous decision? The journey seemed infinite but when I pulled up at the allotted spot some five hundred metres from the Citidome gate, I gasped at the sight of five TravelPods, fifteen horses and a small army of people, all armed with makeshift weapons of sorts. So many people at risk, and this was meant to be the easy one! The danger of the situation, a fact I'd ignored until this minute, hit me with unbearable force. I looked at Michael and saw the fear behind his eyes.

"Michael …" I began. But my words were taken from me

by a kiss of such ferocity it took away my ability to think at all. How long since he'd last kissed me like that?

"I love you Cathy."

"I love you too. Stay safe," I whispered, and with that we exited the TravelPod.

"Cutting it fine weren't you?" said one of the community leaders.

"It's 6:58 – I'm 2 minutes early." Michael grinned.

"Cathy, we weren't expecting you," another leader said.

"Daisy's sick," I said.

"Remember what we agreed, that the drivers only move forward if no-one comes this way three minutes after the signal," Michael said. "I know this is selfish, but I want Cathy to be an exception."

"Of course, the children. We'll make sure nothing happens to her."

I felt that I ought to protest but didn't, moved by the immediate compliance of the others.

"What do we do now?" I said.

"Stay in hiding until we hear something," said Michael. "Remember to look in all directions. Once the alarm's raised, guards could come out of the other gates. I reckon we have two or three minutes, tops, then we need to retreat. Drivers, stay here. Fighters, time to advance. Each driver stood by their vehicle, whether TravelPod or horse.

Time moved with agonizing slowness. 7:15 came and went. Then, at 7:19, a furore made my muscles tense in preparation to move. I heard the shouted word, "Green," the codeword to indicate that the group's exit had been achieved. I peered out from behind our camouflage of shrubbery to get a better view of what was going on.

"Over here," shouted Michael.

The crackle of footsteps on undergrowth heralded the arrival of the escapees. Around twenty people ran towards us. An explosion of gunshot. Someone fell – not Michael. Then Michael pulled a young man to his feet and both ran in my direction. I scanned the landscape and screamed. No-one had noticed the CE approaching on a HoverCycle from the left – he must have exited by another gate. He fired a weapon.

"Michael, other side!" I shouted.

I could never clearly remember what happened next. Gunfire seemed to emanate from all directions. A CE fell. Michael pointed to the TravelPods. Five young men and women ran towards us. One fell, clutching her face. Someone disarmed a CE, knocking his stun gun from his hands and sending him crashing to the ground. Then Michael and the young man both fell and I couldn't tell from whom the fountain of blood spurted. I closed my eyes, and only when I opened them and the young man leapt into the TravelPod, carrying a body, did I know the truth.

CHAPTER 19 - JOY

I went to the bathroom yet again. What time was it? Surely the bell would sound at any minute? I removed two rocks from our weapons store; was it safe to arm myself now? Huh, rocks wouldn't be much use if we couldn't override the door system. No, mustn't think like that. Aki had confirmed that the system of arming the doors was the same as that in the Citidomes, so Stage One of the plan was to enable him to access the control room and disable all the locks. There was no reason why this stage shouldn't work, as long as the guards didn't fire on us first.

As I walked back to the bed, I shot a glance at Ryan. I'd missed our conversations but was frightened to even look at him. I'd heard that he and one of the Heroes had been working in Unit three yesterday and had loosened the tops of the storage vats. A throaty cough told me that Mala was also awake. The feisty Citidome escapee had been caught in a nearby village and dragged to the camp last week, fighting all the way. She'd killed a guard by strangling him with her bare hands. It was exactly the sort of skill we needed; we'd recruited her to the gang. Unfortunately she'd arrived with a stinking cold that had spread around the camp. I was no stranger to colds so was one of the few to have survived unscathed.

I'd barely made contact with the bed when the now-familiar bell rang. Adrenaline coursed through my body. I jammed on my leisure shoes and looked across to Aki, already on his feet.

"Time to overcome. Follow me, everyone!" Aki roared.

Ryan grabbed my hand and I squeezed it. "They're not separating us this time," he whispered. Mala and another recruit followed us. Others scratched their heads and muttered, "What's going on?" Almost immediately, a female officer confronted us.

"Back to your beds!" she shouted. "Backup!"

Without hesitation, Aki slammed his fist into her face, flooring her. Mala stamped on her neck. A sickening crunch and her body lay motionless.

"Nice one," said Aki.

I swallowed the bitter fluid that had risen in my throat, the memory of the hammer crashing into Peter's skull filling my mind. Could I do that? Don't think, just act. As the others dashed to the bathroom to arm themselves, I handed a rock to Ryan. A deafening siren sounded and the scenes of chaos became hard to process.

"Keep hold of my hand," Ryan said.

A scream. A surge of people emerged from another of the sleeping rooms. About ten metres to my right, facing away from me, was a guard armed with a gun. I tiptoed across, raised my arm and brought the rock crashing to the base of his skull. He fell. Ryan stamped on him, mimicking Mala's action. All around was fighting and falling as the guards stunned as many people as they could. But our strength of numbers soon floored them. Was that all they were armed with? Where was Kell?

"Joy, over here!"

"Kell!" Keeping a tight grip of Ryan's hand, I ran to Kell. He thrust us deep into the crowd that had gathered around the front entrance, but it remained shut. Some people were ineffectually kicking the door and beating it with rocks. From my position among the throng I could no longer see what was happening, buried among taller bodies, but Ryan didn't release his grip and kept up a commentary.

"Woah, there's another one. Veez, what's that? That looks like the gun they used when I – oh no, it is. It's taken the skin off someone's face."

Every nerve and muscle fibre tightened at the sound of shots and screams. The shots ceased, but the screams and moans continued.

"Someone got her from behind. That's at least five down. No … here comes another one. What's happened to Aki? Surely they've got to the control room by now?"

More shots. More screams. Again, the shots ended. The room span. The human shield that protected me was becoming thinner by the minute. Then a huge push almost knocked me over. The doors were open!

"Don't let go!" Kell gripped my other hand.

I ran, my legs struggling to match Kell and Ryan's speed, towards the open outer gate. A surge from behind pushed me over, then a heavy weight forced my head to the ground. Agonising pain shot through my spine. People were running over me!

"Stop! You'll trample her to death." Ryan's voice.

Two hands hauled me up. We rejoined the surge. But where were our rescuers? And what about the explosion?

And then it happened. The first blast brought everyone to the ground. The second made me think that the world was coming to an end. The noise shook me to my core. A ringing in my ears – had my eardrums burst? Then came the heat. Everyone stared, mesmerised by the scale of the blaze. And then all was movement and a throbbing wall of sound. We ran towards the inferno, treading on burnt bodies along the way.

"Shit, if you hadn't fallen, we might not have survived the blast," Kell muttered. I shivered despite the heat. The explosion must have extended much more than a hundred metres; could anyone throwing the explosives have survived? Could Harry have survived?

Must keep running. Adrenaline tore at my muscles. My lungs burnt, as much from the effort as the heat and smoke. Then we saw them. A huge group of rescuers. There must have been fifty or more people, most armed with guns, but no-one I recognised. No Dad. No Harry. No Helen. Where were they? How did I have any hope of finding them among this madness?

"Line up over here," called a familiar voice.

"Gill!" I ran towards a woman I knew from the Bakewell market.

She let out a cry, and held out her arms. "Joy, I don't believe it. Everyone's frantic. No time to talk, we need to be quick." With a swift movement, she sliced through my ear. The frenzy of pain and blood made me unable to think for a few minutes but Gill was already working on Ryan when I found my voice again.

"Where's Dad?" I said.

"I don't know," said Gill in a way that convinced me she was lying.

"Helen's meant to be doing this, isn't she?" I said.

"Yeah. She couldn't be here, so she sent this young man instead."

A Marked man with a healing lobe was already working on a woman's ear. The screams round me told me that there was no time to make sense of Gill's words.

"Is there a spare scalpel?" I asked. "I know how to do this."

"You're kidding? There's two spare. Here you are," she said, and handed me one. "But keep some pressure on your own lobe for a few minutes."

"I'll do some," said Kell, as she took the other scalpel.

"OK, I'll do you first," I said. "Bend down." I brought the scalpel to his ear and met with resistance; Kell's fleshy lobe was much harder to cut than the pig's ear, but I persisted, ignoring his yelp. Slice, pinch.

"Veez, this is madness," Ryan muttered.

"Next!" I shouted. I remembered Helen's words, "After a while you'll forget what you're doing; it'll become automatic." But the screams were a constant reminder. I was mutilating humans. At first I gave each terrified face a reassuring smile but as the cold bit into my flesh, numbing my hands, I increased my pace. Soon one lobe resembled another, another lump of flesh, like skinning a rabbit. The screaming and gunshot became white noise.

"You're doing brilliantly." Ryan's voice reassured me.

Fresh blood warmed my fingers, its metallic smell pervading my lungs. But despite my focus it was impossible to ignore the heat, smoke, fumes, and the cacophony around me – the endless siren, the gunshots, the shouts, the screams. A man lying on the floor grabbed me by the ankle, crying for help. I looked at him and gasped. His mouth was a gaping sore, his lips burnt away. And then I heard something else – horses! People were getting away! And I still hadn't seen any of the people I wanted to see.

Then an unfamiliar sound filled the air and I looked upwards, the shock almost causing me to drop my scalpel. What on earth was that? A huge metal monster filled the sky, drowning out any other sound. Even in our picture books, I'd never seen anything like it. Kell tugged at my hand.

"Woah, what's that? We'd better get out of here."

Streams of fire rained down from the monster. Bodies fell like toppling dominoes. I finished the ear I was working on, shot an apologetic glance at the endless lines of people snaking away from me, handed one a scalpel and ran as fast as I could. Then a scream made me turn. Escapees surrounded a CE, one hand in the air, her weapon in her other hand.

"Please, you can have my gun. I want to come with you."

Hearing the desperation in the woman's tone, I turned and gasped. The eyes, the mouth, the colouring. It must be!

"Suna?" I said.

She frowned, nodded and handed me the gun. I gave it to Kell.

"Hurry up," Kell screamed

Was Suna for real, or was this a trap? But she was my sister. I had no time to think; better make sure she couldn't be traced. "Open your mouth," I said.

Suna obeyed, her face a mask of terror. I put my finger inside her cheek. Ah, her disc wasn't fastened all the way through. I withdrew my finger, gave a swift tug to the disc, and it was free. Blood gushed from a hole in her cheek.

"Follow me!" I yelled.

I ran blindly, not knowing whether she was following or not. Then Ryan yelled and fell.

"Ryan!" I stopped but Kell grabbed my hand.

"Leave him!" he shouted.

"No!" I bent over Ryan, who was crying out in pain. His pants were torn, and I could see a huge hole in his leg, from which blood was oozing.

"You don't make this easy, do you? Take the gun." Kell handed it to me and threw Ryan over his shoulder.

And then I found myself being squashed into a TravelPod with Kell, Ryan, Suna and another woman. Could so many people fit into one tiny vehicle? The door closed and the vehicle moved away as flames continued to rain from the sky, merging with the fire that was now tearing into other parts of the complex.

I pressed my hand against Ryan's wound, his blood seeping through my fingers. But there was no skin beneath my hand; I was touching Ryan's raw flesh. I looked at his wound with horror. The damage appeared to be superficial: the bullet had dissolved a patch of skin about the size of the palm of my hand. But blood was pouring at an alarming rate from a tear to the right of the wound. He must have fallen onto something – the area was littered with rocks. No-one spoke at first, the car filled with Ryan's moans.

"It's OK, I'm here," I soothed, then to the others, "I have to stop him bleeding. I need something to tie around him." I looked around me. The blue bodysuits we wore at the camp were of a hardwearing fabric that resisted any attempts at tearing. "Driver, do you have a shoelace?" The villager wore handmade boots fastened together by leather thongs.

"Yeah, but sorry, can't stop."

"I'll hold the steering wheel, you untie it," said Kell.

"I'll have your shirt, too," I said.

"Bossy isn't she?" said the driver but after some awkward wriggling, handed them to me.

I placed the thong around the top of Ryan's thigh. How tight? I searched my mind for what I'd read. Must stop the bleeding but not for too long that we damaged the tissue. I took a deep breath, tightened it until he gasped, then pressed the inside of the driver's linen smock against his leg to stem the flow of bleeding.

"At least your legs are skinny. This wouldn't have gone round mine," I said to Ryan. "I think I've done it. The bleeding's slowing. Ryan?" I turned to Kell. "Oh, I think he's fainted."

"Just as well. That's a hell of a wound," Kell said. "Jesus, what are those bullets made of?" Then his voice rose. "Stop the Pod!"

"No way. Are you mad?" said the driver.

"What's up?" I said.

Kell had turned in his seat. What had he seen? I saw people running in all directions, but no-one I recognised. "Harry," he said. "I'm sure it was Harry, running in that direction, a bunch of people behind him."

My stomach relaxed – Harry must have survived the blast!

– and then clenched, remembering that Harry was as good as dead to me.

The vehicle continued its tortuous progress, lurching through dips and crevices along a path not designed for traffic, until we entered the edge of vast woodland. The TravelPod stopped by a tree and the driver nodded towards its base. I gasped; there was an open trapdoor. We leapt out.

"Bloody hell, Joy. We did it!" Kell threw his arms around me.

"Yeah, well we can celebrate later. Let's concentrate on getting Ryan down those steps."

We hoisted him out of the vehicle.

"He needs assessment first," said a man at the door. "Turn left when you reach the bottom of the steps, then register." The man did a head count, recorded the numbers with chalk marks and looked up, eyebrows raised at the sight of Suna. "You, get out."

"No, she's an escapee. She's my half-sister."

"Joy? Don't tell me you were in the camp?"

I recognised one of Dad's AOC colleagues. "Hey, Dai, have you seen my dad?"

"Yeah, he's inside."

"But that wasn't the plan. I thought only those who got injured were staying here."

And then I saw Dai's pained expression and my heart constricted. What horrors faced me now?

CHAPTER 20 - CATHY

"Cathy, how are you today?"

I opened my eyes and saw a row of horse brasses on the wall. I must be at Anna's house. But how did I get here?

"Come on, drink this." Anna lifted the mug of dandelion coffee to my lips. It burnt my tongue but I was barely aware of the sensation. A scuffle outside turned my attention to the door.

"I don't care. I want Mum!" The words increased in volume until Scott burst through the door.

"Mum, they keep saying I can't see you!" Scott leapt onto the bed next to me. Why had he been kept from me?

"Oh, sweetheart." I gathered him in my arms. "Where's Adam?"

Mary came into the room, and placed a wriggling Adam in my arms. He was by now crawling and didn't like being carried, but rested against me with a surprising lack of resistance, fear paling his huge hazel eyes. I kissed the soft skin of his cheek and for the first time, felt something for him that wasn't mixed with irritation or guilt.

"Let's give them a minute; it might bring her to her senses."

Did I hear that correctly? What had happened? How long had I been here? And then it came to me in a rush: Michael, the unknown escapee.

"Where's Dad?" asked Scott.

I took his face in my hands. "Dad's going to be away for a few weeks, six or seven. It's official business." I took a deep breath. Should I say more, prepare him? No. The young man had said he'd detected a pulse. But the expression on Helen's face at the bunker entrance had told me two things. Firstly, that her feelings for Michael were more than platonic. And secondly, Michael's condition was very, very grave. No, I mustn't think like that. Helen was the best health worker I'd ever met. If anyone could save him, she could.

Mary entered the room. "Time for bacon and eggs, Scott," she announced, and winked at me, "and something gooey for your baby brother." Hoisting Adam upwards, she left me to the pleading eyes of Anna. I was overcome with shame. Why had I fallen apart like that? What must Anna be going through?

"How long have I been here?" I said.

"Three days." Anna's words were faint.

"*Three days*?" I leapt out of bed. "How is that possible?"

"I didn't know what to think. You turned up on our doorstep on Wednesday morning and passed out. When you woke up, you couldn't speak, didn't appear to see or hear us. Alex has been here but he said it was nothing physical. So …" Anna's lips trembled, unable to form the painful question.

"M-Michael was injured. I left him with Helen in the bunker. A few people were shot, and everything happened so quickly. Guess I went into shock."

"Injured? Oh, I thought …" Tears trickled down Anna's face.

I drew her towards me. What benefit would it be to tell her that her son was almost certainly dead? Surely it was best to keep everyone's hopes alive?

"He was shot, in the shoulder. Must've hit an artery though, blood was spurting out. It … didn't look good. But Helen's with him."

"So we're clinging to threads of hope." Anna's eyes seemed to pierce straight into my soul. She hadn't been fooled by my false optimism.

I stretched and wrinkled my nose: I hadn't washed for a few days, judging by the smell of my armpits. After a quick bath, I joined the boys downstairs.

"Where's Daisy?"

"Wherever everyone else is." Mary's shrug held a touch of irritation. "Whatever this big secret is, the one that I'm not in on. My guess is it was to do with the noise outside."

My throat constricted. Of course! Outbreak-4! It had been this morning! I exchanged a look with Anna.

"Sorry. You know the rules about secrecy. What noise?"

"You sleep deeply, don't you? About fifteen minutes before Anna woke you, we heard a massive boom, then a cloud of smoke, but coming from quite a way away. Must've been a hell of an explosion if we heard it from here. Come and see."

I followed Mary to the back yard and rubbed my eyes in disbelief. From the south, plumes of black smoke were billowing into the sky, forming a dense cloud.

"I need to check the DataBand," I muttered.

"You need to eat," Mary insisted.

"B-but – "

Mary placed her finger on my lips. Of course, Scott mustn't hear.

I wolfed down the bacon and eggs, and had barely finished when Anna shouted, "Come outside!"

I heard the noise first, then looked to the sky and couldn't make sense of what I was seeing.

"It's a giant bird!" said Scott, pointing to the alien black object in the distance.

What was it? It looked nothing like any pictures of aircraft I'd seen. And – oh no – streams of fire seemed to be falling from it onto the ground below. It must be connected to Outbreak! I shivered – would anyone have survived it?

"I'll wait with you until Daisy gets back. I need to go home first, check the DataBand, then no more secrets, I promise."

Once home, I removed the DataBand from the hiding place that Michael had revealed last week – the gap under the skirting board. Damn, no messages. I looked at my watch and frowned: 09:15. It should have happened two hours ago. Surely there must be some news by now? One of the AOC members was meant to transmit a message, giving some idea of the numbers in the bunker. But as I walked back to Anna's, mesmerised by the surreal scenes in the sky, the DataBand buzzed. A message from Dai! I opened it with trembling hands.

Outbreak-4 achieved but many casualties. Final numbers 228 in shelter.

Was that all? What had happened to everyone else? How many bodies lay dead on the ground? I took a deep breath. It was time to tell the villagers. I sent Scott to knock on everyone's door and alert them to an emergency village meeting that evening, then returned to Anna's and told Mary the whole story.

"Bloody hell," she said. "So Michael's going to be in that bunker for another three or four weeks?"

"Yeah. I guess closer to four, since they didn't fill the bunker to capacity. But Daisy could be home any time, so we should know more then."

But Daisy didn't arrive. By the time we left for the meeting, I'd concluded the worst. Joy, Michael, Daisy. Why was everyone I loved being taken from me? I gripped Anna's hand as if it were the only thing anchoring me to earth, and tried to dam the flood of grief that threatened to burst from me. Now wasn't the time. The village needed strong leadership.

I took a deep breath, stepped to the front of the room and looked at a sea of expectant eyes.

"You'll all be aware that there was an explosion this morning …" I began. I told them everything, a calm descending on me as I did so. I reached my conclusion without interruption. "So please remain vigilant and refer any strangers to me. The members of the communities nearest the site will look for survivors who didn't make the bunker, and transport them to safe houses. The Barrel Inn up at Bretton is one of them. Although a few people may make it here unaided within the next few weeks, the bulk of the escapees should arrive in around six weeks. We've planned for around twenty-five people aged between eighteen and forty to join the farming academy. They won't become permanent community residents; by harvest time we'll choose two or three and the rest will help out in other communities." I exhaled. It had been easier than I expected.

But – oh no – Margaret was standing, hands on hips. "Now hang on," she said. "Twenty-five newcomers – that's damn near doubling the size of the community. Don't any of us get a say in this?"

My voice remained level. I'd been prepared for this. "I

regret that we couldn't involve the whole community in this decision. But remember the village rule we agreed thirteen years ago? To minimise the risk of betrayal" – at this I gave Margaret a cool, hard stare – "all business of the AOC is to be carried out under conditions of secrecy. The decisions of the AOC are for the benefit of all communities and sometimes they may override individual wishes. I realise that not everyone will see this as a positive development but everyone voted to accept that rule."

"Huh. It seems to me the AOC dictates everything these days." Frank stood up beside his wife. "Trading our children to other communities. Forcing complete strangers on us. Keeping us in the dark. Citidome escapees murdering the villagers. And no doubt we're going to have those Citidome scum running riot in the village again for the next few weeks. Perhaps we should vote on whether we want the AOC running things any more."

Then Anna leapt up. "I've heard enough. You two always have to make it personal, don't you? Well, I've kept quiet for weeks now, but if it's personal you want, you're gonna get it. My son's done nothing but good for this village, but all I hear these days is muckraking about him. And as for your scumbag brother, Cathy was able to put personal feelings behind her and let him live here again, and how did he repay her trust? By sleeping with a fourteen year old girl, trying to pin the blame on her husband and then raping her daughter!"

A collective gasp went down the room, and individual arguments began to break out. I put my hand to my breast as if this would slow my racing heart. I'd lost control of the meeting. Why oh why had I thought I could be a leader? Not only had I lost Michael, I could have destroyed everything he'd been working towards over the last year. My eyes darted to Daniel. How would he have handled this situation? His cool blue eyes remained impassive; a barely perceptible nod of the head giving me strength. I raised myself to my full unimposing height and banged on the table until everyone quietened down.

"Order, please."

Silence was restored.

"If you don't want the AOC to represent this community

any more, we can put it to the vote, but before we do, I want to stress that the AOC has always worked for the greater good of all. Would anyone else like to speak? One at a time please."

Maeve, the baker, stood up. "How will there be enough food to go round?"

"It's all been planned down to the last detail. I was going to tell you separately; we're going to assign extra help in the bakery. Our problem isn't lack of crops; it's lack of labour. Remember, we only have twenty-five people until summer; after that we'll have two new skilled farmers. The other communities will trade for the ones we don't keep – we may get more livestock."

"Huh, we're treating people like our sheep now," Margaret muttered to Frank.

"Can you address your comments to me please?" I said.

Margaret scowled.

Luke stood up. "Do you know how much of the barley crop we lost this year? A third, because we didn't have enough people to bring in the harvest before that heavy rainstorm in August. We lost half the crop of runner beans to frost because we weren't able to pick them quickly enough. We all know about the problems we've had with cheese this year – we need a skilled dairyman. This community is desperate for new blood. I'd urge everyone who doesn't want strangers to think of the alternative."

A murmur passed around.

"Anyone else?" I asked.

No-one moved.

"Let's vote," I said. "Raise your hands if you're happy for the AOC to retain the powers it has."

A number of hands rose, including Matt's, incurring a lethal stare from his mother. More than half? I counted and the tension in my stomach loosened. Thirty-nine. There followed twelve against and seventeen abstentions. The community was fractured, but intact.

"In that case, the decision-making process will remain the responsibility of the AOC. I'll keep you posted as soon as I have any more news."

"I resign from the village committee," said Margaret.

"Me too." Frank joined her.

I bit the lining of my cheek. I wouldn't rise to them.

"Would anyone like to nominate two new members?" I said.

Within minutes, two other villagers had been voted onto the committee. I released a huge, deflating breath, closed the meeting and headed straight towards Anna.

"I'm so sorry, love." Anna's voice was contrite. "I should have kept my mouth shut, but that bloody woman's had it coming for weeks. I was livid – "

"You said what we're all thinking," I said. "It needed to be said."

At that moment a hand rested on my shoulder. Daniel. "Well done," he said. "I knew I'd made the right decision in choosing my successor."

While the war against the Citidomes raged, I'd won my first battle of the lesser village war. But without my husband, my daughter and my best friend by my side, it felt a hollow victory.

CHAPTER 21 - JOY

So this giant subterranean cavern was to become my new home. My eyes scanned the heart of the bunker – a murky, grey-walled expanse containing row upon row of metal-framed beds, and not much else. The whole place stank of damp, and the panels on the ceiling emanated only faint light. Well, I guess I wasn't planning on doing any reading in here. Then I became aware of a cough behind me. Damn, I'd almost forgotten. Suna.

"Follow me," I said. "That cheek will need a stitch."

I pushed and shoved through the line of people whose condition was being assessed. Where was Dad? All I could see was people sitting around, dazed and exhausted. Then I saw the far end of the room. Oh no. All those prostrate bodies. How many casualties were there? Then a familiar voice.

"Joy!" It was Helen, or a diminished version of her. Because she did little outdoor work, her skin never had the healthy bloom of the other villagers, but now she looked ghostly.

"Helen, where's Dad?"

"Joy, Joy, It's a miracle. Your blood. We can – we can use your blood. He was sh-shot. Must have been caught in the crossfire. I removed one of our bullets. He's holding on, but, but he needs m-more."

He was alive! But what had happened to Helen of the legendary cool head? Why was she gabbling almost incoherently? I followed her and fell to the floor beside Dad. His shoulder was bandaged, he was unconscious, and with a deathly pallor worse than Helen's. I took as deep a breath as my tight chest would allow.

"No-one else knew their – what d'you call it? – blood group. Sit on that chair and roll up your sleeve. Quick."

I did as I was told but Helen seemed to be having trouble

locating my vein. I flinched at the prick of the needle, and cried out.

"Ouch, that hurt."

"S-sorry. Let me do Mic – your dad. Have to do the other arm."

Dad's inner arm was covered in huge black bruises. What had Helen been playing at? In our practise sessions she'd never made more than a thumb-sized bruise and I'd done it without bruising at all. After some fumbling, Helen got the needle in and soon my blood was flowing into Dad.

"Dad, wake up. It's me, Joy."

I smoothed his hair. His breathing was shallow. He couldn't die, could he? I'd never been able to make up my mind about religion. I found it hard to believe in God, but now I made a deal with Him. Spare Dad, and I wouldn't think about Harry any more. And then I remembered Suna, who was standing to one side. Why was she here? This was no time to discover a new sister.

"Helen, this is Suna. Her cheek needs a stitch or two but there might be more urgent cases coming through."

"They didn't bring antibiotics." Helen's voice was about two octaves higher than usual.

"Who? Oh, the supplies that were meant to be coming from Sigma-2. Damn, wasn't that top of the list?"

"Yes. Bloody idiots. And they've all got these big wounds … no skin. Can you time yourself with the blood? Look at them all! Oh no, it can't be – is that Ryan?"

Ryan had been placed next to Dad, his moans reduced to whimpers.

"He was shot in the thigh. It's one of these large flesh wounds everyone's got, but it seems deeper than the others. He must have fallen onto something – he bled a lot. I made a tourniquet so he hasn't lost too much blood. No point in trying to stitch it – there's not enough skin to hold the stitches. And we should rinse these wounds – they seem to be getting bigger. Are they from some sort of chemical?"

"They're acid." Suna found her voice. "You need to wash them with as much water as you can spare."

"No. We haven't enough water," Helen whined.

"You have to!"

Alarmed by Suna's urgency, I waved down a volunteer. "All these wounds need washing with water."

"Guess so," Helen muttered. "B-but I'm not treating her." She shot Suna a sour look. "Plenty of our own to treat first."

"OK, wash Ryan's wound, and give him some painkillers. I assume we've got those." I turned to Ryan. "It'll stop hurting soon."

"Over there." Helen was barely focussing so I couldn't tell where she was indicating.

"I'll wash him, you get the painkillers," Suna said to Helen. A rivulet of blood had run from her cheek and down her neck.

"Thanks." I smiled at her. "I'll treat you once I'm free but this'll take about fifteen minutes. Take one of those gauze pads and press it to your cheek for now."

Dad's eyelids flickered.

"Dad, please wake up." No response. I turned to Suna. "So what happened? Why did you decide to come with us?"

"Impulse," she said, looking as if she regretted it already. "We got the alarm call from the camp; we were called out for reinforcements. And when I saw all the chaos, all those people screaming in agony from our weapons, I couldn't do it any more. These acid bullets – OxiBullets, they're called – they're evil." She had the strange neutral tone of some of the people in the camp, almost robotic, but at the last word, I heard the stirrings of passion in her voice. I stared at her. So this was my sister. At first glance she could be mistaken for Mum but there was something missing, as though she were dead behind the eyes.

"How do they work?"

"They have a plastic coating so they don't penetrate very far and then there's a wax plug that dissolves on impact and releases the acid. They're designed to cause maximum pain and disfigurement."

"That figures; typical Citidome," I muttered, then shouted to Helen, "Don't stint on the water."

At that point Ryan cried out.

"Go gently on him can't you?" I said.

"I think –" Suna sniffed around the wound – "I've got all the acid out now."

"OK, we'll have to try the honey dressings."

"Honey?" Suna frowned.

"Yeah, there's jars of it over there. Smear a thick layer on the gauze and place it over the wounds. Then bind his thigh in those cotton strips."

Suna followed her instructions with precision and efficiency, which was more than could be said for Helen, who was attending to a woman with a facial wound.

"More water, Helen," I said.

"OK, but we won't have enough honey. And we can't treat wounds this big." Helen nodded at a large object bound in a sheet. I winced. It must be a human body. "That woman. There was so much exposed flesh; her whole body went into shock. Oh, this is awful, so many. I don't know where to start."

"But Helen," I dropped my voice. "Some of these aren't going to make it. Look at that guy's stomach; there'll almost certainly be organ damage. So we prioritise. We can't save everyone, but we can save some."

"Yes, yes, of course, you're right," said Helen.

Why wasn't Helen thinking straight? Someone needed to take charge and it looked like that someone had to be me. Wounded people were arriving more quickly than we could treat them. I looked around and raised my voice to command the attention of the room. "I need volunteers to wash wounds." A number of people, including Kell, stepped forward.

"Helen; why don't you give each patient an initial assessment?" I suggested. "Then show the volunteers how to wash the wound and apply honey dressings."

Once a relative calm had been established, I turned to Suna. "So you used to shoot people with these bullets? How did you sleep at night?"

"I haven't been a CE for very long," she explained, her voice flat. "I used to be a scientist. I worked in the laboratory that developed these. I was stupid enough to write in my report that I didn't recommend them; they were too dangerous and unethical. So they transferred me to the correction unit. No-one gets dismissed in the Citidome," – she gave a hard, dry laugh – "Instead you're redeployed. My first assignment was to test the bullets for operator safety and optimum firing range."

"What would have happened if you'd refused?"

"I'd have been sent to a correction camp. They made that clear."

"And how – I'm not sure I want to know this – but how did you test them?"

"On Sector F citizens," she mumbled.

I screwed up my eyes.

"They're low status citizens," she explained. "Ones with chronic illnesses, disabilities or low brain scores."

"Shit," I muttered. "I knew that place was evil but …"

"You can't imagine until you live there. If it's any comfort, the bullets went off too soon in the first tests." She rolled up her sleeve to reveal an area of hard, mottled scarring on her arm. "We have protective clothing now."

"I don't know what to say." What would I have done in Suna's place? No, I could never have inflicted pain on the weak as part of an experiment.

"You haven't told me who you are," Suna said.

"I'm your sister, Joy."

"Your mother's the woman who looks like me?"

"Yes and this is my dad. You've met my mum? When?"

"I saw her near the camp a few weeks ago, when I was out looking for an escapee. She looked so like me; it freaked me out. We spoke but I had to go and she wouldn't give me any way of contacting her. I haven't been able to think of anything else since. But living outside … I don't want that."

"Should have thought of that before you threw your lot in with us. You haven't got much choice now."

"But where will I go?"

"Back home to our village, of course. You're family. Hang on, that should be enough blood. I'll disentangle myself and do your cheek." I removed the cannula and went in search of the polymer needles and thread. Helen was at the store cupboard, taking dressings and looking flustered.

"Hey, Helen, I've finished with Dad. So what's the deal with him?" I asked. "How long has he been unconscious?"

"He came in three days ago, after the Sigma-2 breakout. He'd ruptured a blood vessel. I managed to remove the bullet and put a stitch in the vessel wall."

"Three days like this?"

"Took me a long time to stop his bleeding. Had to give him three doses of my own blood."

"Three? I thought we agreed that wasn't safe." I drew my breath through my teeth. That explained Helen's jitteriness and sinister pallor.

"I know, but I couldn't get his blood pressure up. Then he was fine for a day, but he burst his stitches last night. His blood pressure dropped again this morning. That's why I couldn't go out. Had to keep his fluids up."

"I'll keep an eye on him while I stitch Suna's cheek, then I'll get someone to monitor him."

"Why are you treating her? She's one of them."

"Not any more. She's my half-sister."

"Huh?"

"Mum was a stem cell donor in the Citidome." Ignoring Helen's frown, I returned to Suna. "Sorry, there's no way this isn't going to hurt, but I have to save the painkillers for the others. They need them more."

"Of course." Suna sat perfectly still.

The wound was easy to stitch and I'd completed the job within minutes. I looked at my charges with satisfaction. I checked the blood pressure reading on Dad's DataBand, and smiled: 90/60, low for a man his size but not-life threatening. Ryan was sitting in his makeshift bed, looking more comfortable.

"Have the painkillers kicked in yet?" I squeezed his hand.

"Almost," he murmured. "But I can't feel the rest of my leg."

I frowned. Could the bullets have been penetrative enough to sever the nerve? Or was it the way he fell? He must have hit something sharp for his bleeding to have been so profuse; no-one else had bled like that.

"Don't panic. Nerve damage is usually temporary. Try to lie still and take deep breaths. I'll have to get on. Can you keep an eye on Dad for me? I'm hoping he's just sleeping, but he ought to have regained consciousness by now."

"Course I can. I'll shout if there's any change."

"What else can I do?" Suna asked.

I looked around. "Looks like we have enough people washing, but you did a fantastic job on dressing, so why don't you help with that? I'll supervise."

"Of course." Suna set to the task willingly, but I couldn't help being disappointed. After longing for a sister; I'd expected more than an automaton that had maimed defenceless humans. I wandered up and down the growing rows of bodies, adding advice on how to apply the honey dressings, and treating specialist cases myself, all the time becoming more and more aware of our shortcomings.

A voice from across the room distracted me. Ryan. "Your dad's awake. He's asking for you."

I ran to Dad's side.

"Dad!" I thought my heart would burst there and then. "Don't move, I need to check your blood pressure."

"Joy?" Dad screwed up his face.

I looked at his DataBand and breathed out. It hadn't dropped. It seemed unlikely he had internal bleeding.

"You're not to move; don't even raise your head unless I say so. Drink water first. You're massively dehydrated." I tilted his head and put the glass to his lips.

"Bossy madam." He grinned. "Where the hell have you been?"

Thank you, God, I silently said. His speech was lucid. "I was in the camp, but there's no time for explanations. There's so many casualties and Helen's not coping."

"Still? She was bloody useless yesterday. How many did we get?" He tried to raise his head but I stopped him.

"Stop that! Head down or you'll get dizzy. I haven't seen any figures. Plenty, but a lot of injuries, some horrific."

A flash of pain shot across his eyes.

"But Dad, we did it! The explosion was stupendous!"

"I love you, sweetheart."

"I love you too. And look, Ryan's here, next to you. And there's someone else you'll want to see. You won't believe this."

Kell had finished attending to a wound. I beckoned him over and watched Dad's face come alight at the sight of his old friend.

It took several hours to deal with the emergencies but by late afternoon I found myself in charge of an organised health care team. Everyone had assumed I was in charge and, seeing the strain behind Helen's eyes, I hadn't corrected them. While I'd been attending to the casualties, Dai had assembled a catering team. I joined a queue and grimaced at the rations of a drink of yeast extract, bottled fruit and a slice of chewy cured beef.

After an hour or so, the demands on my time lessened enough to allow me to stop. I was able to take stock of who among the Heroes had made it, and it was tragically few. Aki had joined my volunteer team, as had Mala, but there was no sign of the other people who'd become my friends in the last long weeks. Suna was still wandering up and down the rows of people, looking uncomfortable. I'd already stopped someone from addressing her as "CE scum".

"Suna, come and meet my dad."

I took her to Dad's bedside. At the sight of her he broke into a coughing fit.

"I don't believe it. I thought I was hallucinating. You look so like …" Dad seemed brighter; his blood pressure had risen, and he was able to prop his head up. "Cathy told me she'd met you."

"Yes. Joy says I'm to come to live in your village," Suna said without enthusiasm.

"Of course you must," Dad said. "So Joy, are you going to tell me where you've been for the last two months?"

"I've been with Ryan." I glanced across to him. He'd fallen asleep. I told Dad everything, from Peter to finding Suna. In turn, he told me that Peter was dead. I couldn't pretend to be sorry.

"It's a day of miracles," he said. "You, Kell, Ryan, Suna. Was there any news of Harry?"

"No." My eyes fell from his. "But Kell thought he saw him running across the woods."

"And you and Ryan? Looks like you've gotten pretty close."

"Yeah, we have."

Dad raised an eyebrow; it wasn't much of an answer. But what else could I say? Suppose Ryan wasn't asleep and could hear me?

"Joy, the guy over here's having convulsions!" An urgent voice.

"No rest for the wicked," I said to Dad with a wink, grateful for the distraction.

With so many people constantly demanding my attention, I had little time to think for the rest of the evening. Positioning myself in the casualty section, in a bed next to Ryan, sleep overcame me quickly, but soon came the nightmares. That giant metal bird was chasing me, firing flames. I opened my eyes, the pulse in my neck racing. Oh, I was in the bunker. Then I heard a murmuring.

"Michael, my love, you're going to be all right. I'll make you better."

I turned onto my side. It was Helen, and her hand was on Dad's. Anger surged through me. Dad couldn't be cheating on Mum, surely? I knew things weren't good between them, but how could he prefer drab little Helen to Mum? And if Helen wasn't sleeping at night, no wonder she was incompetent during the day. I sat upright. Helen span around. Her eyes met mine and then dropped to the floor.

"What the hell are you doing?" I hissed.

"J-just keeping an eye on him. Don't want him bursting his stitches again."

"We've got people with worse wounds. Why don't you sit with them?"

"He's the leader." Helen's eyes dropped.

"What's going on between you two? And don't pretend there isn't. I heard what you said to him."

And then Helen burst into tears. "Don't tell him, please. I'd never stand it…"

"You mean he doesn't know?"

"No-one does." Her voice was small. "Don't worry, I wouldn't come between him and your mum. And he's never, ever looked at me that way."

"So what, you've got a crush on him?"

"It's not a crush. I was thirteen when he came to the village. I-I've been in love with him ever since."

Surely she couldn't be serious? Was it possible to live with unrequited love for seventeen whole years? Was this why

Helen had never been with a man? I knew pity was the appropriate response but I felt nothing but contempt for her. What a pathetic waste. And in that moment I realised I was running the risk of suffering the same fate as Helen. The boy I loved had found someone else, and I'd let his loss dominate my life.

"You're tired," I said. "You don't know what you're saying. Go to sleep and tomorrow we'll forget we ever had this conversation."

Helen stood up and then fainted. I took her blood pressure and whistled: 60/40, way too low. With a strength I didn't know I had, I lifted Helen to her bed, and gazed at the woman I'd always looked up to.

"Wh-what happened?" Helen came round.

"You're not well. You have to rest tomorrow. Have you been drinking enough?"

"I keep forgetting."

Returning to my bed, I wondered if Helen had eaten, drunk or slept at all. I cast my mind back to what seemed a previous lifetime – life at home. Why had I never noticed Helen's feelings for Dad? And did Dad have no idea? Did Mum? I didn't know whether to be grateful or terrified. From now on, the lives of forty-three injured people depended solely on me. When I returned, Ryan was awake.

"Did you hear any of that?" I whispered.

"Yeah. I'd heard rumours, that she had the hots for your dad, but –"

"Really? I didn't have a clue. I don't think Dad knows either, or he wouldn't have spent so much time with her."

"They're rock solid, your mum and dad, aren't they? You're so lucky to have grown up in a loving environment."

"Huh, don't be fooled. Hasn't been a lot of love, these last few months. Oh, how am I going to cope, with Helen in this state? She looks so ill."

"And so will you be if you don't sleep. Cold in here, isn't it? Why don't you come in with me?"

"There's not a lot of room. I don't want to hurt your leg." But all of a sudden, I wanted nothing more than the warmth of another body next to mine.

"It doesn't hurt; those painkillers are amazing. Push your

bed next to mine, then we'll have more room."

Soon my body was touching his, his hand stroking my bristly head, and I luxuriated in his heat, trying to force images of Harry from my mind. And although the voice of my conscience told me that I was fooling Ryan into believing that my feelings for him were stronger than they actually were, at moments like this I could convince myself that I was in love with him. But lying next to him aroused no more desire in me than when Beth and I had sleepovers together. Soon I was soothed to sleep once more.

***

Life in the bunkers established its own grim routines. Helen refused to rest but accepted a lesser nursing role. I led the medical team, assessed and changed dressings, took blood pressure readings and administered painkillers and goldenseal tincture, our only alternative to antibiotics. And soon the coughs and colds that had been flying round the camp started up once more. It seemed that once I resolved one problem, another replaced it.

After a week, the bunker became oppressive with the smell of human effluvia, and new problems were emerging, horrific situations I'd hoped never to face. One man had lost the skin from half of his calf. Despite my best efforts, the wound had become badly infected. With all the coughing and spluttering, aseptic conditions were impossible to maintain.

"Low blood pressure, fever, looks like septicaemia to me. What do you think?" I said to Helen.

"I th-think so." Helen spluttered; she'd developed a nasty cough. "But there's only one thing we can do for that."

"Exactly."

We stared at each other. Those pictures in the chapters on wartime medicine flashed before my eyes with vivid clarity.

"I'll do it if he's willing," I said.

Helen nodded.

I returned to the patient. "There's no easy way to tell you this. Your leg's badly infected. Bacteria has got into your blood system and that's why you've become so ill. If I don't control the infection, you'll die. But the only way I can do that is to cut the leg off at the knee."

"Tell me you're joking," he said.

"There's no alternative. It's a proper medical procedure; it's called amputation. But I have to tell you, I've never done it before. I only know how from books. We brought a saw; I've sharpened it as much as I can but…" My voice trailed off. "It's your choice."

The man closed his eyes. It was a full minute before he opened them. "I've come this far. I don't want to die not knowing what the outside's like. Do it."

The memory of the operation would haunt me for the rest of my life. The effort needed to tighten the tourniquet. The blood that soaked the floor. The sound of the saw against bone. But most of all the screams that, despite the maximum safe dose of painkillers, filled the vast bunker.

CHAPTER 22 - CATHY

I held a finger for Adam to grab.

"It took a long time, but I've fallen in love with you," I said.

In the last few days, Adam had transformed in my eyes. Every time I looked at him I was reminded of Michael. Sensing the change in me, Adam seemed more content, sleeping more soundly and happy to be cuddled. Anna had moved in with us and her presence was soothing. But no amount of people could silence the voice that shouted inside my head.

Michael's dead.

You'll never see Michael again.

I heard a knock on the door and tensed. It had been like this for days. Who would it be: nosy neighbours, intrepid survivors or a CE? So far it had only been the former. I opened the door and saw a group of six people. I blinked, at first not recognising the smoke-blackened face of the person at the front, and then let out a cry.

"Daisy! I don't believe it!"

They staggered indoors. Daisy's companions were clad in blue bodysuits, with shaved heads and tell-tale ragged ears.

"Come and sit in front of the fire and I'll get you all some soup," said Anna. "We've had a pot on the stove all day. We hoped people would turn up. But sweetheart, we'd given up on you."

I leant on the wall to steady myself, unsure I was ready to hear Daisy's story.

"Oh, it was appalling," Daisy said. "The factory ... the blast was so much bigger than we'd expected. Dan and Gina, who threw some of the sticks and bombs, didn't survive it." She wiped her hair from her brow. "Most of the attacking party didn't, only Harry and Susan. Most of us drivers made it, though. How Harry survived was a miracle. He ran further than the others and dived into a ditch. We pulled a ton of rubble off him, but apart from cuts and bruises and singed hair, he was OK."

"Did he get some people to the canal?"

"Yeah. We couldn't see anything at first – the wall of smoke was enormous. Then we saw them, lines of people – those at the front slicing ears. And then they started running our way, all these people with blood dripping off them. Harry took forty or so. I kept cramming them into the TravelPod, ferrying them to the woods. But soon it was absolute carnage, bodies everywhere, shots from all directions, and then that giant machine shooting fire from the sky."

Daisy took a deep breath and continued. "The guy at the entrance told me to give up and come inside. They were about to close up the bunker; they thought the thing in the air might trace its location. But I said no, there were so many people still outside." She paused and shivered. "He said I'd never get anywhere by road – some people had tried to escape in trucks and there were roadblocks everywhere. They took the TravelPod into a storage unit next to the bunker. B-but I had to try, didn't I? Try to save a few at least. So I walked. Kept finding people along the way. I had to bite off their tags. I left twelve at Bakewell, brought these five."

"You've been walking for four days? Oh, Daisy."

Anna arrived with bowls of soup, which all six devoured.

"Have you eaten?" she asked.

"Not much. Blackberries, well past their best. Found some watercress, managed to catch a pheasant. I've had better meals." Daisy turned to me. "What happened to Michael? Did he …" Her voice tailed off.

"He was injured. He's in the bunker." My voice was high and fast. "So you didn't see Helen, or anyone else we knew?"

"No; I guess Helen was slicing ears but I was too far away to pick out individuals."

I sighed and looked at the weary faces of the escapees. "We need to get you guys warmed up then taken to the safe house, don't we? Ah, no TravelPod. It'll have to be the horse and cart."

Within an hour, I'd arranged for the newcomers to be examined by Alex and took them to the Barrel Inn, an old pub high in the hills around ten kilometres from the village. The pub was the official safe house for the region and had been stocked with food and water for the purpose. But it wasn't empty. Five bald-headed people, huddled around a fire, stared at me with fear-filled eyes.

"Hey, don't worry, I'm a friend. How did you get here?"

"A guy with a horse and cart found us by the roadside and brought us here. Said he was from – what was it – the OAC? He said someone would be here to tell us what happens next."

I smiled. The rescue operation was obviously still active. "AOC. The Alliance of Outside Communities. We'll look after you from now on. I have to leave you here for at least four weeks then we'll find permanent homes for you. But someone's going to check up on you once a week. Who wants to learn how to use a rifle?" I continued to talk to the newcomers. This was good. If I kept myself busy, I could suppress the screaming inside.

It was three more days before the visit I'd dreaded; that of the Citidome authorities.

"I understand you're the village leader," the CE said.

"Yes, come in."

"Fingerprint," she demanded. I proffered my index finger and held my breath.

"You don't originate from the Citidome?" she asked. "Then what's with the ear?"

I cursed my own stupidity. I'd forgotten that I'd tied back my hair. My mind flailed.

"Check deleted records," the woman said, and than gave me a hard stare. "Caia 031954?"

"Yeah." Lying seemed futile.

"It says here you died over sixteen years ago, giving birth?"

"Huh? No, that's not correct. My baby died." I added the latter hastily; there was the grave of Cathy Brewer to account for.

"Strange; this shouldn't make mistakes." The woman screwed up her face.

"The authorities were looking for me, back then. I haemorrhaged during childbirth. I can't remember much about it. Maybe they assumed I'd died." Breathe, Cathy.

"Hmm, I'll update that." She looked up. "It says here that you escaped with Mac 022852 but he was recorded dead on 041772."

"Yeah, that sounds about right. Two days after we escaped," I said.

"The baby you had. Was it his?"

"Er – no. It was someone I went with in the village." Sweat prickled the back of my neck. Why had they asked? Were they trying to find evidence of me having performed subversive activities in the Citidome? Were they going to arrest me?

"Have you seen any strangers in the last week?"

I relaxed. I'd been prepared for this one.

"No, no-one comes out much in winter," I said, my voice deadpan.

"Are you aware of any unusual activity?"

"No." I rubbed my chin, pretending to think. "Except, about a week ago there seemed to be something odd going on south of here. There was a huge black cloud and a strange sort of machine in the sky."

"Huh. I need to search every building in the village. I'll start here."

"Of course. Feel free. My sons are in the living room."

"Sons?" The woman's voice was sharp, accusing.

"From someone I met when I settled down here." I reminded myself to breathe.

"What happened to him?"

"He died too."

"How very convenient." The woman's stare pierced my brain. I followed her to the next room.

"Where's your father?" she demanded of Scott.

"Dad's gone," said Scott in a small, frightened voice.

I could have kissed him.

But the CE seemed unconvinced. After clattering and slamming doors upstairs, she returned, her arms folded across her chest.

"If their father died, why are his clothes still in the closet?"

Think Cathy, think! My mind twisted and tangled. Then my thoughts turned to Joy and Michael, an action that could be guaranteed to free some tears, and inspiration struck.

"He … Peter only died two months ago. Silly, I know, but I haven't been able to get rid of his things." I allowed myself the luxury of a cry.

"I only have your word for this."

"So what? You want to see his grave? Dig up his body? Follow me." In a rush of irritation, I marched to the churchyard, the CE behind me, and pointed towards the fresh mound of earth, at one end of which was a wooden cross bearing the inscription, "Peter Baxter. Died 15th October 2189." I pointed to a spot to the left. "And there's my daughter Cathy."

"OK."

Would I get away with this? I held my breath. Then Milo, back from a rabbit hunting mission and eager to greet a new visitor, bounded up to us.

"Get away!" the CE shouted, removed what look like a gun from inside her jacket and shot the dog. Milo fell to the ground but continued to whimper and writhe. When I saw what the weapon had done to him, my stomach heaved. He wasn't dead but had lost most of the skin between his shoulder blades, a vast expanse of pink flesh exposed. I opened my mouth but the woman still had a hand on the weapon. I closed it again.

"I'm going to search the village," she said. "There's some dangerous people on the loose."

"OK. But we're not harbouring runaways. Haven't seen any for years, and even if we did, we don't want them. Our community's doing OK; we don't want disruption."

The CE nodded and turned away, but the noise had brought Daisy out.

"Fingerprint," the woman demanded.

A synthetic voice confirmed Daisy's former identity. "Veez, can't believe you lot live so long as savages," the woman muttered and continued to the other houses.

Daisy looked at Milo and gasped.

"That's horrific," she said. "What sort of weapon would do that? She looked to the ground where the remnants of a pellet remained. She picked it up, yelped and dropped it, shaking her hand and plunging it into snow.

"It's acid." She gathered up snow and placed it on Milo's back, then looked at me. "That must be what they're using on the escapees – shit, that's inhuman."

"A wound that size isn't going to heal, is it?" I said.

Daisy shook her head. "We'll have to put him out of his misery."

"Let's find Luke. I won't tell Scott."

I walked up to the farm, Milo in my arms, and Luke dispatched him with a clean shot to the head. Afterwards Daisy and I wept in each other's arms, as if the dog symbolised everything we'd lost.

For two more weeks, life plodded on. Morale in the village grew even lower. Scott cried every night for a week when his beloved pet didn't come home. I clung to the boys more than ever. No-one seemed to be enthusiastic about the approach of Christmas. Then came a pounding on my door. It was Matt, carrying a girl little older than Joy, in a blue uniform, with a ragged earlobe that looked infected.

"Found her lying by the riverside," he said. "There was another girl with her but she was dead. This one's in a bad way. You need me to help?"

"Thanks, Matt. Could you put a pan of water on to boil and fetch Alex?" I ushered the young woman, who seemed incapable of speaking, indoors. I pressed my fingers against her wrist and shuddered at its chill. As I suspected, her pulse was weak but racing. Hypothermia. "You must be frozen," I said. "I'll run you a bath. Follow me."

She nodded. I ran the bath to lukewarm, knowing how hot water felt against chilled skin.

"When you can stand it, run some more hot in. That's the tap on the left; you turn it anticlockwise. I'll get you a warm drink." When I returned with the drinks, the girl – pitifully thin – smiled and mouthed the word, "Thanks."

"When did you last eat?" I asked.

"Outbreak," she rasped.

I shuddered. How miraculous the human body was. December had proved unseasonably mild, but the temperatures were still close to freezing at night. How had she survived without food? Alex arrived.

"I'd better get some soup on," Anna said.

"I'll give you a hand," Matt said.

"Thanks." I smiled.

Matt seemed awkward these days whenever I saw him on the street. He'd always been a friend of the family, despite being a Baxter. It must have taken some guts for him to oppose his family in the vote for the AOC to retain its control.

"What are you going to do with her?" Matt asked.

"She can stay here tonight. But beyond that, I'm not sure. We can't take her to the Barrel Inn. She'll need nursing."

"But you've got the boys and Anna, and it's not likely that we'll get another CE visit at this stage. Why don't I see if Mum'll take her in?"

I frowned. The last thing I wanted was Margaret and Frank complaining that I'd dumped a Citidome escapee on them. Then something in Matt's expression made me smile. Of course. The girl looked to be around Matt's age and had a delicate sort of beauty. Why not give him an early Christmas present?

"I'd be so grateful if they could," I said.

Within the hour, I'd dressed the girl in some of Joy's clothes, got two bowls of soup inside her, and Matt had taken her away with him. The next day Margaret knocked on the door. I braced myself for a tirade, but – was I seeing things? – Margaret was smiling.

"The girl seems better this morning. We gave her some eggs. Sweet little thing, isn't she? We've given her a new name – Hope."

"That's lovely. Thanks so much for taking her in."

"It's a pleasure." And with that, Margaret left, leaving me open-mouthed.

"Was I going senile, or was that Margaret being civil?" asked Anna.

"It appeared so. That girl really is a miracle."

Something about the frail young woman touched everyone's hearts. A steady stream of visitors arrived at Margaret's house bearing bread, milk and soup. However short-lived it may be, we were a united community once more. And it was with a renewed optimism that Anna, Daisy and I prepared for a family Christmas and prayed that it would bring the greatest miracle of all.

CHAPTER 23 - JOY

Strange how the human psyche adapts The stench of sepsis, the sight of blood and exposed flesh had become everyday occurrences. The odour of the composting toilets pervaded the entire bunker, but no-one gagged or complained any more. Even the nightmares, the waking in the night to hear others talking in their sleep, not actual words but vague babblings of distress, had lessened. Spirits were high in the knowledge that the end was in sight. Except for mine. My only comfort was falling asleep at night to the rhythm of Ryan's breathing. Strange how I'd come to rely on his presence.

"Take a break, Joy. You look wiped out," Kell said.

"How can I, with wounds not healing? The honey's long gone and we're almost out of the goldenseal and garlic extracts. If any more wounds start turning gangrenous, we're in big trouble." I shivered. Last week I'd sawn off an arm just above the elbow. "There's no others that'd be safe to amputate."

"Can't say I'm sorry. Don't think I could stand to hear screams like that again. But bloody hell, you're a miracle worker."

We looked across to where a man and woman were sitting up, eating breakfast, their stumps bound.

"I can't believe we pulled off one, let alone two. It was touch and go for a while."

"But you've got to rest. You're no use to anyone if you make yourself ill."

We looked across to Helen, who was unconscious, as she was most of the time these days. Her cold had settled on her chest. I suspected pneumonia.

"Keeping going stops me from thinking," I said. "Helen's in a bad way. Ryan's wound looks like it's becoming infected. And I'm cold and hungry."

"Me too. At least there's one person you don't have to worry about." Our gaze turned to Dad, now propped up, his arm strapped against his chest. As usual, he was talking to one of the escapees.

"Can you believe we're talking about getting out of here?" Kell's face was alight. "We should be home for Christmas. Dai's going out tomorrow to have a look around, see if the coast's clear."

"And you'll get to see Dee and Harry within an hour of us leaving here. The canal's only a kilometre or so away. They should be waiting there with the boat." Would I ever be able to speak his name without a twinge?

"It still doesn't seem real. Listen, I'm sure you're desperate to get back home, but why don't you come back with me first? See if we can't sort out this business with you and Harry, that's if he's still the one you want." He gestured towards Ryan.

"You've forgotten, Harry's with someone else."

"That was months ago. Tell me the truth. Gonna stay with Ryan instead, are you?"

I took a deep breath. "Not in the way you're thinking."

"Hmm," Kell's expression was unfathomable. "But he's obviously nuts about you. Is it fair to lead him on?"

"It's not that type of relationship. He's a close friend, that's all." I lowered my eyes. How would I describe my relationship with Ryan? We were physically affectionate with each other but he'd never made a single move on me that could be interpreted as sexual. He must have thought about it – each night, the sounds of men and women, discovering each other for the first time, made me blush. But I remembered him saying that sexual attraction wasn't a driving force in his life. And maybe he was more aware of his disability than he was admitting.

"Is there something you're not telling me?" Kell frowned.

"I … checked his reflexes; there's some nerve damage. He might never be able to use that leg again. I brought all this on him. I'm going to stay in the village and help him rebuild his life. I owe him that much. And there's Helen. It'll take a long time for her to recover, if she ever does. The village needs a health worker."

"Woah, hang on. So you're going to sacrifice your whole future?"

"It won't be a sacrifice." I smiled, knowing with absolute conviction what I wanted to do with my life. "These last few weeks – they've been hell, but they've shown me something else. For the last year, people have been telling me that I'm bright, that I should use my brains for the benefit of the village, but every job they've tried to fit me in hasn't worked. And now I've found my fit. I'm a good health worker. Admit it."

"Good? You're bloody brilliant. But you still haven't mentioned Harry."

"Harry …" I shook my head. "He seems part of another world. For my entire life, there hasn't been a single day I haven't thought about him. He used to be part of me. When I found out about him and Caroline – I can't begin to describe how bad I felt. You know, the guys over there are still getting pain where their limbs were. I read that it's a normal response to amputation. I think that's what happened to me. When Harry cheated on me, he amputated that part of him that lived inside me. I felt the pains for a while, but now, I accept that he's not there any more. Maybe he and I were a childish idyll, and now I've grown up. I'm not the person I once was. And in these last few weeks, no I don't think about him any more."

I hadn't quite spoken the truth. Admittedly, during the days, when the demands on my time were relentless, I didn't think of Harry. Besides, I'd made that deal with God. He'd spared Dad. No point in telling Kell of the deranged dreams. Those nights when I dreamed that Harry and I were together, racing up to Monsal Head. Deranged was the only word for them.

Kell and I stared at each other for a long time. Then he spoke. "That's a real shame, but I understand. Whatever happens, let's always be friends."

"We will. Don't know what I'd have done the last few weeks without you."

"And what about your sister?"

That was another good question. It was hard to see how Suna was going to fit into our family. "I still don't get her.

Dad says to be patient, but I don't feel I know her any better now than when I first met her. She's complaining about the smell now but she keeps on volunteering, partly because hardly anyone speaks to her. I think she's regretting escaping."

"Give her time. This must be a hell of a culture shock for her."

"I guess so. Anyway, I'd better check on Helen."

I walked by Helen's bed first, where Suna was sitting. I frowned. Helen's breath seemed more laboured than usual.

"Any change?" I asked.

"Her breathing seems to be slowly getting worse. She woke up about half an hour ago and I forced her to take a drink but she seemed confused. Still no urine."

"Thanks. Let me know if there's any sudden deterioration."

I walked on with heavy steps. All the signs were pointing to heart and kidney failure. It was hard to see how Helen would pull through. I wandered down the rows of beds, when Dad beckoned me to his bedside, Mala and Ryan sitting beside him.

"Mala wants to become one of our farmers," he said

"A woman farmer. How very progressive of you, Dad." I raised an eyebrow. But Mala was well-built, stronger than most of the male patients I'd treated. And I liked her enormously. She had the most animated face I'd ever seen on a Citizen, the creases of her dimples deepening as she spoke. Life must have been difficult for her in the Citidome – she was no beauty and had a purple Mark on her cheek that had caused her to escape.

"I've been trying to place people all day. Reckon Mala's the right type, don't you?"

"Definitely." I smiled. Why couldn't feisty, fearless Mala have been my long-lost sister, rather than Suna?

"I've been telling her about the way we take on new names. Would you like to help her choose one?"

"Hmm, how about Hazel?" I turned to Mala. "It's also a type of tree that grows around the village."

"A tree, yeah that suits me." Her mouth lurched into a grin. "I can't wait to see the village."

"Anyway, Dad, I warned you. No more than three hours of

AOC business a day. You still need to rest. And drink more." I lifted his dressing and smiled; no signs of infection.

"You might want to change your mind now you've realised what a bossy little madam she is." Dad winked.

My heart did a somersault. I'd known that Dad was going to pull through as soon as he'd started winking again. Not that I should be too optimistic. The bullet had torn through the muscle of his shoulder; I wondered whether he'd ever regain full use of his left arm.

"And what about you?" Dad said. "I heard Kell telling you to rest but I don't see you taking his advice."

I perched on his bed but leapt to my feet when I heard Suna call my name, and ran to Helen's side.

"She's stopped breathing!" Suna whispered.

I put my fingers to Helen's wrist: no pulse. I shook my head.

"Shall I –"

"No thanks. I'd like to do this one myself."

And as I wrapped the sheet around the sixth and last person to die in the bunker, I couldn't stem the flow of tears for a woman who had given her life and received nothing in return. The woman who had helped me find my vocation. And now another reason why I could never leave the village.

I spent a few minutes in silence, head bowed. When I got up, I saw endless pairs of eyes looking my way. The natural move would have been to fling myself into Dad's arms, but as one of them was immobilised, it wouldn't be easy. But Ryan spoke first.

"Come here, sweetheart," he said. Did I imagine it or was that inclination of Dad's head a nod of assent? Ryan's arms encircled me and I sobbed against his chest.

"That poor girl," said Dad. "I feel responsible. She'd always been so good in a crisis; that's why I chose her for this job. But you don't die of overwork, do you? She must have had some weakness none of us knew about."

I smoothed his sheets, trying to busy myself so Dad wouldn't read anything in my eyes. No-one had told him that Helen gave him three doses of blood and I hadn't told him about Helen's feelings for him. Why burden him with the knowledge? I caught Suna frowning from across the bunker.

She'd been my most able assistant; having no natural emotions was an advantage when people were suffering.

"Sit here a while; you must be shattered," Ryan said.

"Still plenty to do," I said. "Has anyone changed your dressing today?"

"Not yet. Actually, it's a bit sore." He winced.

I lifted the dressing and drew in my breath. The area around the wound was still red, and looking angrier by the day. Today, yellow pus oozed from its corner.

"Maybe you should jump the treatment queue. It does look sore, but nothing to worry about." The lie twisted in my stomach.

I beckoned Suna over.

"Hey, sis," I said. "Can you do Ryan's leg?"

"Yeah, no problem. I'll be about five minutes." Her glance darted from Ryan's leg to my eyes, where it lingered. When she left, Ryan tightened his grip on my hand.

"Just think. We'll be home for Christmas." It was hard to think of anything positive to say.

"You've forgotten one vital point," Ryan said. "I murdered someone. Can I go back?"

"Of course you can." But panic flooded me. There'd been so much to occupy my mind that I hadn't considered this. I couldn't abandon Ryan now; if he was banished, I'd have to go with him. I called across to Dad. "Dad, will there be any issues with us going back, after what we did … to Peter?"

"You say there were no witnesses?" he asked.

"No."

Dad lowered his voice and spoke to Ryan. "In that case, Peter made a lunge for you when you tried to protect Joy. Self-defence. There'll have to be a vote, and no doubt Margaret will shoot her mouth off, but you'll have plenty of support. If they don't vote you in, I'll make sure one of the communities around Bakewell take you in."

"Not going to be much use to any community like this, am I?" Ryan tapped his leg.

"Maybe you could train alongside Joy? There's always a demand for health workers."

"Sounds wonderful." Ryan smiled and I became filled with a new optimism. Perhaps this was how I could repay Ryan; to give him a new direction in life. I'd enjoy training with him. I could give him a future to look forward to. The plans gave us a new topic of conversation for our last days of confinement.

It wasn't until our final day, the day on which Dai searched the forest and made contact with the rest of the AOC to prepare for our relocation, that things turned uncomfortable once more. I was sitting by his bedside, chatting about medicine, when Ryan gave me That Look.

"Joy, I thought you were an exceptional person before this. Now I know. I love you so much." His hands framed my face, his blue eyes boring into mine. "When we go back, will you marry me?"

CHAPTER 24 - CATHY

Three days before Christmas, the message arrived. But it didn't tell me what I wanted to know. The heavy frost had transformed the village into an enchanted festive scene. I took in the view with a growing sense of hopelessness and gloom. I wasn't ready to celebrate.

> Area around bunker searched this morning. No sign of recent activity; snow undisturbed except for animal tracks. Rescuers meet in arranged locations at 09:00. Tomorrow is Day 1. Estimated numbers as follows:
>
> Day 1: Hest Bank 19; Ashford 17 + 1 deceased.

Deceased. I stopped reading and tightened my shawl around me. It had been agreed that casualties would be returned for burial only if they had family in their home villages. So the worst was confirmed. I handed the DataBand to Daisy, who handed it to Mary.

"Oh no. B-but it could be Helen," Mary said.

"I don't think it's likely, knowing that Michael was shot. Do you?"

Daisy and Mary enveloped me in a three-way hug. When we released each other, their eyes were shining with unshed tears. "Should we tell Anna and Scott?" Mary said.

"Not yet," I said. "Let them have another day of hope."

"I'll arrange the horse and cart," said Daisy.

"I want to come," I said.

"No!" Daisy stood up. "Now listen, for once in your life. After you saw Michael being shot, you came back catatonic. How are you going to be when … if, the worst has happened? Stay with Scott. He knows something's wrong, you know."

"It's all getting too hard." I dropped my head to my hands. "I'm not sure I can be strong for anyone any more. And as for being leader … I didn't even tell you what happened yesterday. Keep this to yourself, but Tia came round. Elsie's pregnant."

"Oh shit." Daisy shook her head. "Everyone's been saying it but I didn't want to believe it."

"Me neither," I said. "Tia wanted me to arrange to get rid of it."

"I can see why," Daisy said. "Elsie's too young to have a kid, even if she had the ability to raise one."

"She's not too young," Mary said. "My mum was only fourteen when she had me. And Grandma was fifteen when she had her."

Mary rarely spoke about her mother, who'd died of a fever three days after giving birth to her. I chose my words carefully. "But think what she'd have given up if she'd raised you."

"Grandma was there to help. Why can't Tia raise her?" Mary shrugged.

"Remember, Kate was still under thirty when you were born," I said. "Tia's fifty-one. It's a lot to ask."

"But getting rid of it? That's evil." Mary's mouth was a tight line. "Besides, is it even possible?"

"I had a chat with Alex," I said. "There are things we could try, herbal concoctions and the like. But I agree with you, Mary. How can we kill a baby? Think what a gift new blood is to around here. Elsie and Peter aren't blood relations; there's no reason why the child shouldn't be normal and healthy. And Elsie's physically capable of bearing a child. It'll be difficult for her on an emotional level but there are plenty of people to give her support after it's born. Let someone in another village adopt the baby."

"Phew, that's a moral dilemma." Daisy blew out her cheeks. "Let Elsie give birth and then take the baby away from her? Did you tell Tia this?"

"Yeah," I said. "But I tried to point out the benefits for Elsie. I told her an abortion was potentially more dangerous than adoption. She wasn't happy, but I'm learning that being leader means sometimes you can't keep everyone happy;

sometimes you've got to go with your instincts. I wish I'd realised that before I let Peter back in."

"You can't torture yourself with that for the rest of your life," Mary said. "What a week. That and the relocations."

"Yes, that wasn't easy." The refugees at the Barrel Inn had been unhappy to discover that they were to be relocated to separate communities. Over their time in exile, they'd formed a strong alliance. We'd allocated them in groups of two or three to each of the communities centred around our market town. "But my idea of having regular socials based around Bakewell seemed to appease them. We're becoming a more mobile population. In future people are going to have friends in different locations. It's important they're encouraged to maintain those links."

"You're right. And sixteen newcomers coming back with Helen. It's going to change things around here. Michael would have been so proud of you," Daisy said.

"Yes." I rubbed my chin. "I think he would."

This is how it would be from now on, wouldn't it? Speaking of Michael in the past tense, as we did about Joy. I remembered how it felt last time, seventeen years ago, when I believed he was dead. At the time, the pain seemed too great to bear. But this would be infinitely worse. Back then, we were still at the passionate beginning of our relationship. If he'd died then, all my memories of him would have been good ones. Even a year ago, the same would have been true. I thought of the last months, of bitter recriminations and non-communication. Would they become my abiding memories? Then I realised that Daisy was still talking.

"– and letting Hope stay. That was a smart move."

"Yeah, Beth's pleased to have a new friend," Mary said.

"It's brought out a new side to Margaret, hasn't it?" I returned my focus to our conversation. "She even asked me if I'd heard any news of Michael yesterday. I have to admit, letting Hope stay was my one soft-hearted decision. She doesn't look much of a farmer, almost certainly not capable of bearing children, but have you seen the way Matt looks at her? He's smitten." My throat tightened. "How are we going to handle tomorrow? I mean, I'm going to get the roads guarded – best be careful – but what about once they all arrive? I feel we ought to have some sort of welcome party for the newcomers but knowing that…" The rest was lost as the tears I'd been suppressing gushed out with full force.

"Hey, it's OK," Daisy said. "Let it all out. Better now than tomorrow."

"Our last months together," I sobbed. "We were tearing each other apart."

"Hindsight's a wonderful thing," Daisy said. "But you've had more than seventeen years together. What you and Michael had, few people get in a lifetime. Hold onto that."

"I'm trying but I might unravel tomorrow. Not the stuff of leadership, is it?"

"You're always strong when it counts," Mary said. "And you'll have us two and Anna with you, and your boys. We all love you."

"Anna. This is going to destroy her."

"She's stronger than you think," Daisy said. "Put yourself first, for once."

I blew my nose. "What would I do without you two?"

"You'd cope. You always do."

"So, tomorrow. We need to prepare people."

"Perhaps it's best to keep it low-key," Daisy said. "Spread the word that the newcomers are arriving, arm the guards and make sure everyone's alert, but at the same time say there'll be no celebrations until we know that Michael and Helen are back safely."

"I'd better tell Maeve in the bakery, then alert Julia and organise the catering," I said. One of the older village residents had volunteered to be warden of the new academy.

"Ssh, I think that's Scott coming in."

I wiped my eyes and prepared to be the strong mother and leader everyone would expect of me.

"Will Daddy be home for Christmas?" Scott asked.

"Let's hope so, sweetheart," I said.

At least after tomorrow there'd be no more pretence.

CHAPTER 25 - JOY

I glimpsed daylight for the first time in weeks and breathed deeply, my shoulders heaving as I drank in the cold air, the pine aroma cleansing my lungs of the stench of human waste. I smiled at the white clouds of my breath. Crystals of frost coated the leafless trees, shimmering in the pale morning sun.

"I was prepared for one of those depressing white-skied midwinter days, but this is perfect," I said. "It's as if someone choreographed it."

"I ordered it. One picture-perfect day to mark our release." Dad winked. "See you soon, sweetheart. Ridiculous, me getting a ride in the TravelPod. I can walk, you know."

"No point in taking risks. You're still not strong. There's room for you to sit next to Ryan. And it'll cheer him up to have you on board. It's not going to be a great journey." I looked inside the TravelPod. At the wheel was Hazel, next to her, Helen's body and then Ryan, who gave me a look of such longing it twisted my gut. I blew him an inadequate kiss. I still hadn't given him an answer. Time to think. What a pathetic excuse that was. "I wish I was there to see Mum's face when you arrive though. If she saw you get shot, I can imagine what she's going through."

"I saw what she went through, what we both went through, when we thought we'd lost you. Her face when she sees you, now that'll be worth seeing."

Dad hugged me, climbed into the TravelPod, and they were gone. I turned my attention to the expectant group around me.

"Follow me, everybody," I said.

A group of people strode behind me and I heard a constant buzz of excited chatter. What would the future hold for them? I, on the other hand, tried to suppress my rising nausea. Why hadn't I realised that the meeting point for the Hest Bank and

Ashford escapees was within a kilometre of each other? My task was to lead the group to the canal, where the Hest Bank recruits would be picked up by a narrowboat, then continue to a road junction where someone from home should be waiting with a horse and cart. But my thoughts hadn't strayed from the narrowboat. Would I see Harry? And how safe were we? I'd have felt more secure if the ground was blanketed in snow. No-one ever came out of the Citidomes then; it blocked the roads. The gnarled skeletons of the forest trees exuded suspicion, as if intending to recapture us. The frosted carpet of decomposing leaves crunched with every footstep.

"You're unusually quiet. Are you worried about Ryan?" asked Suna.

"A little." It wasn't a lie. "And about Helen's family. Helen's younger brother died a year ago; it'll be tough on them."

"What family does Helen have?"

"Her parents and an uncle. Half the village are related to each other. You'll get used to it."

"When I get to the village, where will I live?"

"With Mum and Dad, of course. You're family."

"But you hardly know me."

"We will, soon." I doubted my own words. Apart from the fact that she'd been forced into a job she hated and performed evil experiments, I knew nothing about this sister. She shrank from the slightest hint of intimacy.

"The others are living communally in a large building, aren't they?"

"Yeah, while they're training. But no-one's decided what you're going to do, have they?"

"No. But I might feel more comfortable with them. It's what I'm used to."

"Suit yourself." I couldn't hide my annoyance. "But you might hurt Mum's feelings, not that I expect you to understand that."

"It seems more logical for me to live with them, that's all," Suna said, her voice that maddening monotone that gave you no idea what she was thinking. "But I don't want to train to be a farmer. I don't like the idea of raising animals for food."

"There'll be a lot of things you won't like out here," I

snapped. "But you'll have to work on the land or make babies. Get used to the idea."

"M-make babies. What do you mean?"

"I mean meet a man and couple with him and get pregnant then push the baby out of your vagina."

"You're kidding?" Suna's face seemed to fade to three shades paler.

I softened my voice. "Don't worry; it's not the Citidome. No-one can force you to do anything you don't want to. But you'll have to earn your keep somehow. And chances are, you'll be able to conceive naturally, because you're similar in build to Mum. Most Citizens can't, you know."

"I couldn't … do that. But I'm willing to work."

"I don't want to have children either," I said. "We'll find you a job."

"But I have nothing except the clothes I'm wearing. And surely the CEs are going to be scouring the villages for months yet, looking for survivors?"

I looked at my followers, all still dressed in their blue correction camp outfits with blankets draped around their shoulders, their heads covered with stubble, their ears mutilated. Their origin was obvious to any fool. Could we keep them all safe? We'd have to keep them in hiding for a long while yet.

"Don't worry about clothes," I said, because it was the only reassuring comment I could give her. "We've been stockpiling knitwear and raiding the dumps for ages."

"I thought the canal was only a kilometre away?" Kell called from behind us.

"It is," I said. "We must be near the edge of the woods now. I bet it's at the bottom of this bank."

We descended a steep path, inexpertly negotiating the mulch of leaves and partly-frozen mud. At the bottom, Kell broke into a run. I'd barely reached the level towpath when I smiled at the sight of the familiar boat. Then I stopped. There were Kell, Dee and … yes, Harry, all enveloped in each other's arms. Harry. My Harry. He hadn't seen me, oblivious to everything being with his dad again. I felt a surge inside, knowing that joy would be bursting inside him at this moment. I thought of the plays on my name he used to say to me, and realised I was trembling.

I turned to the group behind me.

"Those who are going to Ashford, turn left and start walking along the canal side. I'll catch you up soon. Those going to Hest Bank; there's your transport."

A murmur of excitement and wonder grew at the sight of a means of transport that none of the Citizens could have imagined. People paused to thank me, then they swarmed towards the boat. I started to follow them; I needed to speak to Harry. The right thing was to marry Ryan but the way my pulse had gone out of control had told me what I'd been denying for months. I could only truly love one man. I took a step forward, then stopped. A young blonde woman had emerged from the cabin and spoke to the escapees.

"Hey, everybody, climb on board. My name's Caroline."

Harry, Dee and Kell were still locked in embraces. I snuffed out the flame of hope, swivelled around and sprinted along the path until I'd regained my position at the head of the group.

"Was that Kell's family?" said Suna as I caught up.

"Yeah." A sob caught in my throat.

"You seem upset. What is it?"

"Nothing, just an emotional time. I haven't seen my family and friends for over two months."

The path opened into a clearing and I saw the horse and cart and someone standing in front of it. My shoulders sagged. Of course it wouldn't be Mum; she couldn't leave Adam. But a familiar voice shouted, "Joy! I don't believe it!" and I threw myself into Daisy's arms. It took me a while to disentangle myself, and then I became aware of the mutters of the escapees and turned around.

"This is Daisy. Climb on board, everybody," I said.

"Your dad …" said Daisy, her eyes misting over.

"Dad's ahead of us, in the TravelPod. He's doing OK."

"B-but we thought … We heard there was one deceased coming home."

"Helen." My voice dropped. "I'll tell you all about it on the way home. And see that girl getting onto the cart now? She's my half-sister. Can I ride behind you? So much to tell you, and I can't think of anything nicer than being on horseback right now."

"Course you can; I don't think I can wait to hear all this. But wear these" – she handed over the knitted hat and cloak – "and put the blankets and hay over the others before you jump on." She smiled apologetically at the escapees. "Can't be too careful. Doubt anyone's out at the moment but we need to hide you in case anyone passes."

The journey was slow and as I updated Daisy, my momentary happiness faded. Harry was still with Caroline. And I'd almost believed what I'd said to Kell – that he was no longer part of me. Who had I been kidding? The pain of seeing Caroline – a physical being rather than a concept – had been like a knife wound. No, not a knife. That would have been quick and clean. More like being stabbed with a gnarled branch that was still twisting inside me.

"Oh shit – a TravelPod," said Daisy, seeing a stationary vehicle on the road ahead.

We held our breath as we passed but I saw a familiar person looking at the engine.

"Stop!" I shouted, and jumped down.

"Hazel, what's wrong?"

"I drove through that puddle too fast, fell down an enormous hole in the road, and the freaking engine died. Can we have a lift?"

Daisy had already leapt off the horse and had opened the door.

"Michael! We all thought you were dead! Ryan, sweetheart. How are you doing? Oh, is that … " At the sight of the shrouded body, she fell silent.

We carried Helen's body out of the car and placed it on the cart. Michael climbed up, then Ryan shuffled out of the vehicle, trailing his leg behind him.

"I'll help him up, but can we have a minute first?" I said.

"Hey, sweetheart," he said.

The look he gave me was like a warm, comforting blanket. I strengthened my resolve. I had to say this now, before I changed my mind. I opened my mouth and then closed it again. Maybe I should have rehearsed it.

"Did you see Harry on the boat?" he asked, his face a mask of pain. Of course. He wasn't stupid. Ryan was worth ten of me. Why couldn't I love him the way I loved Harry?

"Yeah, but not to talk to." I forced my voice to remain level. "Didn't want to interrupt the big family reunion. You should have seen Kell's face. It really was something. But that's not what I wanted to talk to you about. Let's not tell the family until we're all together but I wanted to give you my answer. I'd be honoured to marry you."

"Are you sure this is what you want?" His hands gripped mine. "Joy, you never say you love me."

"Emotional eloquence isn't my strong point. But yes, Ryan, I love you." It wasn't a lie, was it? I did love him. It wasn't the all-consuming passion I'd felt for Harry. How could it be? I wasn't capable of experiencing that intensity of feeling for anyone else. But Harry had chosen someone else and I had a chance to put right some of the wrongs I'd inflicted on Ryan.

"Thank you. I know I wasn't your first choice, but I'll make you happy; I promise."

His chaste, dry-mouthed kiss wasn't unpleasant, but it didn't cause my heart to spin. Perhaps in time it would. And as his arms drew me against him I wondered how many more people I was going to deceive.

CHAPTER 26 - CATHY

As the chill bit into my bones, I prepared for the hardest day of my life.

"Is someone guarding the south road?" I asked.

"Course they are. Stop fretting, sweetheart." Anna's voice failed to reassure. I'd wanted the return to be inconspicuous but Helen's parents, Will and Virginia, had been unable to resist waiting by the bridge to meet the arrival of the cart. Luke stood behind them, shotgun in hand. Should I have insisted that Anna stayed indoors? I'd packed the boys off to the care of Mary, wanting to spare them the sight of Michael's body.

"There's no way the CEs will come out today. It must be about ten below zero," said Luke.

"You never know with CEs. They can turn up when you least expect it," I said and the rat that had been gnawing at my insides started chewing ferociously. Last time I was taken unawares by CEs in winter was just before I gave birth for the first time. My little girl would have been seventeen in a month's time.

"They're taking an awful long time. Surely it can't take more than an hour by horse?" Virginia checked her watch for the hundredth time.

"She'll be taking it easy. There might be injured people. Anna, are you sure you want to stay here? You'll freeze."

"And miss the first sight of my returning hero? Not a chance," Anna said.

"Anna ..." I looked at the woman I thought of as a mother. She was looking every one of her fifty-nine years. Time to prepare her.

"Stop right there. Of course it's occurred to me that he didn't make it. I've thought of nothing else for weeks. But the sooner I know, the sooner I can rest."

"Listen." Luke raised his gun.

All eyes turned to look towards the source of the clip-clopping sound – yes, it had to be – a horse and cart. As it came into view, the waiting group spilt into the road. Then they stopped and someone leapt off the horse from behind Daisy, a too-thin girl with only a thin fuzz of dark hair covering her skull but an unmistakeable face.

"It can't be!" Anna was the first to speak.

I blinked. Was I hallucinating?

"Mum!" the girl yelled.

Then everyone moved at once. Joy leapt into my arms and I crushed her against me, breathing her in, unable to believe she was real. Then a scream drew my attention over her shoulder and my blood chilled. Luke was lifting a body, bound in a white sheet, from the cart. But why was Virginia screaming?

Then I saw him.

Michael.

He looked older, frail, his beard long and one arm in a sling. And I let out the tension of the last month, calling his name over and over. Releasing Joy to Anna, I ran to him and stopped short of rushing into his outstretched good arm, fearful of hurting him. Our kiss was more a collision of lips.

"I thought…" I whispered.

"Don't get rid of me that easily." He winked.

I leant into him but the moment was too brief. Anna had reached us, tears streaming down her face. The hugs and kisses seemed to go on forever and I longed for the world to disappear, for there to be nothing but me and the ones I loved.

"Ugh, what a journey," Daisy was gabbling. "The TravelPod broke down just outside Bakewell; we had to get them up on to the cart; it's been tough on Ryan."

I looked up. Ryan was here? Where had he and Joy been, all this time? Oh no, I had a fresh battle to fight, didn't I? Margaret would be bouncing off the walls with outrage if I let Ryan back in without punishment, that's assuming he'd been the one to strike the fatal blow. And then I saw him, his arm around Joy. He looked older, gaunt, but rather more handsome than he used to. Cropped hair suited him. So Joy and Ryan really were together. Then Daisy's voice dropped, and I discovered whose body was wrapped in the shroud.

"Helen, no!" I ran to Virginia, but the woman was hysterical by now, and Will was shouting at Michael.

"My little girl … You were meant to look after her."

The whole scene was too much to process at once. I leant against Michael's good side, feeling dizzy. It was some time before I saw a young woman standing alone on the periphery. It couldn't be. What was Suna doing here? Oh no, had the CEs turned up without us noticing? Then I noticed the scar on her cheek and smiled.

"Hey, Suna." I said.

"Hey," she said.

"Let me meet you properly."

Suna allowed me to embrace her but her body remained rigid. I pulled away, realising how alien the whole experience must seem to her.

"Helen was the most heroic woman I ever met," Suna said. "She gave too much of her own blood to save Michael."

"No!" I looked to Michael.

"Too much?" Michael frowned.

Joy glared at Suna.

"Yeah, I didn't want to tell you," Joy said. "She gave three doses when we'd agreed only one was safe."

"Stupid … why?" he muttered. He turned to me and lowered his voice. "Self-sacrifice isn't so noble when others need you. You were right about Helen. You were right about everything, come to that. Helen wasn't up to it. Lost the plot. Didn't eat, didn't drink, didn't sleep. I should never have chosen her … too late now." An agonised expression shot across his face. "But our Joy, she was the true hero."

"Joy? How?" My brain couldn't process the onslaught of new information.

"Why don't I take everyone home, and you settle this lot in, then we'll tell you everything," Michael said. "They're all dying to meet the village leader. Where are Scott and Adam?"

I took in the group of crop-headed young men.

"With Mary, just in case …"

"I'll collect them along the way. Ryan, rest on my good shoulder, and Daisy, you grab his other arm."

They propelled Ryan forward and I noticed that he was dragging one of his legs. In an attempt to clear my head of the riot of questions, I turned to face the newcomers. I scanned their faces with a smile. Their expressions ran the full gamut of emotions – fear, excitement, relief – with the exception of Suna, whose face remained devoid of animation.

"Welcome to Ashford-in-the Water," I said. "I'm Cathy, the village leader. I'm going to take you to your accommodation first. We've got some soup warming on the hob; I guess you're all hungry."

A chorus of appreciative murmurs greeted this comment.

"For the next few days we want you all to rest; you've all been through quite an ordeal," I continued. "You'll have a warden, Julia, to answer most of your questions, but I'll pop in to see you every day. And on Monday, you'll have an induction course on how things work around here. Everything from how to cut an animal up for meat to how the rainwater plumbing systems work. But I won't leave you in the cold any longer. Follow me."

Another wave of excited mutters.

"Suna, walk with me." I noticed Suna hanging back. "I'm guessing you're not part of the farming academy."

"No but I wondered if I might live there?"

"Er … yeah, I guess you could." I rubbed my nose. Where was Suna going to live? What was she going to contribute to the community, if she wasn't going to train as a farmer? "But would you like to come to meet your half-brothers once I've settled everyone in?"

"Yes please."

We had little more opportunity to get acquainted. One of the newcomers turned out to be a lively young woman called Hazel who bombarded me with questions about the village. I liked her instantly and smiled, remembering an old argument I'd had with Michael. I'd argued that Citidome women were for the most part as strong as men, and there was no reason they couldn't join the farming academy. He'd disagreed. But much as I enjoyed Hazel's enthusiasm, I longed to be with Joy and Michael. It was another frustrating hour before I was able to return home with Suna, who had said little so far.

"I guess you'd had enough of being a CE?" I said.

"Yeah. It was a snap decision. I was in the right place at the right time. I didn't think it through."

"Well, I'm sure you won't regret it." I tried to inject some warmth into my voice but it was hard to feel much for this cold stranger, whose face said she was very much regretting it. I tried to cast my mind back to the wave of maternal affection that had engulfed me when I'd seen her in kindergarten. Now her presence seemed intrusive. The only people whose stories I wanted to hear were those of Joy and Michael.

I heard the riot of voices as soon as I opened the front door. Daisy was telling a story that involved a lot of gesticulation. Ryan appeared to have become part of the family and was seated on the armchair with his legs raised, Joy perched on the chair arm with her hand on his shoulder.

"Scott, this is your half sister, Suna," I said.

"Another big sister?" Scott wrinkled his nose. "You might have brought me a big brother."

Everyone laughed.

"You two look alike," Anna said, which raised a smile from Suna. In fact, she appeared to be interested in her younger brother. "Time for some celebratory wine, I think. Suna's first taste of alcohol." Anna poured four glasses of the musty liquid, and raised her glass. "To new beginnings."

Suna failed to hide her grimace at the first taste of the wine but soon the alcohol flowed as freely as the stories and I heard every detail of Joy and Ryan's missing weeks. Ryan's hand remained in hers, as if afraid to let her go. Then Joy silenced the group.

"I've got an announcement to make. I'm going to marry Ryan. And we want to get married the day after Christmas."

"If I have your permission." Ryan turned to Michael and me.

"Of course," Michael said. "You two kept that quiet. But why so soon?"

"We'd be doing it eventually, so why not sooner than later? Besides, we need something cheerful after Helen's funeral." Joy bit her lip. "We don't want a big fuss though. Just us, Daniel, Alex, Matt and Mary's family. Is that OK?"

"Yeah, why not?" I said. Was that the real reason? Joy's

expression was unreadable.

"So Suna, if you want to move in here, you can have my room," Joy said.

"Thanks." Suna's expression was half-smile, half-frown. I suppressed my own frown. I wasn't sure I wanted Suna living here.

"Congratulations. You make a fantastic couple." Daisy was the first to recover herself and give an appropriate response.

"I think another drink's called for, to toast your engagement," said Anna.

Glasses were raised and the conversation resumed its previous volume. Then I noticed Joy chatting to Scott. Without warning, she started crying, great heaving sobs.

"What is it, sweetheart?"

"S-Scotty told me about Milo."

I frowned. Joy had never been as attached to the dog as Scott had been. It seemed an extreme reaction. Something was wrong. I needed to speak to Joy alone.

"She always has been a softy where animals were concerned," I said to Ryan and then to Joy, "I should heat up some soup. You must be starving. Come and help?"

"Yeah, sure."

"I'll help too." Michael followed us in. As soon as the door closed, Joy sniffed.

"Get the impression I'm about to have an interrogation," she said.

"Why are you crying? Surely it's not just about Milo?" I said.

Silence. And then I got it.

"It's what Milo represents, isn't it?"

"W-what do you mean?"

"He's your last link to Harry. I'm not stupid. I'm not convinced by this romance with Ryan. So be honest. What's the real reason for the rushed wedding? Are you pregnant?"

"Hell, no." Joy wiped her eyes and laughed, a hollow, empty laugh.

"So what is it?"

Joy bit her lip. "Ryan's leg's never going to fully recover; he'll need someone to help him around the house. So it's best that I move in with him as soon as possible."

"I knew it." Michael shook his head. "Look sweetheart, I've grown to like Ryan a lot in the last few weeks. He's a decent guy and it's obvious he adores you. But don't marry him out of pity."

She shook her head. "I can't win with you, can I, Dad? I'm staying in the village and marrying a village boy. Isn't that what you wanted all along?"

Michael's head dropped. "There's something else I need to tell you. After I forced you to break off communications with Harry, I sent a message to Dee and said you were with Ryan. I'm so sorry, sweetheart. It was inexcusable. Your mum told me earlier this year that I was turning into Fin, the guy who kept her prisoner because he was obsessed with new blood, and she was right. I've messed up, this last year. I was so focussed on trying to fix the wider world that I didn't see what I was doing to the people who matter most. If Harry's the one you want to be with, go to him."

I saw the flash of pain in Joy's eyes and braced myself for the explosion, but there was none.

"It doesn't matter any more." Joy's eyes were focussed on the floor. "I've made my decision."

"Tell me you love Ryan the way you love Harry and I'll never mention it again," Michael persisted.

"Dad, don't push it. The village needs a health worker and it has to be me. And Harry has someone else, remember? Caroline. She was on the boat with him this morning."

"He's still with her?" Michael frowned. "I assumed it was a rebound thing."

"I'm going back to Ryan now," Joy said. "He'll suspect we're talking about him."

"Hang on, Joy. One more thing," I said. "Offering Suna your room? Don't you think you might have discussed it with us first?"

But Joy turned around and left the room. So much for happy reunions. My eyes met Michael's.

"Thought I'd never get you to myself," I said. "But what are we going to do? Is it worth sending a message to Harry, to see if we can stop this?"

"When could we ever stop her if she's made her mind up?" he said. "And Joy and Ryan … they were close in the bunker.

But not like she and Harry used to be. I don't know, maybe Harry's settled for this Caroline instead. I'll send him a message later. Now, come here."

His good arm pressed me against him. We kissed with renewed intensity, and for those precious moments the anguish of the past and the challenges of the future were forgotten.

"What happened to us?" he whispered. "What made us say such unforgiveable things to each other?"

"Let's just say we had a row that lasted too long. And now we've got a lot of making up to do."

"I don't think I'll ever be able to make up for what I've put you through. But I'm going to have fun trying." He gave me that wink that I'd never been able to resist.

It proved to be a Christmas that none of the village would ever forget. I sent Joy away to rest, not telling her about the difficult visit to Margaret. When we told Margaret what had happened in the dairy that day, and that Ryan had acted in self-defence, she collapsed in a fit of silent crying that was harder to take than the fury I'd expected. On Christmas Eve we buried Helen in the churchyard next to her brother, and shed tears for the lost young lives and for the parents who had outlived both children. Christmas Day was a family day, although we shared ours with the new residents, cooking six roast chickens for dinner and drinking Anna's mulled wine. Michael sent Harry a message, but got no reply. There was no way of talking Joy out of marrying Ryan.

And so, on Boxing Day, I prepared for the wedding in the village church.

"Do you need any help getting ready?" I called from outside Joy's room. Joy emerged in her normal sweater and pants.

"Not yet, thanks. It won't take long. But first, I need to change Ryan's dressing. Back in half an hour."

It didn't seem worth mentioning that it was considered bad luck for the bride to see the groom on the day of her wedding. Never was a wedding less fitting for a girl named Joy. But she no longer seemed a girl. Even though she could be maddening, I missed the old Joy. There was a knock on the door and Beth and Mary came in, both in their dresses. I wished I'd been able to persuade Suna to wear my only other dress, but she politely refused. Strained politeness was the most I'd got out of her so far.

"Where's the bride?" Beth said. "We've made her a headdress."

I smiled. The headdress, fashioned from horsehair and fabric flowers, was beautiful. At that point, Joy arrived.

"Matt was with Ryan; he said he'd look after him. Oh … is that for me? It's gorgeous – I was wondering what to do about my head." She put her hand to her stubbly scalp.

"Can I help you get ready?" Beth asked.

"Of course; that's what a bridesmaid does, isn't it?" In that minute Joy was her old, animated self. But it was the first sign of it since her return.

"Why don't you join them, Suna?" I suggested.

"OK."

As Joy and Beth ran upstairs, Suna following more slowly, Mary and I sat down.

"She's a cold fish," Mary said. "How are you getting on with her?"

"With difficulty. She doesn't say a lot but I'm not exactly giving her my undivided attention either. To be honest, she's the least of my problems."

"What else?"

"How would you feel if you suspected Beth wasn't marrying her true love?"

Michael joined us, in his best shirt and pants.

"You two look like you're about to go to a f – " He stopped himself just in time.

"It's hard not to think of Helen, isn't it?" Mary murmured. "She used to idolise me when we were growing up. But she never approved of my market trading, nor when I married Vincent. He asked her out first, you know, but she turned him down. But Cathy, you were saying about Joy … she doesn't love Ryan?"

We'd barely finished telling Mary the story when Joy and Beth came down. My stomach lurched. My once-beautiful daughter was pale and thin, the dress that had accentuated her curves last February hanging on her like a sack, her luscious mane of brown curls missing. Thank heavens for the headdress. Suna followed them, looking bemused by the entire scene.

Michael put his good arm around Joy. "I don't think I've ever been more proud of you." His voice was thick. "Ready to walk an old man down the aisle?"

With a sinking feeling, I walked to the church, and only when I saw the look of adoration in Ryan's eyes did my mood lighten. And so Michael gave our little girl away to a young man who seemed barely able to look after himself.

We both woke with hangovers the next day.

"Ugh, that beer went to my head last night," Michael said. "I'm not used to drinking any more."

"It wasn't a bad day in the end though, was it?" I smiled. "I have to say, they did look happy."

"That's what I thought. Maybe she chose the right one after all. And it wasn't a bad night." He winked. "Not blushing, are you?" He drew me closer towards him.

It was another half-hour before we got up. We still had a lot of making up to do. As was still Michael's habit, he reached for his DataBand. He looked at the screen and gave a long, low groan. I read it and did the same.

> Sorry, haven't been checking my messages, busy relocating the escapees. I sent a message to Joy. Can you make sure she reads it before she marries Ryan? Harry

CHAPTER 27 - JOY

I'd spent so much time imagining my wedding day that I could replay the scenario in my head at will. It would be at the end of summer, everyone happy in the knowledge that the harvest was gathered and the year's hard work was done. I'd have a new white dress, all the way to the ground like those I'd seen in books. Harry would wear a proper shirt and jacket. The whole community would fill the church, the party afterwards would be one of legend, and as the light faded, we'd ride away on a horse and cart before spending our wedding night alone on the narrowboat with no-one but the birds around us.

My actual wedding day was nothing like this. I wore the yellow dress of my sixteenth birthday but it was now way too big for me. Daniel officiated at the short ceremony in the church. Ryan stood only for the vows, his weight supported on a stick. Then we had a modest party in the village hall. After the first dance, I helped Ryan to a chair, biting back the tears. Would I ever have a slow dance with a man I was in love with? He dropped to the chair with a thud.

"You're so stubborn," I said, stroking his bristly hair.

"Couldn't deny you a dance on your wedding day, could I? You sure I didn't lean on you too heavily?"

"I'm stronger than I look." My shoulders were screaming with the pain of bearing his weight, but how could I tell him? His face was alight with happiness, and I was the cause of it. In a rush of affection, I kissed him on the lips. I did love him, of course I did. I just wasn't in love with him.

"Think we can slip off home now?" he said.

"Don't see why not. We've entertained our public enough. Let's say our goodbyes."

We did the rounds of well-wishers, Ryan dragging his leg behind him, using his stick. Maybe I'd make him a chair with wheels, if … I couldn't bear to think what came next. I hadn't told anyone, least of all Ryan, the true reason for the haste of the marriage. Maybe I was being pessimistic. I'd tried different poultices and had found a bottle of goldenseal tincture. I'd be able to get some more honey from the market next Thursday. But would anything work against what was increasingly looking like septicaemia? Only one thing could. But could I amputate so high?

Once home, Ryan fell onto the sofa in front of the remnants of the crackling fire and drew me towards him.

"I love you." His lips sought mine. Even his lips were burning up.

Before the kiss could lead to anything else, I turned away.

"First, I'm playing nurse. Look, Mum had a whole bottle of goldenseal tincture."

I removed his dressing and the now-familiar smell assaulted my nostrils. I knew that the movement of the journey would put stress on Ryan's wound, but hadn't been prepared for the expanse of freshly opened areas, nor the increasing swelling of the surrounding flesh and that impossible to ignore putrid-smelling pus.

"It's much worse, isn't it?"

"It's not pretty, but we knew the journey would give us a setback. It didn't help that Hazel threw the TravelPod down a bloody great pothole. I'm going to boil some water and give this a really good clean. Sorry, but it's gonna hurt like hell."

I tried to dab as gently as I could, but Ryan's mouth twisted up. Finally, he slumped back into the sofa and gave way to loud, choking sobs, and the sound tore at me. For everything he'd been through, I'd never seen him cry.

"Nearly done." I applied a clean dressing, but by now he was sobbing his heart out. I sat beside him and held his head against my chest. We stayed like that for several minutes.

"Dry those tears. It's our wedding day, remember?" I said.

"I should never have asked you to marry me. You don't deserve this. I don't want you to be tethered to a cripple. Go home."

I took his head between my hands, and raised it until he was looking at me. "You heard what Daniel said: for better, for worse, in sickness and in health. This is my home now and you're my husband. And I love you."

"I love you too, so much."

We sat in front of the dying embers of the fire and talked of trivia, of village gossip. The light from the fire cast shadows across his face, accentuating the hollows.

"We're going to have to feed you up," I commented. "You've lost weight."

"Not as much as you. We'll live on cheese from now on," Ryan said. "Anything, as long as I never have to eat a nutribar again. That fire's nearly out. Why don't we go to bed?"

As I helped him up the stairs, my panic mounted. I liked sleeping with him. But to make love to him … how could I? My own words returned to me from another lifetime. "We always owned each other's souls. Now we own each other's body." I helped him undress, trying to conjure up desire for his emaciated, elongated, hairless body, but all I could think of was the rotting flesh of his thigh. In fact, how were we going to do this without hurting him? I undressed quickly. He'd seen it all before anyway, in the camp. But I looked better then. When did my breasts become so shrunken?

"You're so beautiful." A smile crept up his face.

I climbed in beside him, every muscle tensing.

"Joy, I want to. But I'm not sure I can."

I glanced down, saw that he was flaccid, and tried not to show my relief.

"It's OK, love. It's been a tiring day. There's plenty of time for that when you're feeling better."

I nestled my head against his chest, listened to his heart beating – too quickly – and bit on the inside of my mouth to focus my pain into a physical form. I was trapped inside the pages of a novel that could have no happy ending.

We spent much of the next two days in bed, and I finally gave way to the exhaustion that I'd been carrying but not acknowledging for the last weeks. Thankfully Ryan didn't seem to be physically capable of any intimacies beyond kissing.

"This is bliss," he said. "Are we really not meant to be working?"

"No, I spoke to Mum. You're not to do anything until you have your strength back; I'm allowed to be your full-time nurse for now, and when you feel better we're going to start training with Alex to be health workers."

"Sounds wonderful. They're happy for us both to train?"

"Absolutely," I lied. I hadn't discussed Ryan's future with anyone until I was sure he had one. Hope was meant to help people recover from illness, wasn't it?

The following morning, as soon as Ryan rose, he fell to the floor in a faint. I leapt out of bed. Fainting, what caused that? Low blood pressure wasn't it – could that be linked to septicaemia? Damn, I should've gone to Helen's house yesterday to collect her medical books. Alex, the retired health worker, would know. I put on my coat and boots, ran to his house and pounded on the door.

"Hey, what is it?" Alex rubbed his sleepy eyes. "Joy! I wondered when I was going to see you."

"It's Ryan." I garbled an explanation, every word of which knotted Alex's brow tighter.

"Sounds like septic shock," he said. "Come on, let's go."

Ryan had regained consciousness when we returned. Alex looked at his wound, sucked in the air through his teeth, and lifted Ryan back onto the bed.

"Let's have a look at you, young man."

I waited downstairs until Alex returned, his expression grim.

"Sorry, Joy, there's little I can do without antibiotics. We can make him some infusions of detoxifying herbs but I've never seen them save someone with this degree of sepsis. The next stage will probably be gangrene. Then his organs will fail. Amputation is the only thing that could save him."

"I knew you were going to say that; I've been forcing myself not to face it. I amputated a leg and an arm in the bunker."

He whistled. "You're joking? I heard you were a hero out there, but I'm not sure I'd have had the guts to try it. And it worked?"

"Yeah. But they were both lower limb injuries. Ryan's is going to be a lot more risky. The blood transfusions that we did were successful." I paused. "I gave Dad a dose of my own blood without any ill-effects. But Helen …"

"How much did she give?"

"Three half-litre doses."

Alex shook his head then laid a hand on my arm. "It's your choice, and Ryan's obviously. If you want to try it, I'll give you all the support I can. We should have enough blood donors in the village. And Joy, your mum's been to see me. She tells me you want to step into Helen's shoes. I'd be honoured to train you, and there's no doubt you have the brains for it. But think about it long and hard. Helen gave her life to the cause of medicine. You seem so young to take it on."

"I'm nearly seventeen. Helen was only fifteen when you took her on as your apprentice."

"Yes, but Helen …" He smiled. "Helen was never young in the way that you are. She was more serious. You should be out there, having fun, breaking the hearts of all the new young men."

"I can be serious," I protested. Young? I'd never be young again.

I sat alone for a long time before creeping up the stairs to see Ryan.

"What did Alex say?" Ryan said.

"He said … he said I should amputate the leg."

Ryan's shoulders slumped. "We've been kidding ourselves, haven't we? We knew it'd come to this."

"I'll only do it if you want me to." My voice was barely more than a whisper.

"Do you think you can?"

"I don't know. Cutting through the femur, the femoral artery … it's not easy. But I'd try anything to save you."

"No." His voice was strangely calm and measured. "If it didn't work, you'd torture yourself for the rest of your life. If you did … I'm not sure I want to live that way, disabled, the object of pity. So tell me, and don't mollycoddle me. How long do I have left?"

"I don't know. Days, weeks maybe." Panic bubbled up. "No, Ryan. I can't let you die. Let me try."

"No." He blinked several times and then smiled. "So, it's a short-lived romance. But better this than living to be a hundred and never having known love."

And with that, I fell into his arms and gave way to the tears

I could no longer contain.

For the following nights I hardly slept, listening to each of Ryan's rapid, shallow breaths and wondering if it would be his last. But Ryan, it appeared, had no intention of releasing his grip on life. He drifted in and out of consciousness. In his lucid moments, I gave him painkillers, washed down by infusions of nettle and goldenseal, stroked his hair and told him the words he needed to hear, of how much I loved him. There were many types of love, and this one was borne of gratitude rather than passion, but that didn't lessen its intensity.

"After … you will talk to Harry, won't you?" Ryan said on a good day.

"Why should I do that? I can't think of anyone but you." This was true. I was engulfed in the tragedy of Ryan, drowning in it.

"You'll love again, Joy, and you should."

"Don't talk of it."

Touchingly, Suna visited often and helped me clean Ryan. He seemed to enjoy her visits; she didn't appear to be repulsed by his deteriorating condition and he wasn't embarrassed in front of her.

It was a different story when Matt visited on the second week. Ryan was asleep.

"Ugh, what's that stench?" he whispered.

"The gangrene from his leg. It's horrible. And he's losing control of his bladder and his bowel." I shook my head then added, "I'm doing my best but –"

"It's making my stomach heave. And what's that rattling sound when he breathes?"

"His heart's failing; his lungs are filling up with fluid."

"Poor Ryan. Not a dignified way to go, is it?"

"It's hideous. Alex said he could still go on for days, weeks maybe. And when he does wake up, he struggles for breath, like he's drowning." I rubbed my eyes. "Cheer me up. What's been happening here?"

"Mostly worry about you. Joy, I've got to say something. That day, when you walked up to the dairy and called out to me. I heard you."

"I know." I tightened my mouth.

"I didn't know what to say to you. I'd heard what they were saying about your dad … I was embarrassed, I guess. Ever since, I've thought: would things have turned out differently if I'd spoken to you?"

"They might have." I knew I was being cruel. But a million 'what if' scenarios had rushed into my head. If I'd spoken to Matt that day, maybe I wouldn't have seen Ryan, and I wouldn't have confronted Peter. Matt's rejection of me that day had hurt and I wanted to hurt him back. He wanted exoneration and I couldn't give it.

"I'm sorry," he muttered. "I'll never take my family's side over yours again."

He looked so despondent that I softened.

"It's my birthday in a month," I said. "Remember last year?"

"Course I do. Our first dance." He winked. "Seems a lifetime ago. And there's something else I've got to tell you. Remember me saying I'd never been in love?"

"You're not!" I grinned. "Ah, is it Hope?"

"The minute I saw her I was lost. She has the palest skin I've ever seen and her hair, now it's growing back – it's almost silver. She needs a bit of flesh on her bones, but Mum's feeding her up."

"That's wonderful! And how does she feel about you?"

"Gratitude; that's all." He ran a hand through his hair. "But I'm working on it."

At that moment Ryan woke up and spluttered, his eyes wide with panic.

"Hey, Ryan, how are you doing?" Matt made an attempt at cheerfulness.

"Hey, Matt." His words caused a paroxysm of coughing.

"It's OK, love. I'm here." I handed him a glass of water.

"Ryan, mate." Matt laid a hand on Ryan's shoulder, but Ryan looked away. I wiped the tears from his face.

"I'm having to turn away the visitors. You're the most popular guy in the village. Everyone's been asking about you," I said.

"Don't want to …" Ryan's muffled voice faded.

"Well, I have to feed the cows. Take care, mate." Matt got up to leave.

My heart twisted at the sight of Ryan clutching his chest, desperately trying to make his lungs work. I flipped him onto his back and rubbed his chest until his breathing eased, and felt the wet sheets beneath him.

"Let me get you a clean sheet."

I rolled his body one way, then the other to change the sheet. Tears trickled down his face.

"It doesn't matter," I said.

"Yes it does." He couldn't look at me.

I crawled into bed beside him, and laid my head on his chest.

"I'm so, so, sorry," I whispered.

"Why … sorry?"

"I brought all this on you." I swallowed hard, trying to contain the swell of guilt that threatened to gush, geyser-like from me.

"You … gave my life … meaning." His words came out in laboured bursts and the effort of speaking seemed to exhaust him.

"Ryan, what can I do to make it better?"

"Remember … we treat animals more fairly."

"What do you mean?" But I knew exactly what he meant. The thought had entered my head three nights ago and kept me awake every night since. Fear settled on my stomach like a stone. But I had to hear him say it.

"Tell me what you want me to do."

"End … it."

"Ryan, I'm not sure I – "

"Please."

I got up from the bed, gazed into his eyes and saw the pleading in them. I reached for the pillow and knew what I had to do.

CHAPTER 28 - CATHY

"You're full of surprises." I smiled at Michael in bed, where we seemed to be spending a disproportionate amount of time.

"So are you. We haven't been like this for … how long?"

"More than a year." I looked over at where Adam was rousing.

"We'll have to move him in with Scott soon." Michael winked.

"Wakey wakey, birthday boy," I said. Adam sat up and giggled. I lifted him from the crib and onto the bed.

"Da-da," he said, pointing at Michael.

"Yes, that's right, little man, I'm Da-da," whispered Michael, his eyes glistening. "Was that – "

"His first word. Yes."

He turned in the bed, winced, and rubbed his shoulder. "Alex thinks I'll get some movement back in time but I might never have much strength in this arm. I'm scared, Cathy. What am I going to do? A one-armed man isn't much use. Can't ride, can't work on the farm."

"Bet you can drive, though. TravelPods more or less drive themselves."

"Guess so, but the horse might be safer for the next few months. There's going to be CEs crawling around for a while yet. I know I shouldn't complain, could've been a lot worse, but I can't stand the thought that I might never hold you properly again."

"You will. I'll make sure of it. And we're doing OK at the moment, aren't we?"

"Better than OK." Oh, that wink.

"Anyway, we'd better get up. We've got to paste on our happy faces today, remember?"

Michael squeezed my hand. As well as Adam's first birthday, today was Joy's seventeenth birthday but it could have been her seventieth.

"I wondered about telling her about Harry's message," Michael said.

"No. Too soon," I said. "Besides, we don't know what it said. He might have been giving her his blessing. And he hasn't replied to any of your messages since you told him it was too late to stop the wedding, has he?"

"No." He groaned. "Let's try not to screw up Scott and Adam's life the way we've ruined Joy's."

I followed Michael into the bathroom and washed and dried the armpit of his immobile arm.

"At least poor Ryan didn't last long," he muttered. "I know this is a fraction of what he went through but this reliance on someone else – it's not easy."

"Stop that self-pity and let me help you with your top." I kept my voice upbeat, blinking away the tears that Ryan's name invoked. The tragedy of his and Helen's wasted young lives had filled my waking thoughts, and our community was reunited in grief.

I carried Adam down the steps and found Suna in the process of dressing. Since Joy had moved back home, she slept in the living room. At the sight of Adam, she smiled.

"The bathroom's free," I said. "Grab it before the kids do."

"Thank you." Suna went upstairs.

I sighed. I hadn't expected us to form an instant mother-daughter relationship, but the girl was so stilted, so polite. Adam and Scott were the only family members she seemed to enjoy. Whenever I'd asked how she was settling in, she said, "Fine, thanks." It seemed to be her stock reply to everything. What the village needed was a huge party, a coming together, but it didn't seem appropriate in the wake of the latest tragedies.

Anna and Daisy had already arrived.

"Hear you saw Virginia last night," Anna said.

"Yes, we did our best," I said. "But we couldn't get her to eat anything. To lose two children in just over a year … how does anyone get over that? I keep thinking about when I first saw them. Helen, thirteen, but already old before her time. Then Paul, almost twelve, blushed every time he looked at me."

"I don't know what God's playing at these days." Anna

shook her head. "I miss Kate but at least she had a good life. But to take those two, and young Ryan …" She inclined her head upstairs. "How's Joy doing?"

"I don't know. She's shut down completely, worse than she was last summer, after Harry. Doesn't cry, doesn't say much. Eats, but never clears her plate."

"We've been thinking, why doesn't Suna eat dinner with us every now and again?" Daisy said. "You need time together as a family, not that she isn't family, of course."

"That'd help," I said. "Truth is, she doesn't feel like family yet. I know she should but – "

"It's only a biological tie," Anna said. "It's never going to be the same as what you feel for the children you've raised. You may become close to her, you may not, but you've given her the chance of a better life."

"Not sure she sees it that way," I said.

"It hasn't been the best start, has it? With all this grief around, Suna needs space as much as you do."

"Talking of space, do you mind if I have a few minutes with Joy on my own? She should be down any minute."

"Course you can. I'll take Adam." Anna lifted him up. "Ooh, he's getting heavy. We've been saving our eggs and bacon for the last few days; thought we'd make a big birthday breakfast."

Joy trudged down the steps.

"Happy birthday, sweetheart," I said.

"Thanks, Mum." Her voice was flat. She allowed herself to be hugged, but didn't hug me back.

"We'll make up for this one," I whispered in her ear. "After what you've been through, it could never be anything other than a shitty time. But it's your little brother's birthday too. One thing you'll learn now that you're a woman is that sometimes you have to keep smiling, even though you're screaming inside. For some unfair reason the same doesn't apply to men."

"I don't think I'll ever stop screaming." Her eyes met mine.

"You will. I'm so proud of you. How many women would have done what you did? Ryan died happy, thinking you loved him. But you didn't, did you?"

"Actually, I did … We were inseparable, these last few

months. And I miss him. I never imagined I'd miss him so much. But it wasn't the right kind of love. Not the way a wife's meant to love a husband." She gave a world-weary sigh that seemed inappropriate in one so young. "I've had it with men, Mum. Think Helen had the right idea on that score." Her colour rose, causing me to frown. There'd been so much to think about in the last months that Helen and Michael's relationship had been the last thing on my mind, but now I wondered what Joy knew.

"Apart from being in love with your dad and then sacrificing a valuable young life for him, you mean?"

Joy blinked.

"Don't worry, I'd worked it out," I said. "And while you were away, Margaret tried to persuade the rest of the village that there was something between them."

"There wasn't; you know that, don't you? Dad didn't have a clue about the way she felt. Neither did I until I caught her sitting up one night by his bedside while he was sleeping. She said she'd loved him since she was thirteen years old. It seemed such a waste."

"So she died never having known love." I shook my head. "But Ryan knew love; you gave him a precious gift. You'll love again, Joy. You're too much like me to be able to help yourself."

"Huh, maybe I am." The corners of her lips twitched upwards. "Funny, I used to hate the fact that I wasn't like you. Everyone adores you; you always knew what you wanted out of life. And then Suna – she looks so like you. It made me feel weird at first, jealous, I guess."

"You've got nothing to be jealous about. Suna doesn't feel like a daughter. I'm trying to be understanding. I remember how I felt when I first left the Citidome. I was freaked out by the open way everyone talked and hugged each other. And I thought they smelt. But when I try saying this to her, she clams up."

"I know what you mean. I found her odd in the bunker. It's not that she's frightened of emotion, more like she doesn't feel it. I suppose that's why I suggested she live here; thought she'd learn more quickly." She rubbed her nose. "Sorry, I should have run it by you first."

"You did the right thing. And you're right about the lack of emotion. It's not unusual in Citidome people. But she's not learning as quickly as the others. So what do we do to get through to her?"

"I was wondering, maybe she should read your journal?" Joy said. "It might help more than talking about it. She's not unhappy, you know. She likes working at the bakery."

"The journal; that's a brilliant idea." I smiled. "How did I raise such a genius?"

"Not sure I'm that. I couldn't save Ryan," she murmured. "How are the newcomers settling in?"

I felt something loosen inside me. This represented progress. Joy had taken no interest in anything for weeks. "Pretty well, though I think they're all fed up being cooped indoors. All they get at the moment is lectures about farming; they're desperate to get outside."

"Probably for the best. Any news from the Citidomes?"

"No sightings of CEs since the latest dump of snow. From what we hear on Out There and Doodlebugs, they've done a few local raids but we're getting pretty good at getting people into hiding places, and there's only been a handful of arrests. Apparently there's been a record level of arrests inside the Citidomes – I guess they need new people to work in the factories."

"Poor devils. The camp was hideous. I wish … I wish I could bring the whole system down." Her eyes flashed and for a moment she looked exactly like Michael when I first met him. "Seems ages since I saw anyone. Beth never visits these days – I don't think she enjoys my company any more."

"Give her time. It was hard for her when you ran off with Ryan."

"Guess so. Poor Beth. What happened to Elsie?"

"Of course, you wouldn't know. After we found Peter, Elsie wept and wailed so much at the funeral that most people guessed the truth. There's been nothing but rumours and muck-raking around here for months now. And then, in case anyone was in any doubt, Nanna blurted it out in a village meeting. But now Elsie's pregnant. Tia wanted her to get rid of it but … what do you think? Would you have done it? Why are you smiling?"

"That's what I told Peter – that she was pregnant and I could get rid of it. I tried to bribe him: I'd spare him the scandal if he told the truth about Dad. Told him the baby would have red hair and everyone would know the truth. Never imagined at the time she actually was pregnant. But no, I wouldn't have done it. A human life's too precious around here."

"I'm glad you said that; I wondered whether I'd made the right decision. I've spoken to a couple in the Chatsworth community, an ex-Citidome couple in their late thirties. They're not able to have children of their own and they'd like to adopt the baby."

"Mum." Joy's hand linked with mine. "Why weren't we always like this?"

"Like what?"

"Friends. You tell me everything now."

I grinned. We'd made the transition without realising. But the Joy that left the village was a child. A delightful, idealistic, headstrong and occasionally selfish child. The Joy that had returned was an adult. And once I managed to get her to smile again, her transition into womanhood would be complete.

"Promise me you'll always tell me everything too."

"I will, I promise. It's just that I don't feel anything anymore. I don't even think about Harry any more. I just feel numb. Does that make sense?"

"More than you know. I've felt that twice. When I returned to the Citidome after first coming here. Then when I was living with Fin, believing your dad was dead. Each time, I didn't think life would ever get better. But it did."

After breakfast and the exchange of presents, Joy slipped the journal into my hands. Beth arrived with a present and I took the opportunity to speak to Suna.

"Suna, how about a walk by the river?" I said.

"OK, thanks," said Suna. Did the girl ever say anything except please and thank you?

"Ooh, my back's aching this morning." I stretched. "Don't you sometimes long for your RestPod?"

"Oh yeah," said Suna, then bit her lip. "But everything's lovely here."

"It's all so alien though, isn't it? The food, the behaviour codes, the disgusting toilets."

Finally Suna's eyes smiled. "It's a lot to get used to," she admitted. "I mean, it's good to have found you all, but now I realise that there's no going back. I like the work here, and what Daisy does in that factory … it's incredible what she achieves with such limited resources."

"So what's the most difficult bit?"

"The dark," Suna said.

"Weird isn't it, after only having two types of light in the Citidomes. Does it frighten you a bit?"

She nodded.

"It's perfectly normal. Scott used to be afraid of the dark. But it's something you'll overcome in time. Is there anything else bothering you?"

"Uh, not really." She chewed on a nail, unable to meet my eye.

"The emotional side?" I prompted.

She raised her head and gave the briefest of nods.

I turned to her then placed the book in her hands. "Suna, here's something I'd like you to read. It's the story of a woman a couple of years younger than you, who looked just like you, and how she discovered the truth of the Citidomes and adjusted to a weird life." I smiled. "You even get a namecheck in it."

"Oh… thanks."

We reached the grassy expanse that led to the river. The beginnings of a thaw had made the grass squelchy underfoot.

"Look, signs of new life." I pointed to the long, yellow tails dangling from the hazel trees.

"Mmm, what do they remind me of?" Suna was clearly entranced by the catkins. "I remember, I had a unique outfit once – it was a dress covered in metallic yellow tails. It was scratchy and uncomfortable."

"These are soft; touch them," I said.

Suna reached to feel one of the tails and smiled.

"Nature always wins out over any of the hollow imitations of the Citidome," I said. "But come over here; this is what I wanted to show you."

The riverbank was filled with short, stiff, green spikes

which shot out of the soil, some with white flowers.

"Flowers! At this time of year! They're wonderful."

"They're called snowdrops. I call them little darts of hope," I said. "Hope that the winter will end before we freeze to death, and new warmth will enter our lives."

"How lovely. Daisy was telling me about the spring flowers. I can't wait to see them."

"Imagine that small bolt of joy you felt just then, multiplied by a million. That's how it feels when you form genuine relationships with people."

Suna's smile filled her face, and in that moment she was beautiful. And as I walked back with this strange new daughter, I felt my own stirrings of hope.

The thaw was gradual, for the land as well as my family, but a sunny week at the end of February made everyone smile except Michael. What he called our 'making up and making out' phase was as strong as ever. But I'd noticed his lapses. He'd retreat into his own world and when he re-emerged he seemed sadder than when he'd gone into it.

"Do you think I should resign as AOC leader?" he asked one day.

"No way." I shook my head. Where had this idea come from? "Look what you've achieved."

"What did we achieve though? Around three hundred survivors; that means around four hundred people died. You were right all along. Is anything worth that level of human sacrifice?"

"I've been thinking about that and I've changed my mind. While you were gone, I read about those great wars," I said. "Millions lost their life in the cause of freedom. But the world would have been a poorer place without those victories. Those Citizens who lost their life were prisoners. You've heard from Joy what a hellhole the correction camp was. Every single one of the people in there would have given their life to overthrow the system that took away their souls."

"I don't know. When I saw those hideous wounds in the bunker … Ryan …"

"Our only mistake was not knowing about their weaponry. Next time we'll be better prepared. Daisy's already talking about how we might be able to make acid-resistant clothing."

"I guess you're right. But there's another reason I'm losing the heart for it all. I didn't like the person I was turning into. The AOC was starting to take away my soul. It nearly took away the most important thing of my life: you."

"Maybe you need to step back? Remain as leader but delegate more, especially until you're able to ride. Lighten your load a little."

"Hmm, that's not a bad idea."

We sat in silence for a moment.

"The next stage scares me even more," he whispered. "We need to tell the world, to send the whole system crashing down."

"Scares me too. But I believe something for certain. Our grandchildren will live to see a different world."

"Grandchildren? It's going to happen in our lifetime. Why are you smiling?"

"It's back."

"What?"

"That fire in your eyes. You'll never give up the cause. And I don't want you to. That passion, it's what I fell in love with in the first place."

"This time it'll be more balanced. Adam might be the last child we have. I want to be there to see every milestone."

And as his mouth moved towards mine I felt it again. That sense of compressed excitement that I'd had in my first months in the village. That our future was full of possibilities, some terrifying but each one exciting.

CHAPTER 29 - JOY

"Mum, you look amazing. Though being thirty-six seems like the most tenuous reason ever for a party." I put down my book as Mum came downstairs, trying to unwrap my brain from mitral valve regurgitation.

"I'm not sure it's something I want to celebrate." Mum grinned. "Your dad's daft idea. Truth is, we were desperate for an excuse for a party. The village needs it – all those newcomers haven't had a chance to integrate. And it's time for you to come out of mourning and get your nose out of those bloody medical books. I'm going to reinstate a full social life around here – the movies and the Saturday socials. We can't hide forever, and from what we hear, the authorities have stopped searching for survivors. Now, don't tell me you're going out like that? I thought you could wear your yellow dress."

"I guess so." I shrugged. "But it's still too big for me. Besides –"

"Don't you dare say 'What's the point?'" Mum's voice was too emphatic for me to bother arguing. "The point is that seeing my daughter looking beautiful will make me happy on my birthday. And it might even make you happy. It's time to start living again, Joy. You're starting to turn into Helen and it scares me. Remember, too much reading and you'll ruin your eyesight."

"OK, just for you. I'll hardly be beautiful though. Look at my hair, for starters."

"It suits you like that."

I looked at my reflection. In no way did I look as good as I had last year, but the hollows under my eyes had started to fill. My hair was still boyishly short but long enough to curl.

"I'm going for a walk, then I'll get ready."

I put on my coat and went to the churchyard, stopping first to pick a handful of wood anemone and aconite. I arranged them into a bunch and laid them beneath the wooden cross that bore Ryan's name.

"Hey, Ryan," I said. "Not much choice of flowers yet, but I brought you these."

I rubbed my chest, trying to release the pressure that built up whenever I came here. It was the right thing to do, I told myself. And talking to Ryan helped fill the surprisingly large void he'd left behind. But the part of the grieving young widow was becoming harder to play. Tonight I'd have to run the gauntlet of sympathetic faces and kind words, all the time wanting to scream: he died because of me.

On my way back, Beth greeted me with that half-apologetic, half-embarrassed smile she had when she saw me these days, and I tried to think of something to say to her. We hadn't managed to slot back into our old gossipy friendship. She seemed younger, more insubstantial than I remembered. I guess I'd outgrown her. Too much had happened, and now I couldn't talk to her the way I had to Ryan. I missed him so much. But Mum had become my best friend instead.

"Hey, you been to see Ryan?" she said.

I nodded.

"There'll be someone else for you." She spoke the words mechanically, as if reading from a manual of what to say to bereaved people.

"It's hard to imagine. Anyway, what about you? Ready to knock the new guys dead?" I winced at my own words.

"Absolutely. I even managed to get the wine stain out of my dress. What's your mum doing with Adam tonight? I heard everyone's coming, no exceptions."

"She's bringing him along. Funny, she's besotted with him these days. Mind you, he's more interesting than he used to be. He crawls everywhere and has the cutest laugh."

There was more laughter in our house all round, especially between Mum and Dad. Those two were positively icky together. But it was good to see. It helped me to think that, sometimes, love could last forever.

"What's Suna wearing?"

"A bodysuit. It's what she feels most comfortable in."

"Huh. Oh well, less competition for me, I guess." Beth tossed her hair. "Can't say I've taken to her. Or Hazel, come to that. She looks like a horse. Laughs like one too. And she's already given the Mark to one of the academy guys."

Family loyalty forbade me from commenting on Suna, but I was about to defend Hazel, who'd been the star pupil of the farming academy as well as being lively, intelligent company, when Hope joined us.

"Hey, kitten. Can I get ready at your house?" she said to Beth.

"Sure, we're going to make you so hot that Matt's not gonna be able to control himself."

"Stop it, you're too gross," trilled Hope.

"See you later, Joy," said Beth.

I watched them walk arm-in-arm to Beth's house. Hope seemed to have filled the best friend-shaped gap in Beth's life. It didn't bother me, though I thought Matt deserved better than the silly, shallow ex-Citidome girl. I returned home and dressed for the party, laughing while Mum attempted to get a comb through Scott's bird's nest of hair. Dad came down the stairs and smiled at me.

"You look gorgeous, sweetheart. How about a hug for your old man?"

He squeezed me, a more powerful hug than he'd been capable of for a while.

"Hey Dad, that shoulder's getting stronger."

"It's you and your mum's combined nagging. I've been doing those exercises. I've promised your mum a slow dance tonight, and I want to be able to do it properly." He winked at me, and Scott mimed a vomit.

Nanna, Daisy and Suna joined us.

"Hey Suna, looking forward to your first party?" Mum said.

"Yeah," said Suna with only a hint of enthusiasm. It was going to take time for Suna to become one of us, but every week seemed to bring a little progress.

We reached the village hall, back to life for the first time in months, and saw Matt, together with Hope.

"Hey, you two. How's it going?"

"Great, thanks," said Matt, hugging Hope, while she squirmed in his grip. I'd like to see a happy ending there, but wasn't convinced. Like Suna, Hope didn't seem to have any interest in the opposite sex. Perhaps Citidome and village-born were fundamentally incompatible.

"Joy, good to see you!" Hazel said. "How are you holding up?"

I gave my well-practised 'I'll-get-there-in-time' smile. "Still crazy about the farm?" I said.

"Loving it. Last week we ploughed the top fields. We learnt all about crop rotation today. Fascinating. And fifteen men to one woman. What's not to like? But it's good to have some female company."

We chatted and I realised that, while Beth had found a new best friend, I might be making one too.

As the party gathered momentum, I absorbed the flood of condolences and watched the others dancing. I noticed that Beth hadn't left the dance floor, claimed by a different man every time one song ended. Suna and Hazel had their fair share of offers, too, though Suna turned most of them down.

"Hey, sweetheart," Daisy said. "How much fun is this? All these tasty young bodies on display. If I don't catch one; I'll need a cold shower later."

"It's fantastic to see, isn't it?" I said. "But aren't they a bit young for you?"

"The oldest one's thirty-one." Daisy gave a wicked grin. "He might need an experienced older woman to show him the ropes. There's a few that are a good age for you, though."

"Not sure about that," Joy said. "I feel older than all of them."

"In some ways you are. Hey our luck's in."

Two young men approached us. One led Daisy to the dance floor, the other stood in front of me and cleared his throat.

"Hey. Joy. I'm Joe. You don't know me, but I remember you from the shelter. I'm sorry about Ryan."

"Thanks." Out came the grateful widow smile again.

"Sorry if it's too presumptuous of me, but would you care to dance?"

"Actually I'd love to. I think everyone's too scared to ask me." I was overcome with an urge to feel young again, if only for a few minutes.

"What do you think of life on the outside?" I asked.

"Incredible," he said. "None of us ever imagined we could

live like this. Your dad's a legend."

I followed him to the dance floor, and for three glorious minutes the burdens of guilt and sorrow fell from my shoulders.

"You dance well," Joe said as the music faded. "Would you like a drink?"

"Thanks, but I need to speak to Dad." I excused myself quickly. No point in giving another boy the wrong idea.

"Hey, sweetheart, good to see you dancing again," Dad said. "Having fun?"

"More than I expected. How's it feel to bask in adulation? These guys think you're a god."

"Don't know about that." But his smile was broader than it had been for some time. Then his eyes shifted to behind my shoulder. "Ah, here's the special guests."

"Huh?" I turned around and a familiar figure lifted me from my feet and swung me in the air.

"Belated happy birthday, honey."

"Kell! I didn't know you were coming!"

"Your dad invited us. Thought it'd perk you up. We wanted to come sooner, but we thought you'd need time." My eyes followed his to where Dee was standing, together with Harry. No sign of Caroline. My feet had frozen to the spot.

"Come on, he wants to talk to you." Kell took my hand.

"I'm not sure what to say to him." My arms and legs had stopped working.

"Do I have to drag you?" Kell said.

But Dee and Harry were walking towards me. For the first time in what seemed forever, I felt my breath quicken. And now my heart was clattering in my chest. I grasped the back of the chair for support.

"You're looking lovely, Joy." Dee kissed my cheek. "Now, if you'll excuse us, I'm dying to catch up with your mum and dad."

And Dee and Kell left the two of us facing each other. I took in every detail of his face, as if reminding myself what he looked like. He, too, had lost weight, his cheekbones more well-defined than ever. A deep scar bisected his left eyebrow and ran up his forehead. Otherwise he was still my Harry.

"Sorry about Ryan," he said.

"Thanks." My eyes dropped.

"I know the whole story. Dad told me half of it, your dad the rest." He shifted his weight from one foot to the other.

"Where's Caroline?" My voice was sharp.

"Haven't seen her for months. She wasn't the right girl for me." His voice was loaded with meaning. Now our eyes met. "Biggest mistake I ever made. I needed my ego massaging, and I wanted to hurt you the way you'd hurt me."

"But –"

"I understand it all now. But you and Ryan – it was so easy to believe. I saw the way he looked at you, that time in the barn. Caroline knew we weren't right together too. We stayed friends. We finished on the day your mum told me you were missing. Nearly killed me, the thought of anyone touching you." He sighed. "We made a right mess of things, didn't we?"

"So why was she on the boat when we got out of the bunker?"

"Helping out. She's a health worker, remember? I didn't even realise you were there, that day. Seeing Dad, it was so overwhelming … course you'd jump to the wrong conclusion. Then I started helping everyone on board. Just before we cast off, Dad said you'd been there. I leapt off the boat and ran down the path but I was too late."

I felt a loosening inside, as if I'd been clenching my fists for months, and had released them. "So why are you here? Come for a haircut?"

"You don't need one." He grinned and ruffled my curls. "No, I heard you hadn't read my message."

"What message?"

"The one I sent after reading one from your dad three months ago. The day you married Ryan."

"Wh-what did it say?"

"It said that a life without Joy isn't worth living." His eyes bored into mine. "And then it said, don't marry him. Marry me instead."

When I didn't reply, his eyes dropped and he put his hand in his pocket, taking out the stone I'd engraved for his birthday. He gazed at it as if it were all he had left of me. I blinked in an attempt to stem the tears that had filled my eyes. And then he looked at me, and the tears spilled over.

"I can't fall into someone else's arms. I'm meant to be in mourning. And Harry … I'm training to become the community health worker." I held his gaze, hoping he'd understand what this meant.

"That's brilliant. Dad told me how you organised everyone, and about the amputations. Sounds like you finally found your vocation."

I traced his scar with my fingertips, unable to speak for a few moments.

"But I won't be able to live with you on the canals. I'll have to stay here."

A broad smile crept across his face. "Well, I was thinking of a change of scenery. I'm surplus to requirements now Dad's back. As a matter of fact, I've had a new job offer too."

"What?"

"Assistant to the leader of the AOC. It'll involve me living round here most of the time and doing some of the travelling. So we don't need to rush into anything. We've got a lifetime."

I caught my breath and my eyes scanned the room. Where was Dad? Ah, a slow song had started, and Mum and Dad were locked together on the dance floor, as were Kell and Dee, but Dad met my eye and winked. I turned to Harry and grinned. "Aren't parents embarrassing?"

He held out his hand. "Come on, Joy. It's time for us to dance."

FREEDOM'S PRISONERS

Book 3 of the Blueprint trilogy

Michael and his army of rebels may have won the first battle in their fight against the Citidome authorities, but will they win the war? The Citidomes are fighting back and no-one is safe any more. When Michael and Cathy finds themselves back in Sigma-2, Cathy must confront her worst fears.

Can Joy and Harry recapture the magic of first love, or have the horrors they have witnessed scarred them forever? Do they have any chance of succeeding in the most ambitious mission that the Alliance of Outside Communities has ever undertaken?

For Suna, this is a time of difficult decisions. Where do her loyalties lie? Is she capable of understanding human emotion?

Will the fractured State Eleven be able to unite and form a new society?

Freedom's Prisoners, the explosive conclusion of Katrina Mountfort's *Blueprint* trilogy, will be available from Elsewhen Press in 2016.

Acknowledgements

Thanks to my husband, Gerry, for your constant love, patience and support, and for humouring me! Thanks, Mam, Alex and Steve for always believing in me and being there when I need you.

I'm grateful to all my friends; not only for encouraging me in this adventure but also for the good times we've spent together. It's easy to become hermit-like as a writer and I so appreciate your company. Special thanks go to Diana McGarry, Sue Johns and all the members of the Word Cloud online writing community. I couldn't do this without your advice, critiques and proofreading.

I'm enormously grateful to everyone who reviewed *Future Perfect*, either on Amazon, Goodreads or book blogs. Reviews greatly increase the book's visibility and create sales. If you've enjoyed this one, please consider leaving a review; every one counts!

To all the new friends I've made through social media, thanks for enriching my working day.

Thanks to Alex Storer for a wonderful cover design; you expressed my vision perfectly. And finally, massive thanks to Peter Buck and the team at Elsewhen Press for all the work you do – you've made a lifelong dream come true and opened up a whole new world for me.

Elsewhen Press

an independent publisher specialising in Speculative Fiction

Book 1 of the Blueprint trilogy

FUTURE PERFECT

KATRINA MOUNTFORT

The *Blueprint* trilogy takes us to a future in which men and women are almost identical, and personal relationships are forbidden. Following a bio-terrorist attack, the population now lives within comfortable Citidomes. MindValues advocate acceptance and non-attachment. The BodyPerfect cult encourages a tall thin androgynous appearance, and looks are everything.

This first book, *Future Perfect,* tells the story of Caia, an intelligent and highly educated young woman. In spite of severe governmental and societal strictures, Caia finds herself becoming attracted to her co-worker, Mac, a rebel whose questioning of their so-called utopian society both adds to his allure and encourages her own questioning of the status quo. As Mac introduces her to illegal and subversive information she is drawn into a forbidden, dangerous world, becoming alienated from her other co-workers and resmates, the companions with whom she shares her residence. In a society where every thought and action are controlled, informers are everywhere; whom can she trust?

When she and Mac are sent on an outdoor research mission, Caia's life changes irreversibly.

A dark undercurrent runs through this story; the enforcement of conformity through fear, the fostering of distorted and damaging attitudes towards forbidden love, manipulation of appearance and even the definition of beauty, will appeal to both an adult and young adult audience.

Katrina Mountfort was born in Leeds. After a degree in Biochemistry and a PhD in Food Science, she started work as a scientist. Since then, she's had a varied career. Her philosophy of life is that we only regret the things we don't try, and she's been a homeopath, performed forensic science research and currently works as a freelance medical writer. She now lives in Saffron Walden with her husband and two dogs. When she hit forty, she decided it was time to fulfil her childhood dream of writing a novel. *Future Perfect* is her debut novel and is the first in the *Blueprint* trilogy.

ISBN: 9781908168559 (epub, kindle)
ISBN: 9781908168450 (288pp paperback)

Visit bit.ly/Blueprint-FuturePerfect

Elsewhen Press

an independent publisher specialising in Speculative Fiction

LiGa series

Sanem Ozdural

A thought-provoking series of books in an essentially contemporary setting, with elements of both science fiction and fantasy.

LiGa™

Book I

Literary science fiction, LiGa™ tells of a game in which the players are, literally, gambling with their lives. In the near-future a secretive organisation has developed technology to transfer the regenerative power of a body's cells from one person to another, conferring extended or even indefinite life expectancy. As a means of controlling who benefits from the technology, access is obtained by winning a tournament of chess or bridge to which only a select few are invited. At its core, the game is a test of a person's integrity, ability and resilience. Sanem's novel provides a fascinating insight into the motivation both of those characters who win and thus have the possibility of virtual immortality and of those who will effectively lose some of their life expectancy.

ISBN: 9781908168160 (epub, kindle)
ISBN: 9781908168061 (400pp paperback)

Visit bit.ly/BookLiGa

THE DARK SHALL DO WHAT LIGHT CANNOT

Book II

We find out more about the organisation behind LiGa as we travel with some of them to Pera, a place which lies beyond the Light Veil on the other side of reality. There are light trees there that eat sunlight and bear fruit that, in turn, lights up and energises (literally) the community of Pera. There are light birds that glitter in the night because they have eaten the seed of the lightberry. The House of Light and Dark, which is the domain of the Sun and her brother, Twilight, welcomes all creatures living in Pera. But in the midst of all the glitter, laughter and the songs, it must be remembered that the lightberry is poisonous to the non-Pera born, and the Land is afraid when the Sun retreats, for it is then that Twilight walks the streets…

ISBN: 9781908168740 (epub, kindle)
ISBN: 9781908168641 (480pp paperback)

Visit bit.ly/Darkshalldo

Elsewhen Press

an independent publisher specialising in Speculative Fiction

The Lost Men

An Allegory

David Colón

In a world where the human population has been decimated, self-reliance is the order of the day. Of necessity, the few remaining people must adapt residual technology as far as possible, with knowledge gleaned from books that were rescued and have been treasured for generations. After a childhood of such training, each person is abandoned by their parents when they reach adulthood, to pursue an essentially solitary existence. For most, the only human contact is their counsel, a mentor who guides them to find 'the one', their life mate as decreed by Fate. Lack of society brings with it a lack of taboo, ensuring that the Fate envisioned by a counsel is enacted unquestioningly. The only threats to this stable, if sparse, existence are the 'lost men', mindless murderers who are also self-sufficient but with no regard for the well-being of others, living outside the confines of counsel and Fate.

Is Fate a real force, or is it totally imagined, an arbitrary convention, a product of mankind's self-destructive tendency? In this allegorical tale, David Colón uses an alternate near-future to explore the boundaries of the human condition and the extent to which we are prepared to surrender our capacity for decisions and self-determination in the face of a very personally directed and apparently benevolent, authoritarianism. Is it our responsibility to rebuke inherited 'wisdom' for the sake of envisioning and manifesting our own will?

David Colón is an Assistant Professor of English at TCU in Fort Worth, Texas, USA. Born and raised in Brooklyn, New York, he received his Ph.D. in English from Stanford University and was a Chancellor's Postdoctoral Fellow in English at the University of California, Berkeley. His writing has appeared in numerous journals, including *Cultural Critique*, *Studies in American Culture*, *DIAGRAM*, *How2*, and *MELUS*. *The Lost Men* is his first book.

ISBN: 9781908168146 (epub, kindle)
ISBN: 9781908168047 (192pp paperback)

Visit lost-men.com

About the Author

Katrina Mountfort was born in Leeds. After a degree in Biochemistry and a PhD in Food Science, she started work as a scientist. Since then, she's had a varied career. Her philosophy of life is that we only regret the things we don't try, and she's been a homeopath, performed forensic science research and currently works as a freelance medical writer. She now lives in Saffron Walden with her husband and two dogs. When she hit forty, she decided it was time to fulfil her childhood dream of writing a novel. *Future Perfect* was her debut novel and the first in the *Blueprint* trilogy. *Forbidden Alliance* is the second of the trilogy.